Insurrection

Truth Devour

www.truthdevour.com

Published in 2016
by Truth Devour
www.truthdevour.com

Beta Readers
Danni Erbs
Suzanne Learmonth

Interior layout and design
by Publicious Pty Ltd
www.publicious.com.au

Book cover design by:
Artist: Diana Toma
Email: diana@artbydianatoma.com
Facebook: facebook.com/ArtByDianaToma

Catalogue-in-Publication details available
from the National Library of Australia

ISBN: 978-0-9922999-8-9 (pbk)

Also available in ebook
ISBN: 978-0-9922999-9-6 (ebk)

In wisdom gathered over time I have found that every experience is a form of exploration.

Ansel Adams (1902 – 1984)

ALSO BY TRUTH DEVOUR

Soliloquy's Labyrinth Series

Adult Contemporary Fantasy / Paranormal
with a psychological edge

Illuminarium
(1st Book)

Enigma Series

Adult Contemporary Romantic Trilogy

Wantin
(1st book)

Unrequited
(2nd book)

Sated
(3rd book)

www.truthdevour.com

DIRECT
DEVOUR

Contents

Convergence

The clock face positioned at the top of the elongated bluestone bell tower struck midnight as the old fob watches swung in the breeze suspended by varying lengths of chain under the tree canopies. The cloud formed makeshift arms that moved in a jolting rhythm to the ticks and the tocks of the multitude of timepieces scattered across the Salvador Dali mind scape I held in my recurring dream. There was no reprieve from the emphasis on time being of critical importance.

Waking to a cold sweat petering on my brow from the looming significance of today, I stretched my arms out to touch the edges of the suns first light streaming in the window with the tips of my fingers, while I thought about the crew. A full seven days had passed since I had left the boys in San Francisco to fend for themselves. My phone remained switched off to ensure I held no temptation to answer when Liam called. As much as I missed his presence, it was safer for all concerned for me to remain unencumbered by people. The mayhem that was about to be unleashed would guarantee myself to become the interferon's single point of focus.

Thanks to Liam's contacts I had found out that the USA Vaccine Administration Group (VAG) approved a new vaccine called eXileanon for unrestricted trial. The release of the vaccine caught my attention when Liam's sources indicated that the global health outreach program (GHOP) were backing the early release of the drug for human clinical trials exerting their influence and recommending a bypass of the typically stringent research protocols. Their premise was due to the trace markers of the disease's high risk for epidemic spread stipulating it warranted regulation bypass to circumvent catastrophic peaks of the epidermis infestation the media had tagged as Euphoric death.

To date there are only twenty suspected cases reported worldwide of which five people were confirmed to have contracted the disease and all five people had shortly after lost their lives. The patients held the identical symptoms prior to death with the autopsies concluding each subject had varying stages of the same classification for cause of death, vital organ erosion. The newspapers labeled it Euphoric death because the surface skin irritation compelled the person to frantically scratch pleasurably relieving the itch. Under the surface of the skin, the scratching triggers off the bacterium to release a chemical, which causes the hosts blood to temporarily lightly congeal. This forms the perfect breeding ground for the bacteria to multiply. The millions of microscopic progeny travel through the blood stream lodging themselves to the outer surface of the main organs where they relentlessly feast for a cycle of ten to twelve days and then detach to rise toward the skins surface to repeat the process of host irritation to breed.

I reluctantly arose from the comfort of my bed to

head down stairs to make breakfast. Entering the kitchen, I immediately noted the shifting of shadows at the bottom lip of my front door. I paused to watch as the dancing silhouette unnaturally stilled when I released an intentional cough. Quietly, I opened my cutlery draw to retrieve the retractable knife. I had it secured to a halter taped to the underside of the bench top. Placing the handle in the palm of my left hand, I silently walked toward the entrance. When the doorknob clicked the lock over to release, the shadow immediately stilled again. At the thump of my hearts beat I swung the door open to confront the presence.

My eyes scanned the vacant space and then looked up toward the exposed skies from the hallway's glass roof as I saw the edges of a person's feet running away from where I stood. A length of rope was all that remained trailing behind them after the person disappeared from my view. Directly above, the hall way air vent was removed allowing a slight breeze to whistle in the enlarged cavity. The years of dust particles and fragments of building debris expressed their dance of freedom before settling on the next surface landing.

Still half dazed I stepped forward.

"Yelp, mmm, mmm, mmm."

Jumping back, I gasped with the shock of the noise drawing my eyes to the ground. There sitting perfectly still wagging its little tail was a tiny fluff ball puppy in a makeshift bed. It looked up at me with its adorable eyes while releasing a shiver and a whimper. This time it attempted to walk forward waving its right teeny-weeny paw in the air. I glanced around one more time to ensure no one else was present before crouching down.

"Hello" I said in a soft voice smiling at the extreme cuteness of my unexpected visitor.

The puppy extended his neck forward licking the air before connecting to my skin to greet me with kisses. My heart was in instant meltdown. I gently picked the puppy up with both my hands cupped around its body before raising it to my eye level to make a closer inspection. It was a boy. I suspected by the look of him he held a genetic lineage to either a purebred or part bred wire fox terrier. He had a mottle of varying shades of brown on his crinkled fur, an elongated muzzle that transitioned to grey and black across his brow and then back to tones of brown on his ears. The rest of his torso was white except for his rump that had a splash of all the colors present on his face plastered on the centre point of his backside and partially on his hindquarters.

I tucked him under my arm before picking up his bedding to inspect it. I shook the blankets stuffed in the basket to check there wasn't anything hidden between the layers. The outer portion of the container was made of woven cane, which also seemed to be nothing more than a basket. There was an attached layer of bedding on the inside held together by material bows. I looked up once more at the exposed vent before taking the dog and the bedding inside my apartment.

My mind was reeling with a multitude of thoughts as I placed him on the kitchen bench safely nestled back in his bedding. I waited until he stilled before leaving him to enter the pantry to find a container to provide him with some water. Whoever delivered this puppy didn't want to be seen. The stairwell is key coded to an electronic card combined with a handprint and pass code, so the only entrance point without security access required is via the elevator. The architect had a penchant for safety. His surveillance cameras were not only state of the art, he ensured the elevator, and hallway cameras were positioned to overlap so there is no blind spot available to utilize. The system is held under lock and key with an uninterrupted power supply to deter perpetrators from an easy fix. If the electricity fails the entire building switches to the emergency generator, each floor is assigned its own uniquely configured system. The person on the roof must have known there was a degree of complexity to the entry of the building. They could have used the elevator but the effort taken by their choice of entry heightens the emphasis on them not wanting to run the risk of being seen.

I placed the bowl of water in front of the basket. It didn't take long for him to come forward to sniff and lick at its surface. I bowed down with my arms folded on the kitchen bench so my face was resting on my arms while I observed him. Why would someone go to such lengths to deliver me this puppy?

"Who are you?" I whispered.

The puppy responded by lifting his head from the bowl, sitting and once again raising his right paw, waving it in my direction. I tilted my head to look at his action. He immediately dropped his paw then mimicked the tilt with the most adorable gaze directly into my eyes.

None of this made sense. I knew the little fellow must hold significance, but I failed to understand why. Given all of what had already taken place I wondered if the Interferon's were aware of my plans and counter launched using the puppy as a medium. Instantly my eyes widened as I covered my mouth and nose with my pyjama top. I picked up the puppy along with the basket racing them into the guest bathroom where I placed him gently back into the bedding and onto the floor before shutting the door. Returning to the kitchen, I scrubbed my hands and face with disinfectant and ran paper toweling with a generous lathering of germ killing spray across the bench.

"Shit, shit, shit" I said shaking my head. I paced up and down the lounge while listening to the pitter-patter of his little paws at the bathroom door. Fumbling through my kitchen cupboards, I found a high potency chelated mineral booster for my immune system. I took a fresh glass from the cupboard, filled it with filtered water and drank a double dose.

There was a swell of frustration growing within me over the pending possibility of the situation. I knew I shouldn't make assumptions or draw conclusions but I was feeling compelled to mentally kick myself for my obvious gullibility. The whole delivery of the puppy was so extreme it should have alarmed me to greater suspicion. It was as though they wanted to have me feel like I was living on the sharp of the pointed edge of life where their decision to gust the wind left or right would determine my direction. I possess a greater determination to propel forward in the absence of such influences with a 'fuck you' plastered on my forehead. I will not yield or be a puppeteer pawn in their veiled games. My only option as I saw it was to exercise a process of elimination, but first I had to take a shower.

Once freshly dried and dressed I placed on an apron and some rubber kitchen gloves before retrieving the puppy and the basket. I took him to the garage, placed him on the floor of the back seat of my car and headed to the local veterinarian clinic. Inside the room, the two receptionist instantly smiled as they saw him peer over the edge of his bedding.

"He is adorable. How old is he?" Asked the

receptionist to my left while the other answered an incoming call.

"I'm not sure. I guess he is about eight to twelve weeks. I think he is a wired fox terrier."

"What's his name?"

"Actually I don't have a name for him yet."

She frowned as she looked at me seemingly disgusted that I knew so little about 'my' pet.

With a cold tone she adjusted her posture to an upright position and stared at her computer, "Do you have an appointment?"

"No, I was hoping there was a vet available or I could wait to slot in between appointments."

Her right eyebrow rose impressively high as her lips pursed, "We are very busy here at the clinic so you will need to make an appointment."

"It's okay Maryanne, I've got fifteen minutes before my next client is due. If you want to come through I can see you for an initial consult."

I turned to see a man with his hand extended inviting me to head toward the door, he was holding open. I smiled and nodded, "Thank you."

"She hasn't filled in any forms," blurted Maryanne as the door closed.

"Sorry, she can come across as very regimented. I'm Victor." He said extending his hand.

I didn't think to remove my rubber glove before accepting his shake, "I'm Harper and this little fellow landed on my doorstep this morning. I wanted to get a full health check including bloods."

I noticed Victor glancing at my gloves. "Ok then, hello little guy, let me take a look at you," he said while lifting him gently from the basket.

The Vet placed the stethoscope on his chest to listen to the timing of his breaths and the beat of his heart before proceeding to inspect the inside of his mouth. Meanwhile, I looked at the poster on the wall, which held images of dog breeds of the world. Victor felt around the puppy's body pausing when he reached his neck and then leaned in to take a closer look.

"This little fellow has a collar. You said you found him at your door step, this might give us a clue as to where he comes from." He said removing it from his neck.

I watched as Victor looked at the collar and then at me. "You said your name is Harper."

"Yes, that's correct." I responded now fixated on the tiny orange collar he held in his hands.

"Harper Perelle?"

I nodded my head.

"According to this collar you are the owner of Huckleberry."

My heart skipped a beat while the terrier simultaneously released a little bark spinning in a circle at the mention of the name.

Victor laughed extending his hand to pat the twirling puppy, "You know your name little one, don't you?"

I stepped back feeling a well of emotions.

"Are you okay? Did you have a fall recently or some sort of shock to your system?"

"No," I said shaking my head while looking at Huckleberry who was now sitting on the bench facing me wagging his tail.

"You look flushed. There is a chair behind you, take a seat. I'll get you a glass of water."

Victor walked out of the room before I could respond. I was still taken back by the discovery of the collar and more importantly the name. I reached across to lift the blankets on the bedding. Once again, I shook them and found nothing out of order. Slowly I untied the bows that held the final layer of cushioning on the inside of the basket. When it was partially free, I lifted one side to reveal the bottom of the basket. Attached to the underside of the cushion was a note and with an implement. I gently pried it from the adhesive. It was a very ornate tarnished silver letter opener and a folded note, which I immediately opened.

'Everyone needs a friend they can depend on. Happy Birthday Harper from me to you.'

Victor re-entered the room with a glass of water in hand. He glanced at the note as he passed it to me.

"Did you find something?"

"Yes," I said as I put the letter opener back under the bedding where he couldn't see it. "Its a note I found in the underside of the dogs bedding."

"What does it say?"

I took a sip of the water while I held the page facing it outward so he could read it for himself.

"Happy Birthday Harper from me to you."

I glared at Victor while almost choking on my water. When I turned the page to reassess what was written I realized that he wasn't able to see the whole message.

Victor, "Its not my birthday."

"Well whoever left the puppy at your doorstep and wrote you the note certainly believes it is." He said looking at the page again smiling. "I think it is kind of romantic with a dash of irresponsibility. So many people who provide others with a pet as a gift end up at the shelters these days. A puppy is not just for Christmas or birthdays for that matter."

I nodded my head to acknowledge his words but was too consumed by the realities to actually be bothered listening.

"Victor can you please read everything on the note out aloud. I don't have my glasses with me."

He glanced over the page again, shrugged his shoulders and said, "That's all it has written. *Happy Birthday Harper from me to you.* Do you have any idea who this is from?"

"Not a clue."

"Are you going to keep him or place him up for adoption?"

I looked across at little Huckleberry and smiled. "I'm keeping him." I said. "Everyone needs a friend they can depend on Victor." Huckleberry released a bark and began to twirl again while I removed the rubber gloves from my hands and took off the apron I forgot I was wearing.

Victor laughed at Huckleberry's timely response to my words, "I'll give him his vaccinations and make up a card for your records. Maryanne can organize a puppy starter pack, which will include a two-week supply of food, water and feed bowl, some flea capsules and other items you will need. If you don't have anything in your home, you can use for sleeping the pet store across the street has a nice array of bedding to chose from. This little guy is not going to fit in this basket for much longer. There will be some pamphlets on toilet training and the classes we offer as a service for obedience when he is a little older." He said tickling Huckleberry under the chin.

"Thanks, it all sounds wonderful."

Once the bill was settled I loaded the armfuls of supplies into the boot of the car then placed Huck's newly purchased car harness on him in the passenger side front seat. He sat there quietly and watched me the whole way home.

Entering the corridor of my floor, I noticed the vent had been secured back into position. Inside the apartment, I placed Huck in his new bedding where he once again sat quietly watching me organizing a place for his food and water before setting up his temporary toilet space in the guest bathroom.

I took the note he came with and placed it on the surface of my fridge door. It was curious to know that Victor couldn't see the whole message. This made me feel a level of assurance that the gift was not intended with malice. The name Huckleberry just like York's dog in the story of Illuminarium couldn't have been a co-incidence of alignment. Whoever orchestrated this knew things no other has known. The statement 'Everyone needs a friend they can rely on' had connotations supporting the voicemail message I had received from the Italian man at the hotel where he said 'trust no-one.' Would my only confidant and ally in this life be a dog? It was getting increasingly harder to delineate when I was reading too much into the event. Trusting my instincts, I lent towards 'trust no one' being a fundamental truth. It disappointed me to entertain such a narrowest conclusion, but I also was cognizant of the realities of the watchers and their total oblivion to how they participated in the silent wars. The only anomaly, which struck me as worthy of investigation, was my date of birth. My birthday was just shy of two months away or was it?

Entanglement

Driving down the road where I had grown up, I found the memories of playing kick ball in the streets with the neighboring kids resurfaced as a vivid imagery. I could see Danny sitting on the curb with his elbows to knees and hands holding his face as his head turned from left to right watching the game from the side lines. Little Steven always darted between us all, manically chasing the ball. Jasper and I would team up against the others and for the most part, hold our own. The only time we would break from our games was when we heard the approaching sound of the chimes from the ice-cream truck on a hot summer's day.

No sooner had I turned into the driveway my mom opened the front door. Waving with a smile widened across her face, I could tell she was excited to see me. I grabbed Huckleberry nestling him under my right arm while walking across the lawn. I could feel the swag of his hindquarters as his little tail propelled from side to side with a speedy swish through the air.

"Harper, it's been too long," she said as she embraced me.

"I know mom," I replied as I pulled her in with the arm that was free, giving her a squeeze.

As I stepped back I lifted Huckleberry and held him out for her to grab.

"Oh my, he is cuter than you described." She said as she took him to nurse in her arms. "Don't you have any bags?"

"No, I told you I was just passing through to see how you and Dad are."

Mom paused to look at me, "Harps, you rarely do anything without a reason."

I smiled, "I did mention I want to pick up my old college notes for some research I'm doing at the moment."

She looked at me suspiciously as she squinted her eyes and smiled, "Ok, Harps but the birds say otherwise." Mom turned to walk inside as I followed closing the door behind.

"What birds?" I asked.

"Come, I'll show you."

We went straight down the hall to the back section of the house where mom and pop extended the home to create a sunken lounge with a floor to ceiling glass wall overlooking their prized expansive custom designed Japanese garden. She placed Huckleberry on the ground and opened the sliding doors. As the cool gushes of air greeted my face in conflict with the central heating of the room, I felt a flush across my brow as I heard a squawking noise. My eyes glanced to the left where I spied four sulphur crested white cockatoo's sitting on the red Japanese tori gateway entrance to the traditionally styled mini bridge.

"Aren't they native to Australia?"

"Yes, I just looked them up online. They are also

found in New Guinea and areas of Indonesia. They arrived the minute the phone started ringing and haven't left since I spoke to you." She turned to look at me, "Are you sure there isn't something you need to tell me?"

I looked at the cockatoo's watching my every move. "Nope. Perhaps these guys escaped from some illegal collector?"

"Maybe, or perhaps you are planning to go on some trip or relocate and don't know how to tell me?"

"Mom, I think you're reading too much into it. You have been on edge ever since Dylan got reposted to Japan with the air force." I turned to face her, engaging her eyes, "I promise, I have no plans of migrating anywhere. Against all odds I purchased a place to live in remember? I'm as settled as I will ever be."

"Well, Dylan had a house here and was quite happy with Launa until the Ryukyu robin appeared in the yard on the day he received his orders from the air force."

I smiled. It was mom that always looked to animals for signs and had taught my brother and I how to read the messages presented. My dad was also attuned to nature but leant more toward the natural order of things such as the way a tree grew could demonstrate the degree of persistent heavy winds in the area or the quality of the soil indicated by the resulting health of the plants. Both were avid activists for the environment and heavily into the promotion of organic agriculture also known as bio dynamics. They established a charity called Dynamically Global. It focuses on teaching third world farmers how to utilize Rudolf Steiner's principles of bio dynamics with the resources they have readily available in their immediate environment. The primary objective is focused on educating people on how to increase the quality of their native soils to aid in better crop yields with higher nutritional value.

"You and I both know Dylan wasn't happy with Launa. I'm not sure why you even said that."

Mom paused looking down at her weathered hands, "I just miss him and wish that he would come home."

I smiled as I placed my arms around her, "He's the happiest I have ever seen him. You know in your heart he's never coming back. If you miss him, then the solution is a simple one. Go visit him."

"Do you want a cup of tea?" She asked stepping away from my embrace to enter the kitchen. I could see she was attempting to discreetly wipe away a rolling tear.

"Talk to me mom. Let it out. There is something clearly annoying you. What is it?"

She placed both hands on the bench and leaned forward with her head bowed as though she was suddenly asked to support the weight of the world. "I'm never going to be a grandmother."

"That's not true. Dylan and Kichiro may adopt one day."

"Its not the same Harper. I wanted my children to have children. Now that Dylan has chosen to go down that path I've had to come to the realization that I won't be a grandmother. Our lineage stops here. Lord knows you won't settle down so all my hopes were pegged with Dylan."

"Mom, he's happy. I'm not sure it's as simple as *'choosing.'* He and Kichiro are deeply in love. I have never seen him glow so bright with a zest for life. It's a blessing. There is no compromise too great for true love."

"I know, I'm happy for them and Kichiro seems lovely. Its just hard to let go of my dream."

"Perhaps its not the dream you need to let go of rather the rigidity of it being dependent on their progeny being born through blood relations. What if they are destined to adopt the child who was always set to be theirs who had been born through another channel because they couldn't enter this realm via the two of them?"

She went quiet as she straightened up and took in a deep breath. "Harper, look at that."

I quickly turned around. Outside the back door, one of the cockatoos had landed on the ground and was walking up to Huckleberry. He sat patiently watching the bird approach. There was a moment of pause as they faced each other before the cockatoo fanned its yellow crest and made a head tilt while releasing a loud squawk. The other three cockatoo's bounced up and down on their perch eagerly watching over the two of them. Huckleberry slowly rose to a stance wagging his tail. Quietly, he stepped forward placing his torso against the bird who seemed to respond in kind by pushing up against him. Then suddenly the cockatoo dropped its crest, closing its eyes while continuing to lean into Huckleberry. They were greeting each other like old friends.

"I don't know what this means Harper but I can tell you it feels significant."

"It is." I said while continuing to watch.

"Tell me."

"Love endures, love finds a way. No boundaries, limits in space nor time can break the bond of two who hold a love so pure."

"Yes," Whispered the voice in my ear as tears formed in my eyes. 'I miss you,' I said quietly under my breath as I felt the warmth of arms wrap around me.

"Harper, you're crying," said mom as she reached for a tissue to pass across to me.

I smiled, "Its beautiful when old souls recognize each other. No matter their shape or form, air, land or sea bound they are still connected by love."

"You are right. I'm silly for struggling to hold onto the ideals of the one thing I can't have when I am so blessed with all that I do."

"Like I said mom you will receive your grandchildren via Dylan, just not the way you had initially imagined. When the time is right, if he and Kichiro choose to adopt, the child or children who enter into their lives are already a part of them and universally destined to be. We are all interconnected."

She smiled as she reached across to touch the side of my face, "I do hope one day you meet someone who you can fall in love with so you settle down to a normal life Harps."

I lent into her hand and closed my eyes, "I know you do mom. I know you do."

"Beanie Bear, you're home."

"Dad." I said as I swirled with open arms to greet him.

He gave me a big squeeze and then stepped back. "Let me take a look at you." He said inspecting me from head to toe. "You need to eat more young lady, here let me fix you up a naughty but nice bowl of ice cream."

I laughed, "Nice try Dad. Mom has obviously put you back on a restricted diet again. I'm not going to encourage your binging habits. So no to the offer of some ice cream but yes to your next immanent offer of a tour around your garden to see what's new."

He pouted, "She won't let me eat anything anymore

and the stuff she prepares all tastes like cardboard. Stupid high cholesterol."

I patted his stomach and turned to walk outside.

"Go and show her around the garden while I prepare a cardboard lunch for three," said mom poking her tongue out at him.

Huckleberry came running to the door as we walked out. He seemed to have a little skip in his step before twirling around in circles for Dad.

"He clearly likes you." I said with a chuckle.

Dad bent down to pat him. However, Huckleberry had other ideas as he leapt into the air in good faith that Dad would catch him. As he picked him up to his eye level Huckleberry was licking the air frantically lunging forward to connect with Dads face.

"What a cutie and he's full of beans."

"It's Huckleberry."

"Who is this other fellow?" My Dad said chuckling as Huck's licks gave him a tickle.

I looked down and saw the cockatoo confidently trotting toward us. It slowed as it got closer to me and then much to my surprise proceeded to clasp onto my pants with its beak and claws to begin the steep ascent. I placed my hand out as an offer, which the cocky had no hesitation in taking. Once he was perched in the palm of my hand, I raised him up holding my arm extended. The cockatoo fanned his yellow crest and released a squawk bouncing up and down in excitement as Huckleberry joined in with a series of barks. Then it walked sideways up the length of my arm settling on my right shoulder.

"When did you become Doctor Do Little with all creatures great and small?"

"I didn't. I'm assuming this is an escapee from somewhere

in the neighborhood. He's too tame not to be an illegal pet. Look up at your Japanese gate there's three more."

"Well slap me with a feather."

I released a laugh; this is one of the classic statements my Dad defaulted to when he witnessed something he couldn't explain.

The cockatoo on my shoulder stepped into gently nuzzle my face and then bent its head to nibble the end of my earlobe as though it was greeting me with a kiss.

"Thank you." I said when it stopped.

It spread its yellow crest and released a loud squawk, bopping its head up and down before settling in a squatted perch.

"Guess you have made a new friend," said Dad as he stepped forward to lead the way down the cobblestone path into the main portion of the garden.

"It happens." I replied smiling at the delight of the experience.

The first point of call was the Zen garden.

"I can see you have some new rocks."

"Yes, I happened to cross paths with a fellow who mentioned he had a parcel of land filled with mid sized to somewhat largish boulders he didn't know what to do with. I suggested he places pictures of them on the online artists and landscapers page to see if there is any interest. He received such an overwhelming response and couldn't believe people were not only eager to obtain the rocks but willingly paid him for them. He reserved these three and had them delivered to me as a thank you for my advice."

"I like the way you have them positioned. The dried lichen on the surface of that one near the far right edge seems to draw your eye across the rest of the stones and finish on it as the main point of interest. It's a clever layout."

Dad smiled as he raised himself on the tips of his toes and back down again. Huckleberry was happily nestled in the crook of his arm.

Moms voice called out, "Lunch is ready."

"Ok," I yelled in response. Dad went to step further down the path to show me the rest of his creations. "Come on, you can show me the rest of the garden later."

He hesitated for a moment before nodding.

"She will get crabby if we don't. Come," I said as I turned back.

I stood at the entry of the door and leaned my head in. "Mom, do you have any fruit and veggies maybe even some nuts you can spare please? I'd like to feed these cockatoos."

"Sure." She collected the scraps sprinkling some of her seeded and dried fruit muesli on top. "Here you go."

"SQUAWK, squawk, squawk"

"Oh my," she said jumping back with a gasp. "It frightened the hell out of me. How did you get it to sit on your shoulder?"

"I didn't. It chose to come to me."

My mom slowly passed me the bowl while looking at the cockatoo and I. She clearly held some thoughts on the matter but was not forth coming.

"Thanks," I said taking the container from her. "I'll be back in a minute." I walked across to the Torii gate where the other cockatoos were still perched. I spread the feast on the floor in front of them and took my reluctant friend off my shoulder to place him on the ground. At first, he wanted to climb up my leg again but then spied a piece of carrot that he grasped with his claw before commencing to nibble.

I walked inside, seating myself in my usual spot at the table. "Out with it Mom." I said with a laugh.

"The symbolism of the cockatoo is pertaining to the wisdom to communicate, see beauty where it has been shrouded and the ability to survive harsh conditions. They are known for their presence to sunrise, so they hold particular power associations to the early morning. It could be interpreted as striking early or making the first move."

I pursed my lips with a slight smirk and nodded my head.

"What have you gotten yourself into Harper? Something isn't right. I can feel it in my bones."

Dad tossed a carrot stick at me, "She's never been out of trouble from the day she was born and she always lands on her feet. Don't molly coddle her love. If Harper needs our help, she knows we're here for her. Don't you Beanie Bear?"

I picked up the carrot and snapped it in two before tossing a portion in my mouth. "I sure do. Let's eat, I'm starved."

Dad picked up the salad tongs scooping a generous heap of the fresh mixed greens onto his plate before layering the top of it with components from the variety of side dishes. I followed suit while mom sat back to watch.

"I don't know what is going on for you Harper but I know it's immense. Four cockatoos with one on your shoulder suggests you are equal parts contributor and receiver of this experience or journey you are embarking on or having had imposed on you. It evolves exclusively around you."

I stood up to place some food on her plate. She knew I would never lie to her, but she was also aware I rarely spoke of things that mattered until after the circumstances passed. The accuracies of her ability to interpret the signs combined with her instincts were astounding. I possessed countless childhood memories of her reading signals and telling me what was occurring without me ever confirming or denying the preciseness of her interpretation. It was a natural gift.

"Hey have you seen all the protests and media coverage about this new vaccine that has been promoted as the cure for that skin death thing?"

I looked at my Dad and smiled in acknowledgement for his attempt to divert the subject and was equally amused at the topic he had chosen.

"Sounds interesting, tell me more."

"The activists are claiming there is a government conspiracy around vaccinations in general and there is a call out to the community to boycott the use of any vaccinations until investigations are ensued."

"Wow this sounds huge. Do you know what triggered off the issue?"

"Apparently the underground syndicate, Sanctorum Avow released a series of leaked artefacts from the GHOP around their commitment to influence and support the early release of the drug together with an outline of the proposed strategy of how to achieve the bypass of the existing governance protocols. Instead of denying the legitimacy of the documents the media grunt at GHOP suggested there would be serious consequences to the group if they didn't withdraw their campaign of blasphemy. Then yesterday there was a range of articles released stipulating there is a strong reason to believe civilians are being entangled in a silent chemical warfare trial via intentional contamination of intrinsic vaccinations. An announcement was broadcast on the pirate stations that proof would be provided in due course. It's huge and causing massive community outcry."

"Since when do you pay attention to underground murmurs?" I asked

"Are you kidding? I've been keeping my ear to the ground since before you were born Beanie Bear." He said tapping his nose. "Sanctorum Avow are known to be a very reliable source. They don't take their media influence lightly."

"It seems like a fantastical story someone's concocted for attention. Did they provide any indication on how they were going to prove their theory?" I said calmly taking a mouthful of my salad.

"I don't know Harps, it may sound a little far fetched but on the other hand there are some things disclosed that are a little too familiar and close for comfort. We might not have the whole truth revealed to us as yet but my instinct says that these people are onto something."

"What do you think mom?"

"I think you know far more about so many things than you choose to reveal."

I shook my head presenting as unfazed at her challenge. "Now what?"

She used her chin to point as she released a sigh and said, "There is a raven at the door."

I looked at my dad before turning to see an unusually large raven standing in the doorway. It engaged in direct eye contact with me, then reached down casually preening itself. I continued to watch its beak disappear into its plumage only rising up to shift to another section to repeat the same until it finally plucked a single feather from its plume. Carefully the raven placed it on the ground in front of where it was standing. The bird seemed so calm as it stepped backward pausing to glance at me one more time. I smiled when I saw him clearly execute a curtsey and a bow before flying away as silently as it had arrived.

"The native American's believe raven's are the deliverer of light. In some tribes the legends suggest in the absence of ravens humans would be destined to live within the shadows, oblivious to their true calling. Ravens are predominately linked to foretellers of the Oracle and associated to higher intelligence."

I turned to face the table, "Carl Jung suggested that the raven was a representation of the dark within ones psych."

"True he did but you could also consider that the acknowledgement of such a presence within oneself is therefore brought to light."

Dad laughed. "You two need to stop now."

"Its okay dad, this is actually useful. What does the feather represent?"

"A gift."

"What kind of a gift?" I asked.

"Typically a feather from a raven would suggest creation and knowledge but in this instance I am seeing the raven as a messenger. The way he flew in, waited for you to look at him. He took his time to preen before he selected the feather he wanted to present to you. I think it was symbolic of sacrifice. It seems to me, this raven acknowledged your sacrifice with a gesture of his own. Perhaps this is an indication that you are on the right path. Bowing, as you know, is symbolic of respect. There is honor associated to what you have embarked upon."

"I guess we will have to wait and see." I said rather pleased with the banter. I turned to my dad, "Do you have a copy of the magazine?"

"Sure, I'II find it after lunch."

"Are you going to tell us what's going on?" asked mom knowing full well what my response was set to be.

* * * * *

Rummaging through numerous unlabelled boxes in the attic I stumbled across my college yearbooks. Allowing myself to be consumed by the distraction nostalgia brings I sat down on the stale smelling musty laden rough sawn wooden floor with my hands at the ready to peruse the pages of my history. I inhaled deeply before glancing at the first page looking forward to taking my impromptu journey back to the space where life was seemingly less complex than it is now.

The page held the signatures of the students; some whom I still considered friends and others were classmates of the year in question. My eyes gleamed over the names most of which were apportioned fragmented memories within a kaleidoscope of formative years gone by. I didn't give my allotted educational experiences a second thought post graduation. My personality never lent itself towards participating in alumnus activities let alone being present for the numerous reunions held across the years. When my time had been served and my degrees issued, I simply walked away to focus on developing a yet to be determined career.

Thumbing through the pages a beautiful smile caught my eye. I returned triggering a surprise delight to my memory vault. It was a picture of my besties and I adorned in our lab coats about to embark on the Coca Cola Mentos experiment. The caption to the image even referred to our porn star names, Peppy Threadbow, Sam

Esplanade and Fluffy Tallintyre. My heart was warmed with joy. The three of us had so many good times together across the years. It made me wonder how they, and Precious Clint were doing. I would never admit it directly to them, but I did miss them.

A little over an hour had passed while the pins and needles tingled gently up to both my legs as a warning, my circulation was compromised. I closed the last of the books and returned them to the pile then attempted to stand up.

"Are you almost finished up there?"

"Not quite mom, I got a little distracted. Do you have any idea where my notes from college are?"

"They are in the box labeled Harpers notes. It should be close to the back wall near the window."

"Great, I'll be down in a minute."

My legs felt like they were made of jello with cupcake sprinkles flowing through my veins. It is a pleasurable pain that although uncomfortable always seemed to make me chuckle. I managed to shuffle between the piles of storage to manoeuver my way toward the window. The third box in the stack was clearly labeled *Harpers notes*. I pulled the other two aside and lifted the one I needed, placing it on the floor to my left. This box contained all of my key obiter dicta taken while executing my psychiatry observation outplacement in college.

"There you are," said mom as I entered the kitchen.

"Sorry, I got side tracked when I found some of my old year books."

She smiled.

"What?"

"Nothing, I'm just happy to see you."

"I'm happy to see you too. You know you really need

to find a way to get some air circulating up there. The rise of the heat from the house is creating a funky smell in the attic."

"I've told your father that he needs to look at it." She paused for a moment and released a sigh, "I wish you would stay here with us for a while. You always seem to be on the move."

"Mom, I'm here now. Let's enjoy the time we have rather than waste it stressing about the time we don't spend together. It's a redundant exercise."

"You're too clever for your own good. Offering a rational position to deflect from dealing with the emotions presented. You get that from your father."

I placed the box on the bench before wrapping my arms around her for a hug. "I know."

"Can I make you a cup of tea?"

"I'd love one, thanks."

Mom walked around the island bench to fill the kettle with water while I took a seat.

"Where's dad?"

"He said he was taking Huckleberry for a walk but I know that is just his excuse to sneak out and get something else to eat." She said shaking her head.

"Is his cholesterol really that bad?"

"The doctors are saying he is in a high risk factor for heart disease."

"Doctors?"

"Yes, we went for our annual check up and the new GP suggested some additional tests. When we got the results back there was an alarming concern about your father's cholesterol levels so we were referred to a specialist to get some more tests done. They wanted to put him on an experimental drug program to get his cholesterol down immediately but he wouldn't have a bar of it. He told them, he is no lab rat."

My gut churned as she told me this. "Do you know the name of the drug trial?"

"No, I didn't write it down but I can find out for you. It would be great if you could talk to him Harps and make him reconsider. I'm so worried about him."

"What happened to your old GP? I asked. "He has been working there for as long as I can remember."

"I'm not sure, no explanation was provided. It was like he just disappeared," Mom said shrugging her shoulders.

"Hmm, do you have a copy of the test results?"

"No, I wanted to get them but the GP said it wasn't his standard practice to release copies. He just wrote down the core results on this piece of paper, here." Mom passed across the information.

"Its funny, stereo typically doctor's shorthand writing is notoriously hard to read. Yet, this looks to be written by a layman. Is he young?"

"He is. What are you thinking Harper?"

"Nothing much, just a hunch. Leave it with me."

Mom partially rolled her eyes and released a sigh as she began to prepare the tea. "You always leave me hanging. Why do you do that?"

"Tell me something, was I born late or earlier than predicted?"

Mom stopped straining the tea and lifted her head to look at me. "That's a rather random question."

I burst out laughing, "I guess it is."

"You were born five days after the date my obstetrician predicted. Why?"

I looked at mom then hesitated. Knowing the way,

she incessantly worried about my father, brother and I, there was no desire for me to give her justification to sustain the concerns that consumed her mind.

"Harper, you need to tell me or I won't ever sleep again," she barked then stomped her foot in protest.

"I'll tell you on the proviso that you don't add this to your already mammoth collection of concerns."

"Okay, I'll try."

"You have to do better than try."

"I'll trrryyyy, now tell me." She insisted, stomping her foot again.

I took a deep breath and shook my head. "I told you I had adopted Huckleberry. Technically this is the truth, however the way he came to me are the details that link to my curiosity about my birth date."

I watched Mom shuffle her feet and unconsciously lean forward on the bench as though to prepare for it to support her, "Go on."

"Yesterday Huckleberry was left at my doorstep with a note that said: 'Everyone needs a friend they can depend on. Happy Birthday Harper from me to you.'

Mom turned a ghastly shade of pale green as her eyes widened.

"Are you okay? You look like you have seen a ghost."

She cupped her hands and shook her head taking a couple of steps back while saying, "No, no, no, no, no, no, no, no. I thought it was over. This year I thought it was finally over."

"What are you talking about?"

She burst into tears as I rushed across to console her. I could feel her body shaking. Whatever was upsetting her caused genuine fright. I quietly held her securely in my arms while she released deep sobs. Mom seldom cried.

With sadness in her voice between tiny gasps for air she whimpered, "Come, there is something I think I need to show you."

I followed her back up the attic stairs where she switched on the light and headed toward a singular metal box sitting on a bookshelf shrouded in dust. She took the tiny key from around her neck off and placed it into the lock to release the clasp. I had always wondered what that key she seemed to guard, opened.

Peering inside I could see a clump of letters held together with twine. Mom carefully lifted them out of the container and placed them in my hands.

"These are all for you. Every year on the same day, you receive a card delivered from an anonymous person. Yesterday was the first time since the year you were born that nothing had arrived. I thought it was a sign that it was over."

I paused to feel the gentle hum resonating from the letters. They vibrated in my hands evoking a sense of familiarity, bringing me welcomed comfort. I pressed them against my chest and closed my eyes as my heart responded with a series of thuds. The only word brought to bear was 'home.'

"Harper, this person whomever it is has been stalking you since you were a child. Its an obsessed person who the police suspected might have delusions that you are their progeny."

"The police? What do you mean 'their' child? I don't understand?"

"Of course I got the police involved. I received the first card addressed to you on the 1st of May. I thought nothing of it given it only said *From me to you, happy birthday.* Sure it was a bit strange but for some reason it didn't really bother me. By the third year, I questioned the reasoning behind the cards, but still I chose to let it be. On the fifth year, alarm bells went off when I received the card addressed to you. We had only just moved to a new neighborhood and hadn't updated our information anywhere. Your grandparents didn't even know the address. How could this person have known without keeping a watchful eye?"

"What did the police say?"

"They couldn't find a way to trace the letter and the suspicions were that it was hand delivered. This as you could imagine, petrified me. The suggested theory was that there may have been a person in the hospital when you were born who had lost a child and for some reason attached themselves to the notion of you being theirs. This would explain the variance in their idea of the date of birth. I was terrified that whomever it was had notions of kidnapping you."

"Wow, does dad know?"

"Of course Harps. He was the one who hired a private detective when the police decided there was nothing else they could do."

"Jesus, this gets better and better. What did the private detective find out?"

"Nothing. That's just it. Every year a card gets delivered without anyone to witness its arrival. The detective made arrangements for a full private detail to be issued three nights ahead of the scheduled delivery. All the streets were monitored on both sides. There wasn't a single person or vehicle, which entered or left that wasn't accounted for, yet the card was still positioned in the same way on the doorstep, leaning up against the door as it has been from the year you were born. We don't know how it's done, only that it always is."

"Why haven't you told me before now?"

"There are two reasons. My primary driver was to keep you safe from whomever it is doing this. I believed they weren't aware that you were no longer living at home because the letters have always been addressed to you but delivered to us. I think I was also partially still trying to protect you from the need to solve this mystery. I felt if you knew you might start hunting around to decipher a puzzle that didn't want to be solved. I know what you are like when it comes to needing to get the answers to the questions posed before you. This is where I see a lot of me in you, and it scares me. I might have been relentless at times in finding the truth, but you are fearless, stupidly so. I didn't want to tempt you to go on some blind quest."

I pursed my lips as a wry smile betrayed my thoughts of agreement. "Can I assume that the bottom of the pile is the first card and the rest ascend from there?"

"You can," she said with a sigh. "Let's go down stairs. I'll make us a fresh cup of tea."

"Sure, lets do that."

We re-entered the kitchen. Mom resumed making the tea, and I sat back on the bar stool placing the pile of cards on the bench. My heart was racing as I felt the urge to read them all at once. Calmly I untied the bow and flipped the pile upside down so I could begin in the order that they were received.

Mom glanced across intermittently to watch for my reaction.

The cover of the card was engraved with a picture depicting Egyptian mythological characters. I ran my fingers across its surface and felt compelled to smile. "Save me the research time and tell me what they represent. I know you would have looked them up. Who are they?"

"The woman standing to the left is Maat the goddess of truth and justice and to the right is Ammit who is known as a devourer."

"A devourer of what precisely?"

"She is the eater of hearts."

"Oh, I would never have guessed that is a female. It looks like a human hybrid of some kind."

"She is a female demon who is composed of the manifestation of part lion, crocodile and hippopotamus. The mythology indicates that Ammit was set to eat the hearts of the ones found to be lacking purity."

"How was it measured?"

"The heart would be weighted against Maat's ostrich feather, which represented her truth. If the heart failed the test Ammit would consume the heart, which denied the soul any chance of resurrection or immortality."

"Interesting," I said reaching for the next card in line.

Mom lurched across the bench placing her hand on the pile, "They all say the same thing Harps. Year after year identical picture and words inside the card are present. Now that you have seen one you have seen them all."

I flipped the card in my hand open, "Read it to me please."

Mom didn't look at it, she just responded, "from me to you, happy birthday."

I paused for a moment looking at her hand which was still covering the pile. "Why did you keep them?" I asked.

"I honestly don't know. It's such a curiosity that I found myself drawn to saving them yet I was petrified of what they might represent."

"Mom, you didn't just keep them, you hid them under lock and key. I remember as a child when I asked you about the key around your neck you would say it was guarding a secret."

"Yes, you were always fascinated by the key and I often wondered if it was the key or the contents it unlocked that you subconsciously gravitated towards."

I removed her hand from the pile and lifted them to my chest, "I'm glad you kept them. These are far more important to me than you could possibly know. I promise you there is nothing to fear. Only good will is provided by the gesture of these cards."

"Are you sure Harps?"

"I am."

"Were back," said dad with a musical tone, wide grin and Huckleberry trotting along side.

"How was the ice cream parlor?" I asked.

Dad feigned a scowl, "What do you mean? Huckleberry and I went to the park."

I stood up, walked across and looked into his eyes. "Yes, you definitely went to the park. This is true, however you got ice-cream on the way. I am correct and I not?"

He semi held his breath momentarily deciding whether he should try to get away with telling a white lie and then thought better of it. Releasing his breath with a big sigh he said, "Dammit Beanie Bear, how do you do that?"

"I might have suggested that you snuck out for dessert," said mom chuckling.

"Nope it wasn't that."

"How did you know then?" He asked with a sulky tone.

I poked him in the ribs, "Huckleberry has some evidence smeared across the side of his face and drips on his chest of something sticky. Can I assume it is raspberry swirl ice-cream? Hmmm"

Dad picked up Huckleberry to inspect him. "Double damn it, I thought I was being so clever. You gave us up Huckster."

"Huckster?"

"Yep, we are besties now, although he is on notice given his untidy eating habits."

We all laughed as Huckleberry released a series of barks. Using his little legs, he pulsed forward in an attempt to get close enough to lick dads face. They truly had become fast friends.

"Come dad, help me pack this stuff into the boot of my car."

"You're leaving? You haven't even drunk your tea yet." Said mom with a pout.

"I know but I just realized I need to be somewhere and I think dad needs to come with me." I said giving her a wink.

"Oh, yeah, that thing you said you needed to do. Okay. Sure I forgot about that."

"Darling you are no better than me at lying." He said bursting out into laughter. "You have no clue what she is talking about."

"He's got you figured out mom. I'll have him back in no time, I promise."

"Okay Harps. It was great to see you. Don't make it so long between visits, please."

"I'll trrrryyyy my best," I said teasingly. "Bye mom." I gave her a kiss and then collected the letters from the bench before heading off toward the front door. Dad followed suit with my box of college notes while Huckleberry bounced along proudly by his side.

As we approached the car dad asked, "Where are we going Beanie Bear?"

I shook my head, "You'll know soon enough. Get in."

Latent

Huckleberry immediately nestled in his bed upon arriving home. I placed the box, and my bag filled to the brim with the cards on the coffee table then ran to the bathroom to relieve myself. Once I got changed into my jimjams and made myself a cup of tea I nestled into the sofa to begin to read. I was looking forward to this.

I reopened the initial card and stared at the picture until the rest of my peripheral vision distorted to black. I sunk into the imagery tracing the gold etching, which outlined the details of each character's frame. I knew very little about Egyptology but now understood why my mom had always held an interest in it. There was no doubt in my mind that she was trying to figure out the reasoning behind the repetition of the picture.

I released a sigh as I smiled when I began to read the card.

I trust my words fill your senses with warmth unlike any other. I missed having you caress the core of my soul as you read my scriptures Harper. Ensure you are in receipt of all thirty-four envelopes. Heed my instruction, read them in the order they were given. Each one post your tenth birthday contains the pages of details I have been destined to impart and you to read. I assume if you are reading this annotation that Huckleberry has been presented to you. He is the trigger for the release of this series of communiqué. If by chance you have stumbled upon these cards ahead of time, then know that he will be channeled into this life and gifted to you on the 35th year.

Yes, is the answer to the question you pose. He is indeed one in the same. A different vessel set to host but one in the same soul. It was his desire to reincarnate in this form and in this life plane to assist you through the arduous tasks set before you. We are all universally interconnected. Huckleberry feels his debt is best served by gifting this lifetime directly to you. During your journey, he will see the things you will not. There are key reasons why your future is set with a level of intentional blindness. It is safer for you to travel your course this way. We all must occasionally place our faith in a friend. There are times you will be faced with a reality none would wish upon their worst of enemies. I hold no doubt you will not want to accept what is presented, yet to travel forward on the chosen path, you have to resign yourself to the truth. In this life, there is much to achieve and for you an insurmountable amount of sacrifice required. I believe in you. I believe in us.

From me to you, happy birthday.

I re-read the words again and closed my eyes afterwards. In my mind, I said *'I can hear your voice when I read. I miss you.'* As a tear silently rolled down my face Huckleberry leapt out of his bed, onto the sofa scooping it up before it fell off the edge of my chin. He wagged his little tail and looked into my eyes as he released a couple of small barks.

"Thank you." I said to him.

He licked the length of my cheek then twirled in a circle three times clockwise before settling into a coiled ball on my chest. He dropped his head and closed his eyes to rest.

I watched the rise and fall of his torso as he took in his breaths and wondered what karmic debt he was required to repay. In the story of the Illuminarium, Huckleberry was tortured by psychotic sycophants before he was found and freed by York. The tale depicted thereafter indicated good people who loved him, surrounded him, and he loved them in return. Why would he choose this life, me, to be the one he repays for such kindness? Perhaps there are other lives in which he was not so fortunate, and it held a burden to cause the Saint to become a sinner. That could account for another angle for a debt to be repaid. The curiosity to me was two fold, why choose me and why was he allowed to choose at all? I instinctually felt that reincarnation and karmic debt are the gossamer threads interwoven between souls. Hence, any debt to be repaid would be relative to the link in the thread being somehow connected.

All I knew for certain was the realization that the further I delved into the labyrinth more questions surfaced than answers.

I placed the card back in the envelope and reached for the next in line.

Do we choose to see what we want to see or is it that we see only what we need to see at the time of witness? Perception and understanding are an untameable beast in a world where the truth attempts to break itself free from the tyranny of lies veiled to mislead wisdom's path.

From me to you, happy birthday.

Wow, this is a bit deep for a two-year olds birthday card I said to myself with a chuckle. The philosophical question posed, to me, is a Tao variant thought proposition on a simple common experience in life. We don't know what we don't know and what we think we know eventually reveals it self to have been a blinded state of we don't know what we don't know.

I understood that there was a clear reasoning behind what was written in the cards. I just wished this time that the answers would be given simply rather than compelling me to figure it all out. It is exhausting to have to be in a perpetual state of heightened analysis and assessment, especially knowing that most of what I conclude will be proven to be off course or wrong. This message is either a slap in the face by stating the obvious or a challenge to find a way to tame the untameable beast. For now, I am just choosing to read.

I opened the third card.

To know everything would not be befitting for a life designed to be filled with wonder and discovery.
From me to you, happy birthday.

A life designed to be filled with wonder and discovery. I do like the sound of that. The absence of adventure and the joy of surprise would leave me personally feeling lacking. I guess from this point of view alone I am pleased that my ability to retrieve the wealth of information my mind retains from the river of knowledge is tempered.

They watched you from the beginning of time. Not able to prevent your existence, they studied you, interacted with you, where possible they have recorded your every move to create an assessment of who you have been and who you are. Tell me Harper, is this their advantage or, unbeknown to them, their greatest handicap?

From me to you, happy birthday.

I'm predictably unpredictable. I see it as my greatest strength. Not even I know what I am about to do at times. I just trust the course of action I lean towards is right in the moment. Even still I find it is hard for me not to become consumed by the intrinsically frustrating notion that my privacy has been righteously violated as this suggests across my lifetimes. I want them to pay dearly for their insolence. The indicator of the term 'where possible' holds a curiosity for me. This alludes to there being places where they can't watch, study and or record me. If I knew where this place or places are, then I could use it to further my advantage. I must find the spaces where I lead that they cannot follow. Regardless this has provided me with a great idea.

I opened the fifth card.

Isolation, withdrawal, containment is believed to be their strongest allies. Develop these into a single strength.

From me to you, happy birthday.

Hmm, it would be easy to assume the literal definition of the words and associate them to the traditional default descriptions. Isolation is all about being alone, yes, but what most people wouldn't immediately consider is that a person can be isolated in the presence of many. If I'm surrounded by a multitude of watchers then I am still alone, contained within the perception of company. Knowing this and having the ability to identify whom the watchers are, naturally causes me to want to withdraw from the environment. I'm going to have to ponder the concept of containment more deeply. I don't see how they can contain me, I would have to yield, concede my will to this. A price so high I am unable to pay, for the cost I know if far greater than myself. I guess kidnapping and being held against my will could also be a consideration.

Isolation, withdrawal and containment are believed to be their only allies. This holds to my advantage and gives valor to my choice maiden move in my game of silent wars. Which reminds me, I stuck my hand in the bag and rummaged around until I found the copy of Sanctorum Avow, my father kindly left for me to read. I flipped to where he used the raven's feather as a marker. The write up began on the third page with an impressive full two page spread devoted to the growing underground conspiracy theory regarding the illegal chemical trials on humans.

Chemical Warfare — Guinea pigs 'r' us

Recently, we received an anonymous tip about the alleged collective government bodies involvement in bypassing safety protocols to expedite the receipt of approvals for immediate human trials of a largely untested synthesized chemical labeled **eXileanon**. The underlying urgency for the release was driven by concerns that the

spread of the new disease Euphoric
Death could become pandemic. The
informant's claim is that there is
a sub component within eXileanon
consisting of an unauthorized
chemical called **Anathema**, which has
already been leeched for decades
into our systems by piggybacking
its introduction, utilizing the
standardized vaccine issuance
channels to children globally. In
theory, this indicates that anyone
who has had a commercial inoculation
of any sort has been, for want of a
better word, infected with anathema.

The first paragraph already has me smiling. I needed
to create a name for the drug and decided to use the
word anathema as a 'fuck you' to the interferons. The
dictionary definition of anathema is 'a person or thing
detested or loathed'. It was my way of telling them that
I absolutely loath all that they are doing and detest
what they stand for. The fact that the writer described
the leeching of this chemical into people's bodies
as, us being infected is stellar. We have indeed been
contaminated by these spineless weasels who seek power
while they pathetically remain hidden from the world. I
want the interferons to feel what it is like to be exposed
and hunted.

The team at Sanctorum Avow gets a
multitude of reports of a similar
fantastical nature daily, but none

have provided a foundation of evidence to support the allegations in a somewhat irrevocable factual manner, until this one. The confidential Global Health Outreach Program (GHOP) emails, top secret reports and transcripts of illegally taped phone conversations which were disclosed in the previous issue of our magazine remains unchallenged. Any governing body worth a pinch of salt would be set to immediately deny the authenticity of such evidence. We had our lawyers on standby expecting to receive an intervention order demanding Sanctorum Avow cease any further discussion on the topic. Instead, there was silence.

I knew before I launched into releasing the information that my best strategy was to leverage off the fact that the interferons want to remain a clandestine society. This is why I chose to single out GHOP as my first target. It's not that I thought they were guilty of anything I could prove, however, I had to utilize a scenario which supported the plausibility of my story about anathema. I falsified all the GHOP documents, then supplied them to Sanctorum Avow along with some phone tap recordings I had a hacking for hire crew obtain. My focus is set on stirring the hornet's nest to observe who reacted and who skulked away. When the company chose to remain silent, I added pressure by delivering a falsified threatening message under the guise of representing GHOP, out to the media channels that were now carrying the story. In my mind, the only way forward was to try to play the interferons and their alliances off by using their own game. It was risky but at the time I saw no other choice.

A short while after the dust settled from the publishing of the first article, we began to experience a threatening variant of corporate bullying that had our senses alarmed to the plausibility of the anon's tip. The open threats delivered to us, and other media crew supported the theory that we may have stumbled upon what I suspect is only the prelude to a nightmare that is yet to be unveiled. The GHOP's narcissistic domination tactics stating there would be consequences to the continuance of such discussions or investigations pertaining to anathema, initially held no bearing for us. It was an open threat, we had thrusted our way by many companies before. The cease and desist statements were received by Sanctorum Avow with such a frequency that we placed it as a measure of our success in pushing the right buttons on any given topic. Initially, we considered it

> business as usual, that is until a
> plethora of inexplicable anomalies
> started to occur. Our staff reported
> suspicions of being followed; some
> confirmed their homes had been
> compromised with the detection of
> illegal surveillance and listening
> devices found. Even our heavily
> encrypted network was hacked
> with the perpetrators specifically
> targeting access to our files marked
> with references on eXileanon,
> anathema and GHOP.

I'll admit the Interferons and their puppets threw me out of kilter when they chose not to refute the legitimacy of the documents. I wasn't expecting this, in fact I was prepared for an onslaught of retaliation. Their reaction here was key, they chose to state there would be consequences to the continuance of such discussions, it seemed so weak, almost pathetic. It just made me want to go harder at them. I knew that the staff would be feeling on edge because my communications with them always suggested that they should be on the look out for strange behavior. I created subliminal triggers that heightened their awareness of their surroundings so the interferons couldn't easily have their minions hidden in the shadows.

> If this doesn't scare, you already
> sit down and be prepared to be
> petrified. Anon had warned this would
> be a possible approach and suggested
> that we implement a controlled

emergency protocol prior to the release of the publication. The condition applied to the execution of the protocol was only the staff, which were confirmed as non vaccinated could be privy to the instructions and must ensure that the implementation of the protocol was subject to confidentiality. Added to this anon had provided the non infected team which included myself with a tool that could be used to assist in identifying markers for carriers whose anathema strain had become unbeknownst to them, activated.

What I witnessed will give me cause to lay awake at night for the remainder of my days. I from first hand experience can confirm staff, which have been working in Sanctorum Avow, some of whom are long standing personal friends altered in behavior within hours of the media frenzy taking hold. The others and myself used the tool provided by anon to verify what we had been asked to look for as the marker of anathema being activated. We all agreed that we felt like we were trapped within a scene straight out of an apocalyptic horror film as we noted

> 100% of the staff who had been
> vaccinated all presented with the
> mysterious mark and were completely
> unaware.

Reading this gave me flashbacks to when I first saw the mark on the girl at the hotel front counter, Marla. I had no idea that the discovery of this would lead me to a new level of consciousness about the world I live in. The comparison to an apocalyptic horror film resonated with me. Walking out of the Hipster store with my ridiculous ravers on, to be confronted by countless people bearing a mark in their left ear had me feeling truly alone. I am yet to identify the meaning of the symbol as I have failed to find anything like it. I'm certain it is a merger of a hieroglyph, satanic symbol, and something else. I'm secretly hoping this article will cause people to go on the hunt for its meaning and do some of the work for me.

> The opening words written by Anon
> *"Welcome to the silent wars, where
> the truth realigns you to a reality
> we all live but were never meant to
> know exists,"* now held me in a state
> of awakening to the fact that a
> large portion of what we have built
> our lives upon may be a solidified
> foundation of lies.
>
> The picture on the left is a style
> range of the party goer's glasses
> known as ravers. Admittedly they
> look ridiculous but it is what you

need to use to identify the marker, which only appears typically on the inside of the person's ear when activated. It still isn't known how the chemical is triggered to shift from its dormant state nor do we have access to any information, which conclusively indicates what the full impacts are of the activated state. Anon simply explained it as a channel receptor for subliminal messaging communication to be absorbed more readily so the host is receiving and executing instructions without realizing they are being manipulated to do so. Anon suggested it was initially designed to infect the enemy and then have them triggered to turn on each other thus reducing the need to fund expensive warfare and manpower to the cause. Anon further stated, the government and secret agencies convened to look at how this could be used in other applications and suggests this is what led to it being merged into infant vaccinations.

Who drove the decision to distribute the strain globally to a majority of the populous is something we would all like to know? Anon has confirmed

that a covert team are in the
process of developing a deactivator,
which will be made available for all
in due course. In the meantime, we
urge you to buy some ravers and to
be aware that if you or your loved
ones bear the mark, then you are
a target for heightened subliminal
messaging absorption. We need to
support each other through this.
Turn off your televisions, switch off
your radios, limit your activities
on the internet by staying away
from social media where advertising
promotions can be flashed on
your screen and boycott reading
magazines. These are the confirmed
channels they have been seen to be
using.

This is great. I need people to protect one another
from being subconsciously manipulated by the
interferons. I'm so worried that there will be wide
spread panic where people start ostracizing each other
for bearing the mark when now is the time to begin
the journey towards uniting humanity. Releasing the
information on anathema is about knowledge, awareness
and empowerment. Reclaiming our free will is the only
way we stand a chance to win.

We urge you to go and get some
ravers, pay attention to your
surroundings and look out for one
another. We may not know precisely

whom we are fighting or what we are
fighting, but I do know it is time to
fight.

Anon, on behalf of us all I want
to thank you for everything that you
have done and are proposing to do.
You are not alone. This, I promise
you, will no longer be a silent war.

A shiver ran up and down my spine as I read the
last sentence. The article was far better than I had
expected it to be. I'm not proud of the fact that I had to
manipulate people in order to gain a foothold advantage.
In essence, I recognized to some degree I am no better
than the interferons themselves. We were both leveraging
off the human spirit to manipulate our environments
for a stronger position. The only difference being my
intentions are set to empower people to become aligned
to the strength within themselves while the interferon's
motives are driven by their insatiable obsession to squash
the human spirit in order to gain power over them.

I sat up, grabbed the remote and switched on the
television to the 24hr global news channel. There it was
on the screen, anathema, anathema, anathema listed
over all the major networks across a range of countries.
Reports, interviews, protests, banner updates confirming
that ravers have sold out worldwide in under twelve hours
since the announcements were made, this was better than
I hoped for as a start. The crucial kick off to the first part
of my plan was well and truly underway.

I switched off the television and headed to the
kitchen to make myself another cup of tea. It was

amusing to imagine the look on the faces of the interferons when the media latched onto the story. Thanks to the support of the veritable smorgasbord of underground networks that Liam put me in contact with, I was able to pre-emptively provide information suggesting what was coming. The premise being that when news about anathema hit the media, key people had already heard whispers and were therefore, more inclined to feel there was validity to what was written. My hopes then fell upon trigger fingers to piggy back thoughts causing a viral reach into a vast social media prowess. It was a suggestive, semi-directed, multi-layered spruik across the network. This improved the chances of the news truly going viral within minutes of Sanctorum Avow releasing the online version of their paper. There was a risk I took by leaking the information, as I was not able to affect a stranglehold on how people chose to utilize the information. That's why the synchronicity of the leaks to the release of the article series were crucial. Timing is everything. I also knew it gave the interferons a heads up that something was coming their way.

The best part about this whole plan was the fact that I leveraged off the truth and orchestrated the rest. I am hoping the interferons would have looked up the definition of anathema. I wanted a word not readily utilized within the English language to be the tag name of the drug while having it indicate a message of my thoughts on them as an entity. A perfect silently masked message from me to them now adopted by the world as a reminder that their actions will not go unpunished.

It was curious that the GHOP didn't call out that the information previously published by Sanctorum Avow was falsified. I intentionally created the material to encourage their voice of protest with a hope to cause a purpose for further investigation. The artefacts although visually authentic were most definitely not genuine. The fact that they chose not to call out or have anyone step forward to lead a charge means something. I don't know what yet, but I know I have to find a way to understand why their move wasn't as predictable as I was expecting it to be.

Hacking into the Sanctorum Avow computer network was also a necessary evil on my part. I know the interferon's have at their disposal long standing watchers online who were no doubt already using some ninja hacking devices to seamlessly monitor and download information undetected. This is why I had a group of half-baked hackers set off to trip the alarms, creating a clear auditable infiltration trail leading to a dead end.

The staff being followed was a combination of simple subliminal suggestions that I had placed in my disclosure pack to the team together with a few street performers hired to execute certain behaviors that would be seen by any of the staff who were in transit on their way home from the office. The interferons would have them tailed, but this added action implemented by me allowed for the workers to feel that they were being watched. The paranoia places them in a heightened state of awareness, which therefore increased the likelihood of the interferon's stealth tails being identified or at the very least compromised. They would no longer have the luxury of oblivion on their side. I wanted them to know what it feels like to be invaded and assaulted at all levels, hence I used their tactics against them. Now they had no way of containing the situation.

I slapped my hand down on the kitchen bench as the

words flashed through my mind. *'Isolation, withdrawal, containment is believed to be their strongest allies. Develop these into a single strength.'* Of course the statement in the card isn't about me per say, this is about them. <u>Isolation,</u> no one knows they exist. <u>Withdrawal,</u> never reacting to circumstance or inviting unwanted attention. <u>Containment,</u> historically they mastered the control over any situation with ease through the manipulation and use of watchers. Now that the watchers are watching each other completely aware of 'something' happening, there is no ability to contain it.

Turning to the fridge I grabbed the water-soluble marker from the top of the bench and wrote four words: isolation, withdrawal, containment, strength. They were now there, as a reminder of what my future strategies should continually embrace.

I looked toward the sofa and wondered if I should continue reading or whether it was time to migrate to my bedroom. My mind was hyper stimulated, but my body was exhausted. I took a couple of quick sips of the piping hot tea before tossing the rest down the drain. As much as I held a hankering to finish the beverage, I didn't want the trade off associated with drinking before bed. That is, to constantly get up to relieve myself. I scooped the next five letters in my hand and took them to my bedroom while Huckleberry remained on the sofa fast asleep.

Tucked in my bed, nestled against the overabundance of pillows, I piled the cards on top of my duvet. Looking up at the stars now glimmering in the dark I felt blessed to have the support of the mystery person who as it appears has been by my side since the beginning of my entry to this lifetime, possibly longer. It was clear from all the effort taken that there is a profound connection, which is founded by love. I could feel it from the moment, I laid hands on Illuminarium. A sense of longing and familiarity resonates from all the writing, making me beam with pride. I've been present to a growing sense of how much I love myself since this all began.

I opened the sixth card.

Laughter is the best medicine and it also pisses off the enemy. Never loose sight of your genuine smile.

From me to you, happy birthday.

The envelope from the seventh card seemed to be more worn on the edges than the other cards I had opened so far.

Control is an illusion. It is advantageous to feed their need to lull them into a false sense of security. Watch the puppeteers feast in their false bounty of manipulation using their leverage of trias. They are heaven's keys bound.

The reality does not alter but perception shifts when you strike to tend to the needful once in a blue bird moon.

Free will is always the true governor of thy soul.

From me to you, happy birthday.

PS: The phases of a blue bird moon hold a unique frequency for you.

There is a fable not well known which refers to the telling of the significance of what is mentioned here in regard to a blue bird moon. I'm not familiar enough with the content. I will have to look it up when I am spared a moment. I'm unsure if the reference here is supposed to be metaphorical in regard to striking at the right time or whether the literal is applicable.

I pondered the use of the word trias meaning three

in Latin. It is traditionally set as a representation of the triad, which is symbolised by the triangle. There are three points to the triangle. The triad in current terms is associated to organized crime. This message would suggest that the interferons held access to the utilisation of established corrupt organizations or at the very least hold associations to them. I see the interferons as the puppeteers, their false bounty would be them believing they have 'control.' The spiritual guides, Bahrain and Zivah both confirmed there are seven interferons so the relationship to the trias (number three) would be what?

The fifth card stipulated 'Isolation, withdrawal, containment is believed to be their strongest allies.' These seem to be noted as the three key strategies for the masking and execution of their manipulation. Could it be that this is applied to the touch points of the keys of heaven? The Holy See coat of arms provides a depiction of two keys crossed and bound. The key made of gold represents the power of the kingdom of heaven whereas the silver key is the spiritual ruling of earth channeled through the papacy or from my perspective human form. The rope binds the two keys in a position providing a bond between the two planes, heaven and earth. Holy See itself is akin to holy chair or seat. It is a position of power. Is this suggesting that the interferons, and the trias are bound or worse that they have masked influence over the heavens?

The enormity of what appeared to be revealed from this card alone was hard to fathom. My eyes kept gravitating to the tattered sides of the envelope. I wonder why this card was removed enough times to compromise the structure of its edges when no one other than me, I assume holds the visual capability to read the contents.

The eighth card was sealed. This could indicate it took my mom seven years before she decided there was no point in opening the cards. Yet, she kept them. It is a testament to the way she holds true to her primal instinct. Despite not understanding the purpose of them, she still recognized on some level that they were of importance. I carefully opened the envelope and removed the card.

Don't be fooled by their charms and graces. Know what it is you hunger to strive for, the entitlement to love and be loved in return. It is impossible to lose your way if you are always honest with your heart.

From me to you, happy birthday.

I looked at those words and felt a desire to shut down my thoughts. Internally, I always knew the one I sought was not here in the flesh with me. This life cycle was mine alone to bear. It is this undeniable feeling of aloneness that caused me a sense of inexplicable sadness. I always presented an air of nonchalance about the absence of love in my life yet internally I was at times, when I allowed, completely gut wrenched with an ache that brought me to my knees wanting to silently chant for a quick death, so I may meet with my one again.

The dialogue I had with Vernon Wreath all those years ago, where he razzed me in regard to how I felt inside, was a silent trigger. I knew what I associated to his conjecture related to my deep sorrow for the absence of the love of my lifetimes. I'm not certain whether he knew what it was precisely which drove me to struggle to breathe but he most certainly knew I was prone to psychologically visiting a space where I felt lost.

I needed a distraction from this thought train to divert

from my potential spiral down. I wasn't expecting to have such a strong reaction to the words but I knew my sadness loomed. Slowly, I reached for the ninth and final card for the night. This too had been left intact, so I assumed from here on the remainder of the cards were mine to open.

You live in this life protected by the realms of both good and evil for there is a mutuality in cost associated to your failure to complete all that is destined to be mastered. United they stand to ensure you are enabled for success for influence and sway to either side. This is not extended to any other. Yes, you hold freedoms will to reign but the cause and effect from actions taken may not go untainted. Careful where you choose to tread and whom you target to break. Some hold no concern for life and will aim to temper you by readily punishing others. Money is no object, and control is the ultimate desire. No price for either side is too high to pay.

War forces the reaction to sacrifice. This is indeed the greatest battle of the ages, prepare for war.

From me to you, happy birthday.

I was none too pleased to read this card either. I recognized when I held my session with Bahrain and Zivah that my lifetime holds its greatest currency by being neutral. I'm teetering on an invisible equator, swaying to neither side with any set permanence, at least not right now. This was a clear request to be mindful that there is a cost associated to all that I choose to do. Uncle Ben in the Spiderman series said it best, 'With great power comes great responsibility.' My lot in life may not have been set to become a superhero but the sentiment held true regardless. I need to exercise caution on how I execute my moves in the silent wars to minimize casualties. It is hard to predict a person's reaction in the absence of knowing them personally. I will need to establish a way to benchmark the interferon's patterns of behavior so I can better predict their actions. From what I have seen so far, I know I cannot afford to underestimate them.

I returned the card back in its envelope, collected the rest of the pile and placed them on the bedside table before switching the light off. My eyes were drooping as my body stilled in position ready to follow suit. Thankfully, all the stimulus of the day held my mind at a point where it beckoned me to shut down. It was time to get some well-earned sleep. The morning would be here soon enough with a full day of reading ahead.

Manifesto

My mind was in a swirl of jumbled thoughts trapped under the mutli-colored hue of clouds raining numbers in one's, zero's and letters, with only some forming words. *'Illusion, control, truth, fight, flight, balance,'* were repeated the most. A string of zero's and one's fell vertically down to the ground and then skulked to form a swelling pool across the floor before reforming into a connection of lines surging upward. It swayed in a wave that made them look like a nest of wriggling worms climbing against the grain. They appeared to repel each other, causing their paths to cross with the falling letters. The nudges merged the letters into one another to produce words. It felt as though everything was in competition, and nothing was assured. Stepping back to see the landscape from a wider angle I realized there was once an assumption on my part of a certain synergy of alignment to the flow when in actuality, there was none. The struggle is real for each element, and the movements are random adding to the complexity of predictable behavior theory being applied. Could this complex messaging be a reinforcement of the dangers in making assumptions or becoming complacent? Every action has an equal to or greater reaction due to interconnection.

My head hurt from trying to make sense of it all. There was this innate whimpering in the background that made me feel like I was being called to consciousness. As I slowly opened my eyes, I could hear the whimpering clearer. It was Huckleberry at the bottom of the stairs. He had not mastered the art of how to climb them yet. I smiled. My bundle of cuteness was calling out for me to fetch him. Only days into being in my life, and he was already entrenched in my every beat, as though he had always been.

I took a moment to extend my arms and legs for a welcomed stretch releasing an unplanned squeal as the blood rushed to my extremities. Huckleberry started to bark as if to call out, 'helloooooo, helloooooo, you're awake, helloooo.' I laughed as I jumped out of bed, placing some slippers on before descending down the staircase. My heart skipped a beat when I saw the excitement travel the course of his body. He released a high-pitched yelp and spun in circles. I couldn't stop smiling as I watched him express his delight. Picking him up for a cuddle, I whispered "Morning Huckleberry." He energetically scrambled into my hands licking any bare flesh on my arms he could find to reciprocate my pats. "Thank you," I said as I pulled a face at him when he licked the length of my wrist to my elbow. You would think it was covered in honey the way he was frenzied to mark the portions of skin exposed with his smooth little pink tongue.

My first point of order for the day was to get freshened up. I quickly placed some food down for Huckleberry before returning upstairs to have a shower. There was certainly an air of excitement about today.

The discovery of the cards yesterday was an unexpected gift that made me appreciate the extent of the planning which had clearly taken place for me in this lifetime. In a sense, it re-emphasized the importance of the journey.

The flow of signs, which occurred during the afternoon visit with my parents were now flittering about as images in my mind layered with background visuals of the dreamscape from last night. Yesterday's bird experiences felt as though they were positive messages. Having them now represented as translucent snaps against an array of moving numbers and letters I wondered whether the signs destined for me to witness were being manipulated. I brushed my teeth in front of the bathroom mirror while I pondered on the possible answers to my new question; are wild animal's clear channels providing untainted messages or are they subjected to the same capacity for manipulation and influence as humans?

Before heading back down the stairs I made my bed and collected the cards. I placed a clean pair of jimjams on because I held no intentions to venture out today. There was a rising internal urgency drawing me to read the remainder of the cards. I had consumed nine already so I knew twenty-five remained. The first suite of messages clearly encouraged me to set my train of thoughts in a particular direction. Most of it was known in a sense by me already, perhaps familiar is a better term. Even though there's an underlying frustration I held from all the cryptic messaging, I was eager to proceed forward rather than ponder what had been covered.

Settled on the sofa, Huckleberry by my side, with a cup of tea at the ready, I took the tenth card in my hand to open it. This envelope was different. The sizing was slightly larger, with the contents thicker, and it had been fused in place by a wax seal. I smiled as I jumped to attention, that's why I have a letter opener I thought to myself. Ferreting around the hallway cupboard I found Huck's original bedding and retrieved the beautiful ornate knife. It was satisfying to have another mystery solved. When I first discovered it, I recognized it was an oddity given the note it came with was only folded paper. In truth, I had forgotten all about it. I guess the opener was meant as a subtle hint in relation to these letters. I shook my head and laughed. Whoever orchestrated this held an amazing capacity for detail.

I settled onto the sofa once more, wrapped the orange faux-fur blanket around my toes and carefully slid the dulled metal edge in the gap to pry the envelope open. The first surprising delights of floral scent arose from the paper as I disturbed its bedding. In between the pages, there were dried petals, which had stained the parchment with indicators of what was once vibrant hues. I shifted across slightly to accommodate for Huckleberry to rejoin me. When he nestled in a ball between my feet, I unfolded the wad of pages, then began to read.

There are experiences in this world, which can never be appreciated until you have taken the journey of miles with your own wits to guide. I want to protect you from the realities of a life I wish I had not lived but know in the absence of imparting the wisdom obtained you too may fall into the same. The cycle must be broken, and the story cannot be forsaken for it exists still, beyond the realms, where ethereal threads yearn to draw upon the unforgiving.

The things you have been told in the past to now will pale in comparison to the adventure you are required to embark. All the while knowing that nothing I impart can prevent nor appease the ones who hunt for your favors. You may question my choices and method to act upon the cause I held as my burden, but I can say with certainty that you would have become the same as I. One day, you will understand why this is my known truth.

Time is of the essence and there is much to cover. The criticality of your understanding is what is paramount. Listen without judgement for I did the best that I could. I possess no pride in what has transpired yet under the weight of the same circumstances, I would retake my footsteps with the exacting precision once more.

They thought delivering me into this life within this skin would be set to be a disadvantage. A mere femme whom the Gods assume is now disarmed by the rule of the natural order. Foolish were they to think form alone could be the delineation between strength and weakness. The oppressive dominion exits but they failed to recognize there is nothing, which can make me yield.

I assure you, time may progress, but the ancients hold little true wisdom. Their thoughts are still so antiquated. Can you believe the strategy implemented to sway the advantage in their favor was thought to be best attained by forcing the shift of fate off its axis so my reincarnation to karmic flesh would be served as a woman? A form divined according to their scriptures as bound by servitude.

Let me tell you a little story …

I peered over the pages to look at Huckleberry. His head was resting on his two front paws. Quietly, he lay there watching me. I leant forward and gave him a pat while he remained in the same position. Only his tail shifted to wag. I wasn't sure what it was about the letter that irked me but I could feel my apprehension gaining presence. I took a sip of my tea then recommenced reading.

The nuns in the convent could be heard in whispers throughout the course of the night. Each eve would begin with silence before the strokes to the twilight of a new day could be timed to a cacophony of sounds channeled as expressions of tears, sighs and prayer.

I was no more than eleven when I began to notice the change. It wasn't just how my body was evolving but also the way men looked at me during the course of my transition to bloom. There was a presence of longing in their attentions, which seemed to overshadow any semblance of moralistic rationale. Although I didn't hold the wisdom to comprehend the appreciation of their desires, I held instinct enough to warn no man held proper business to gaze upon a child in such a manner. This is why I was told, for the most part, they kept me hidden.

Little was known of my origins. Variants of a fable had been told to me since I could recollect my first words regarding the matter. I was an infant left upon the kitchen bench buried beneath the morning's selection of seasoned stone fruit picked from the orchard. It was not known who placed me there or when, but it had been suspected that the travellers along the road saw it opportune to leave me nestled within the wicker for the Sisters of the Holy Heart to find.

My discovery was made only upon the eventual removal of the layers of contents from the basket. I had silently lain there still for the duration of my burial with no demands to be freed. It was said when Sister Maud removed the peach, which exposed a portion of my left eye, that I gazed at her with a smile. The others came to Maud's aid as she screamed while pointing to the basket. 'Twas Sister Lydia who doth retrieved me, placed my naked body in a swaddle made from a kitchen apron and then nursed me while the others gathered at the news of an orphan child being found.

The Sisters left me un-baptised, and with no name as they believed it best not to hold reason for me to stay any longer than it required for me to be raised to self-sufficiency. When they sought my attention they would merely say, "Child pass me this, Child come here."

I grew up within the confines of the convent walls and was mostly hidden from the view of the countless guests of nobility who entered to receive prayer. Occasionally hoards of the Kings men arrived at the grounds unannounced to make inspection, collect the taxes and ensure the faith of the order was being upheld to the lord's standards. These were the only times I was encouraged to leave the grounds dressed in a commoner's attire, entering the woods with Nathaniel the gatekeeper's son to help him hunt for game.

'Twas deep within the forest one eve post my sixteenth birthday when Nathaniel watched me successfully hunt an aged stag that I received the name Patience. This is where my story begins.

"What made thee choose this stag to kill above all the ones that passed?" asked Nathaniel.

"The young need a chance to grow. The mothers are purposed to breed and nurture. There are some of the junior stags, which could be portioned to sacrifice for our plates, but they are yet to establish their order. Once it is known, which is the lead, I will cull a selection of the others for our storage for winter supplies. This stag I chose to greet the stealth of my aim has had a life fulfilled. His absence quickens the need for the others to establish their hierarchal ruling."

"Patience," he said in a whisper.

"What doth thou mean patience?"

"You watched, assessed and waited to establish thine focal point of the hunt. This takes skills in observation and an enormous amount of patience. Most whom I hath hunted with hold no regard for the creatures themselves. They massacre, indiscriminately with no consideration to what thee hath just counseled. 'Twas I who taught thee the skills passed from my father to me for knifing and gave thee the taste for the bow and arrow, but it was thee who skulked out, night upon night to practice thine archery to the point thee hath mastered."

"You knew I was leaving the grounds?" I asked perplexed that I had never seen him.

Nathaniel released a laugh, "No, it was father who quietly distanced his witness to your regular folly. Upon my eighteenth, he charged me with the cause to keep night watch over thee."

"In all these years, how did I not detect a presence?"

"Thou intent held repetition so there was little deciphering required. The strength from the light of the night's moon determined whether you would venture beyond the walls to practice by the old riverbed. Come rain or tepid eve on these nights I would camp upon the branch of the tree across the way sheltered by the dark from view to watch over thee."

I looked around the forest, "What is there to fear out here?"

Nathaniel stepped in and placed his hand gently on my shoulder. "Thou art yet to understand what is contained within the walls of where thee lay, let alone hath preparation for what lurks beyond its structural confines."

My body jolted as the sound of Huckleberry's bark

broke the silence. He leapt up in the air growling at the skylights. The dancing shadow cast denoted there was something hovering overhead. It appeared to be a bird jutting in an odd configuration.

Searching in the hallway closet, I found my digital camera. Just as I zoomed in to take the shot it zipped away out of view. I only managed to capture a blur in the direction it trailed before it fell out of the frame. Huckleberry immediately ceased his barking trotting across to where I stood looking rather satisfied that he attended to the matter. I bent down to reward him with a pat, but something set him off again before I could connect. Huckleberry ran to the sofa leaping up onto the cushions toward the highest point while his little eyes fixated upward growling and barking. The noise of the hovering presented louder this time as it reappeared. I aimed the lens pressing down on the button so my camera would take a continuous series of shots while I attempted to keep the fast zipping bird centre of the frame. The only breed I knew of in the area with movement like this is the ruby throated hummingbird.

My curiosity peaked when I flicked the switch to change the ceiling glass from transparent to semi block frost, feeling that perhaps the bird's interest was akin to a reflection on the panes. Much to my surprise the flying object stilled to a controlled hover then within moments rose directly upward into the skies and seemingly disappeared. I wasn't sure whether it was a coincidence but the reactive timing was uncanny and the capability of such vertical motion was rather remarkable. Huckleberry jumped off the sofa, lapped up a considerable amount of water from his bowl before resettling in his bed.

I fetched my laptop from the back room, transferred

the images and maximized their size on screen to take a closer look at our alien visitor. A surge of anger flooded my senses as I realized the bird was actually a remote control flying toy with a camera mounted eye. Someone was either video taping or taking aerial view pictures of my apartment. I closed my eyes as I cringed at the reminder that no space I occupied was private. There is always a way to gain access for those who choose to find it. The reality was infuriating.

Scanning the room I looked for what might be revealed in the images. My eyes widened as I saw the pile of letters on the coffee table.

"Damn it."

The way the unit was tilting in various frames gave suggestion to the possibility that a mighty amount of detail could have been obtained from its quick surveillance expedition. I placed my portable IP encryption scrambler device on before switching live to the internet. One of Liam's intelligence connections had provided me with the unit, which had been commissioned as a design and build for exclusive purchase by the secret service. It held the smarts to ensure no back traceable marker to me or my PC could be found. Not even the interferons could find me on line. The problem was they were still able to watch everyone else, and I knew they did.

Unsure of what I was looking for I searched the word's surveillance hovercraft. The volume of returns, were too high for me to bother delving. I switched across to the image zooming in on the blurry logo to decipher but could only clearly see two words, Flight Flo. I returned to the browser, entering it into the search engine. In milliseconds the top three hits aligned to a company called, ZeonMark. They specialized in camera systems and mounts with a range of limited edition new release mini stealth spy drone called Flight Flo. Judging by the design I could see the model series Z2300 were a likely match to what I saw. The positive news was it held a traceable marker. In theory the likelihood of being able to track who purchased the units sold in this range would be relatively easy. The unfortunate part was not having a serial number or anything else distinctive as an identifier to narrow down this particular unit to an owner. Still it was a solid lead.

The site gave examples of the camera's capability. The images were impressively clear with a fifty times magnification option. It boasted the use of custom designed bleeding edge software to assist in the micro enhancement of the image detail. As impressed as I was at the unit's specifications I cringed at the results. Whoever owned that drone now had a focal view of everything in my apartment. I switched off the internet connection, I'd seen enough to appreciate that there were clearly no secrets between my inquisitive foe and I.

My head was consumed with thoughts as I walked into the kitchen to get a glass of water. While pressing the button on the fridge door to release the cold filtered water out I realized they may have recorded an image with the words plastered on the panel that I had written the night before: *isolation, withdrawal, containment, strength.* No doubt I was in some of the images showing my camera taking photos of the drone. My biggest concern at this point was whether they would make a connection between the book Illuminarium and these letters. Were they smart enough to associate a significance?

My body jolted as the sound of my cell blaring the tune to midnight special broke my train of thought. I rummaged through my bag and saw it was my dad calling.

"Hey Dad."

"Hi Beanie Bear, have I caught you at a bad time?"

"No, I can talk."

"Great, well the doctor you had check me out yesterday afternoon confirmed the results this morning. I'm fit as a fiddle with no signs of high cholesterol. I did the fasting test overnight as advised and went in to get a new series of blood extractions for further examination just to make sure the current results hold true. No more cardboard dinners, I can hardly wait to tell your mother." He said with excitement in his tone.

"Wow, that is fabulous news. I am pleased to hear it."

"I'll know with absolute certainty when these latest tests are return but it seems very positive. There's more, the new doctor made several attempts to call the other GP to get the original tests but never managed to speak with him. This morning I tried calling myself and got greeted with a recorded Telco message stating the phone has been disconnected. I decided to swing by on my way to the office only to discover the whole medical centre is shut down. How weird is that?"

The words from one of the cards came into the forefront of my thoughts.

'Careful where you choose to tread and whom you target to break. Some hold no concern for life and will aim to temper you by readily punishing others.'

"It sure does sound weird but it might just be a coincidence." I said trying to dull his curiosity.

"I doubt it. First, Dr. Stengleton leaves without so much as a goodbye, then this young whipper snapper comes in telling me I have serious health issues, which turn out to be completely wrong and suddenly the place is closed down practically overnight. Something smells rotten."

"Now is not the time to go on a Hardy boys sleuthing mission dad. Lets just focus on what is important, no more cardboard meals."

He laughed. "Ok Beanie Bear, yes this is a relief. I wasn't sure how much more green leafy goodness I could eat without feeling like I have turned into one."

"It doesn't do you harm to eat a little healthier."

"You sound like your mother."

We both laughed.

"I must be going now I have a meeting to prepare for with a team of lawyers reviewing the current allegations against us around a suspected bio security breach in Africa. How is Huckster?"

"He's simply gorgeous thanks for asking."

"If you ever need a puppy sitter I'm the man."

I laughed, "You two really like each other don't you?"

"He is a special fella. I'm not sure what it is about him but he makes me feel uplifted."

I smiled, "Next time I have to travel I will be sure to engage your services. I know you need to head off, can you just give me a quick thirty second insight into the situation you are facing."

"Sure Beans, the government officials have received an anonymous tip that the work we are doing over in Africa is a front for introducing bio hazardous bacteria into the country under the guise of charity exploration via Dynamically Global. It's now blown out to suggestions of warfare testing and other ludicrous statements. We need to address this quickly before they close down our work. Initially I wasn't too concerned but it seems to be fueled by someone who clearly wishes to sabotage our charitable efforts. I just have no clue as to why."

"I thought you were focused on using local resources

to scout for the potential farms to trial bio dynamics and were getting all the soil tests executed in country to avoid complications like this."

"We are. I even have the farming community leaders flown out of Africa for training at our various global facilities so we don't have the added risk of our own experts being subjected to local politics or caught in the cross fire of civil war outbursts. A translator accompanies the farmers for the full duration that they are assigned to shadow and learn from other successful biodynamic farmers. This approach increases the overall probability of success ten fold because it provides them an insight and hands on experience of how it works. All the participants are educated and practiced in the principles before returning home to get them established with what they have learnt. We have made sure that while they are acquiring their new found knowledge that we use our own labs here to experiment with similar local materials, which the farmers have readily available in their home towns to identify the best combinations for high yield results leveraging the same bio dynamic principles."

"Wow, I really should pay more attention. It seems like you have advanced a lot since we discussed this last."

"We certainly have come a long way. I honestly feel like we are on the precipice of making an enormous notable difference from the ground up. I'm not sure who is driving this suite of allegations but I am comfortable that we are going to be able to address it."

I paused for a moment to consider how best to frame my thoughts. "Do you think that people are trying to link you to this vaccination conspiracy? The suggestion of bio warfare is giving me real concern dad. I think you need to squash this as quickly as you can so it doesn't get out of hand."

"The thought crossed my mind too Beanie Bear. I'm doing what I can to get the air cleared on this one."

"Okay Dad, I'll let you get to it. Call out if there is anything I can do to assist."

"Sure thing Beanie Bear, I love you. Don't make it too long between visits and call out if you need a hand with whatever is going on with you."

"Now who sounds like mom?" I said with a laugh

He chuckled, "She does tend to carry on but I know that she is onto something here, I can feel it. If there is anything you need, tell me and I will do it."

"Sure dad. Say hello to mom."

"I will, bye sweety."

"Bye dad."

With this, the phone clicked to silence.

I looked across at Huckleberry who was fast asleep in his bed. I smiled when I saw the little flick of his paws, which I assumed was an indication that he was dreaming. I wonder what the remainder of his life with York was like. When the words in Illuminarium drew to a close I was sad I never got to know more about their journey. The story seemed to simply end, with pages upon pages left empty. Perhaps one day I might feel compelled to write mine in the remainder but for now the book would stay safely hidden.

It was time to settle back on the sofa to continue as my day had been planned, I would need to arrange to track down the owner of the drone, but I refused to allow it or anything else to continue to distract me from reading the letters. There was much for me to learn from this new story about Patience. She intrigued me. I have no idea of the era she lived in but…

"You forget I am no longer a child Nathaniel."

He released a laugh, "Thou art a child and will always be to me."

"I hath heard the whispers of the nun's preparing for my coming of age celebration set for the fall. Three days post the first fruit when the moon is on its dimmest light they talk of a journey."

"How did thee acquire this knowledge?"

"The walls are made of stone, but it carries the echo of all voices through the channels."

Turning his nose in disapproval he said, "You listen through the holes where the bodily waste of the night is discarded?"

"Aye, what of it?"

He swung his left hand in a delicate swirl, "Oh, Patience and here I thought you were a lady."

"I've never professed to be such. Doth a lady wear this attire?" I said stretching my musty top forward. "Doth a lady, hunt, climb trees, sneak out on an eve cloaked by the skies silhouette alone?"

Nathaniel laughed, "T'would appear I hath caused thee an affront my lady. I did not mean to offend thee." He said with an extended bow.

"Stop it Nathaniel." I said pounding on the length of his shoulders to the crook of his exposed neck.

"What ever hath I done now?" He asked stepping back using his arms as a shield from my blows.

"Thou art well aware of what thou hath done. 'Tis what thee always do. Tease me to the point of madness by looking upon me like a child."

His expression changed as he clenched his teeth and stepped forward catching my fisted hands with his tightened grip, thrusting them by my side while his face towered down over mine. "And what would thee hath me look upon thee as? Is thine wish for me to leer as others do? To ponder what spoils lay beneath thou tattered cloth?"

I struggled in an attempt to release my hands as my blood surged to my face in fury. "No, release me at once."

"Answer me why doth thee insist on being acknowledged for an age that warrants thee court worthy of heathens minds and their filthy bed chambers?"

"I want none of this that you speak of. I shall never be betrothed to another."

His hands were still clasped tight as his face rose toward the skies to release a laughter that made me feel awoken to an unfamiliar sense of vulnerability.

"Thou shall not be given the choice if thou art found, nor will thee be granted the honor of being wed. The darkness hath thee marked to lure the sinister from their spoils to seek thee as their prize. Did thee not sense the oddity of the command to not leave the grounds yet upon entry of the King's men thou art each time ushered in secrecy to remove thyself from the convent? Is it not strange that within the walls my father and I are barred from holding thine presence and still we are charged with the role to escort thee on a hunt?"

I all of a sudden felt naïve as my response squeaked past my lips to a whisper of the word "No."

"When you were a whip the nuns made a grievous error by not cloaking thee from the Cardinal's visitation. They considered nothing of it until his eye would not travel past thee to any other. He had marked thee by thought and immediately sought to acquire you. If it wasn't for the quick wit of Sister Lydia, you would be the mistress of a cardinal who has since been revealed to hold a reputation for his unashamed penchant for promiscuously brutalizing young girls."

"What doth thou mean? Explain further." I said straightening my posture.

"Sister Lydia interjected with a proposal that you remain on the grounds for a full cycle of the seasons rotation to be groomed in the proper ways of pleasing. It took her personal deliverance of certain favors to demonstrate what could be taught. He reluctantly agreed to hath thee remain for one full rotation of the seasons but no more. The Sisters hath hidden thee ever since."

"Did he not come looking for me?"

Nathaniel relaxed his grip and stepped back, "Aye, of course he did. Upon the completion of the annual cycle of seasons, he was at the convent's door accompanied by two personal guards in readiness to collect thee. Sister Lydia with the corroboration of the others spoke to thee being taken with fever and shortly thereafter buried in the graveyard of the dammed. This ensured he would not insist upon the witness of your remains, as the risk of sickness was too great to force the challenge. Instead, he left quietly only to return two day's post with a charge of the Kings men set to search the grounds. Doth thee recall that first venture beyond the walls was achieved with thee strung to my fathers back, his overcoat and pack obscured thou tiny body from view?"

"I do, 'tis been by my count six winters past."

"Seven winters, they came to collect thee when you were nine."

Nathaniel allowed me a moment of silence as I sifted through his words. "'Tis a lie, thou art set to mislead me toward a farce. Why would the Kings men be present still? I know it only to transpire for the retrieval of taxes."

His lips pursed as he lowered his eyes to the ground,

"Aye, there are the taxes born of the Kings desire to punish the convent for withholding thee. The Cardinal was so infuriated that he could not hath thee within his grasp that they say he implored the King to present his arms in search for the most beautiful blossom, he had laid eyes upon. It took him two days to sway the King to the cause, and it was only done by his own depraved curiosity developing a need to savor the taste of such a creature. He held no intent in passing thee across to the Cardinal, you were forthwith destined for the Kings bed chamber."

"What right do any of them hath to claim another?"

Nathaniel kicked the dirt, "Land, titles, power, riches."

"Is it because I hath no origins known that they sought to claim me like a wilder beast?"

"No, this is how thee are treated because thou art a girl."

I looked down toward the crest of my bosoms and watched them heave as I released my breath, "Why do they continue to punish the convent with taxes? Surely by now they must determine my absence is faith toward the word of the Sisters."

"Doth thou recall I stated the Cardinal was given special favors by Sister Lydia to entice him to hath thee remain?"

"Aye." I said not completely present to the full understanding of what was spoken.

"The Cardinal passed knowledge of this to the King, who in turn afforded his leverage to demand the same of the entire convent as payment for newly imposed taxes. Those who attempted to deny the servitude were slain. They no longer look for thee when they attend the convent, this is true but there would be certain death for many if thou were sighted by any who had cause to tell."

"All of this resulting from me, an orphan girl of no learnings to speak of or known titled value?"

Nathaniel stepped in once more, this time gently lifting my chin to hath our eyes greet as he softly spoke, "An orphan girl who possesses eyes of emerald, skin of fawn, long tussled hair that glimmers in the presence of the suns light with an array of shimmering hues such as spun gold. Hath thee not looked upon the waters reflection to glimpse thou own presence?"

"I hath, but know of no other child to quantify a measure."

"There is no measure, thy beauty is captivating and distinctly unique. I hath seen many a fair maiden and know of none like you."

I looked at my hands and noted for the first time that my color held variant to Nathaniel's. "What of thy appearance then?"

"I can hold a courtier's interest if I so make it of my choosing." He said with a lift in his heels. "But I am of no such significance as thou art to witness."

I looked down at the earth's soil feeling the weighted burden of knowledge, which had been laid upon me.

"Come, we must collect this buck and return to the convent before night fall. T'will be no moon to guide this eve."

I followed Nathaniel in silence. My mind was now awash with imagery of the tales imparted.

Huckleberry leapt from his bed and ran toward the door before the sound from the bell was engaged. I quickly scooped the pile of letters placing them in the secret panel below the floor underneath the coffee table before heading for the door. My eyes lit up when I saw through the viewfinder who was standing on the other side.

I released the lock and swung the door wide open, "Liam" I squealed as I wrapped my arms around him.

Bind

I couldn't believe my eyes as Liam stood before me larger than life. An unexpected flood of emotions was urging my need to squeeze his hand tight as I lead him into the apartment.

The expression on his face changed when he began to absorb the architectural splendor of the place.

"Take those ridiculous ravers off and let me look at you." I said.

Liam without a word took the glasses off and continued to survey the expanse of the room while Huckleberry curiously sniffed him. "Harper this place is unbelievable."

"I know."

"Wow …" he said stepping forward still looking up at the ceiling.

I walked across to the panel and flipped the switch to revert the glass to clear.

"No way," said Liam spinning in a tight circle while holding his hand to his heart as he simultaneously released a gasp.

"Yes way." I replied, and then chuckled. I was

enjoying his expression of wonderment. "I'm going to brew up a pot of tea while you take a tour around. Off you go."

Liam continued to hold his head toward the skies while he walked. It wasn't too long before his thighs were greeted with a thud at the sofa. He lost his balance and reefed forward using his hands to bridge the partial fall.

"Are you okay?"

He laughed, shaking his head. "I'm truly speechless. This place is fantastical." He pointed to the brick wall, "Look at all the colors projected there. What's doing that?"

"Ah, that would be my bed head. It occurs roughly the same time on a clear sky day and does it on a perfect moonlit night as well."

"I have to see it."

I pointed to the suspended floor and floating spiral staircase. "Up you go."

There wasn't a need to offer twice, Liam was almost half way up the stairwell before I could warn him to refrain from entering my untidy ensuite.

By the time he returned I had everything laid out on the dining table with some shortbread biscuits on the way.

"Take a seat."

Liam seemed hyper stimulated. His mouth was clicking as I saw his tongue repeatedly gliding over his teeth.

"Have you been indulging in some of Sam's experimental hallucinogenic milk shakes? You don't quite seem yourself."

"Oh, yeah, I'm just blown away by this place. It's seriously got to be the best apartment I have ever seen."

I smiled, "Drink your tea before it cools and try one of these shortbreads they are truly delicious."

"Thanks but I don't really eat sweets. I like things to be a little more savory."

I watched as his eyes flittered about the room, looking at everything. I knew something wasn't right. I chose to remain silent in regard to his comment about not liking sweets. Whomever this was, clearly didn't know Liam very well. Something was amiss.

When he finally connected with my gaze and smiled, I could see that it was Liam engaging me. "I have missed you," he said.

"I missed you too but you have no business coming here. I meant it when I said I needed to complete the rest of the journey in the absence of my friends and family. It's dangerous to be associated to me Liam. Haven't you watched the news?"

"You can't do this alone. I have connections, and you need all the assistance you can get. Please trust me. Tell me the plan and what I can do to help."

"I have a direct link to all your connections now and the full backing of the team at the Sanctorum Avow. Practically every news reporter from around the globe is interviewing charlatans claiming to be me. In less than a month, the remainder of my first strategy will be fully deployed, which will mark the beginning of an unknown path given, I have no idea of what the interferon's reaction will be."

"Tell me everything, I can help you," he pleaded.

I leant in placing my hand on his arm, "It's not possible. I have to do this alone."

Huckleberry who was settled by my feet under the table released a low growl as I watched Liam look at my hand gently clasping his arm just above his wrist. He slowly reached across with his free hand and placed his ravers on.

Liam lifted the cup of tea to his lips to take a first taste, "Where did you get the mutt from?"

I noted the tone in his voice changed. "Its Huckleberry, he was given to me by a friend."

Liam's tea sprayed from his mouth onto the table. Huckleberry reacted to the noise with a frantic high-pitched bark between growls. I reached down to pick him up, placing him on my lap. The fur on the back of his neck was on end as I felt the vibration of his growl echo through his exposed teeth.

"Liam, what's going on? Take those glasses off please. I want to be able to see your eyes."

He cleared his throat and slowly removed the ravers, placing them beside the tray of biscuits. Instantly Huckleberry ceased his defensive proposition and began to wag his tail.

I felt a sense of relief, "I don't think he likes the ravers either."

We both laughed.

I had to be on guard just in case Liam is hosting something that is trying to hide its presence. Bahrain and Zivah never hid when they took over his body.

"How are the boys?" I asked.

"Swell, honestly they have been both so welcoming. When we returned home to find you had gone, I offered to be on my way. I felt I held no business staying there without you, after all they are your old college room mates, but neither of them would hear of it. They wanted me to stay. There hasn't been a night since that has passed where the legend of your antics have not been shared. They both truly cherish you, and I can tell, by the way,

Peppy sometimes gazes out the window into the dark when your name is raised that he misses you. More than he would care to admit."

"I know." I whispered while reverting my eyes to Huckleberry. I felt his little body relax again.

Liam cleared his throat again, "Do you have a bathroom I can use?"

"Sure, just over there to the left of the front entry."

"Great, thanks."

I watch as Liam walked into the bathroom closing the door behind without a backward glance. I know he didn't seem to be his usual bubbly self. It made me wonder if he had started indulging in some recreational drugs. Sam could be rather persuasive at times. I couldn't put my finger on it but Liam was definitely not presenting as though he is of sound mind.

Huckberry began to bark when he heard the crash of something falling onto the tile floor.

I jumped to my feet and ran across to the door, "Liam, what's going on?" Knock, knock, knock, "Liam, I'm coming in if you don't answer me. This isn't funny."

I could hear a shuffle and then the sound of a gargle before he cleared his throat, "I'm okay. I will be out in a minute."

Liam's behaviour was alarming my senses. My instinct overtook my politeness causing me to open the door without providing a warning. I needed to validate he was okay. I immediately recoiled at the smell of tepid sulphur, placing my arm across my mouth and nose to deter from needing to inhale it again.

"What the fuck have you been eating? Jesus, it smells like rotten eggs in here."

Liam was slumped over the basin splashing cold

running water on his face. "I know, sorry. I've just been so nauseous lately I keep feeling the need to throw up. My mouth is dry, I'm tired and the boys have been saying that I do some random weird stuff, things I don't even remember doing. I'm scared Harper, I don't know what's happening to me."

A shiver ran up my spine as I adjusted my stance to be on guard, "What kind of stuff?"

"Peppy accused me of putting the hard word on his date one night. God, this is so embarrassing, Sam said that he caught me masturbating over his hook up while she was sleeping in his bed. He woke to a noise in the dark and when he switched on the light, I had my cock out rubbed raw releasing a spray of cum on her face, torso, across the pillows and a bit hit his arm. He freaked out, yelled, threw things at me. She woke and began screaming too, then Peppy came into the room to see what the commotion was all about. Apparently, I walked calmly passed him, into my room and went to sleep. They tried to wake me with no success. I woke the next morning oblivious of what had happened. Peppy and Sam were in the kitchen waiting to confront me. I can't begin to describe how furious they were. Honestly, they pounced on me the moment I entered the room. It began as an aggressive verbal assault but after a while they realized by my reaction that I wasn't lying when I said I had no idea of what they were talking about. Harper, I promise you I don't remember anything."

My arms folded, "Did they throw you out? Is this why you're here?"

"No, they were totally supportive saying that it was clear that I was acting out while sleep walking. Sam made arrangements for me to see his therapist."

"Did you go? What did the therapist have to say?"

"I didn't go to the session. I was on my way and somehow ended up here at your door. I'm not sure what to say except that I blacked out again." He shrugged his shoulders.

Huckleberry moved from his position to sit in front of where I stood with the tip of his hind side positioned on the edge of my toes. He stared intently at Liam.

"Oh how sweet you have a little dog. What's his name?"

My eyes widened as I swooped to collect Huckleberry before slamming the door to the bathroom shut. I pressed the reverse lock to secure it from the outside and stepped back as I watched the person on the other side of the door switch the handle up, then down manically.

"WHO ARE YOU?" I yelled.

There was no response, just a continued focus on the door handle.

The fur on Huckleberry's neck stood on end as his little body vibrated from the release of an elongated deep growl. His teeth were exposed while his eyes were fixated on the bathroom door. Whomever it was ceased making an attempt to free them self. The shadow cast suggested they had stepped away. My heart was thundering against my chest as I attempted to steady my breath while I waited.

BOOM.

"ARGGHHHH," BOOM.

"LET ME THE FUCK OUT YOU CUNT."

BOOM, BOOM, BOOM.

"WHO ARE YOU?" I yelled again. My heart was beating fast. Internally, I felt a rise of anger swelling.

I took a couple of steps back as I watched the door jiggle slightly in response to the persons attempt to break down the door. I had comfort in knowing it would take a lot more strength than a single human to remove the door from its hinges given the re-enforced steel frame was designed to withstand extremes of pressure. The architect may have been considered eccentric, but his vision for this place was to have it withstand the greatest of natural disasters. Nothing in this entire building was designed flimsily.

There was silence. A cast of the person's shadow could be seen concentrated near the bottom lip of the door. "Harper it's me Liam. Set me free. We need to get out of here, you and I. I'm sorry about the outburst, I've not been myself lately. Please open the door. Everything is going to be alright. You need to trust me."

I placed Huckleberry on the ground to continue with his growling.

"Tell me who you are."

"It's me, you saw me, its Liam. Did I black out again? What did I do this time? Please Harper I need help, open the door. We both aren't safe here, we need to go."

My breath was steadied as I stepped forward. "No."

BAM, he hit the door and reattempted to jiggle the handle.

"LET ME OUT."

I chose not to reply. Instead, I walked across to the coffee table to retrieve my phone. Peppy's number went straight to his voice mail, *"Congratulations you have now had the pleasure of reaching Peppy of Threadbow Incorporated, leave a message after the tone and I might get back to you."* There was no success with Sam's either, *"I am Sam I am I am."*

I sat on the sofa and waited to see what his next move would be. Whomever was in that bathroom had already tried to present as Liam to be released. Huckleberry must be able to detect when he is there, which is why he is growling to warn me. Initially, I thought at the dining table, Huckleberry didn't like the ravers but it makes sense now that it was because he had switched. The only driver to wear the ravers would be to cover up his eyes. They change when foreign spirits are active in a host's body. At least, that is what happened when I met the spirits of Bahrain and Zivah. This creature is somewhat altogether different. The smell of sulphur, the nausea Liam described would suggest he is feeling the negative effects of this entity, perhaps even fighting against it. I wasn't sure what it is that I was looking for but panicking was not going to serve me best. My mind needed to be clear in order to gain insight into what the hell was happening.

"Harper, we're running out of time. Open the door, they're coming for me I can feel it in my bones. Please Harper, I need to see you, one last time before they take me away."

I yelled out, "WHO IS AFTER YOU?"

"The interferon's, they know I'm here and have sent people to collect me."

I stepped closer to the bathroom door. "You're lying."

"I need to see you Harper, hurry. I have something very important I need to show you. It will help you on your quessssssssst."

The hairs on the back of my neck stood on end as I heard the slither of the letter 's' roll from the creatures tongue. It was sinister with mal intent. Inwardly mind was firing on all cylinders trying to resolve the familiarity of the reaction my body was having to this entity's presence. Flashes of my face embedded in a frozen moment akin to the art titled, 'The Scream' by Edvard Munch made my blood curdle at the looming truth of what may reside behind the door.

Knock, Knock, Bzzzzz, Bzzzzzzz

"I'm coming." I peered through the peephole to see two men in police uniform were at the door.

I could hear Liam step forward, "I told you Harpuuuuurrrrr they would come. It's a pity we didn't get to fuck. I could have made you cuuuuummmmm."

I froze in position, it couldn't be.

"Yeeeeeeeeeeeessssssssssss. I missed you," he whispered.

Bzzzzz, Bzzzzzzz, Knock, Knock, Knock, "Ma'am open the door."

I mechanically released the latch and opened the door while my mind spun in a daze.

"Hello, are you Harper Parelle?"

"Yes." I said folding my arms not knowing how to hide the discomfort I felt.

"We are looking for a person we believe may have been associated to you by the name of Liam. He's wanted for questioning on a series of murders."

"Murders?"

"Listen to me, your name was found written in blood across the walls with the words I'm coming for you."

I stared at them in disbelief of what I was hearing.

"Ma'am if you know anything in regard to his whereabouts you need to tell us."

Tears welled in my eyes as I started to see visuals of blood on walls. I slowly blinked my eyes and quietly nodded my head while stepping back into my apartment, then pointed to the bathroom door.

The men's eyes widened as they removed their weapons from their holsters and ushered me to stand back.

The voice from the bathroom unleashed a familiar presence I never thought I would have to hear again. "AH HAHAHHAHAHA AHHHH HAHAHHAH HARPER, HARPPPPEEERR, SURPRISE. HARPER, HARPER, HARPPPPEEEERRR, DID YOU THINK IT WOULD BE THAT EASY TO BE RID OF ME? HARPER, HARPEEEERRRR, HARPEERRR ..." on and on he went as the NYPD interjected.

"THIS IS THE NYPD MOVE AWAY FROM THE DOOR, LAY FLAT ON THE FLOOR WITH YOUR HANDS ON YOUR HEAD. IF YOU DO NOT COMPLY WE WILL USE FORCE TO MAKE YOU COMPLY."

"HE'S UNARMED, THAT'S A BATHROOM. I LOCKED HIM IN. THE LATCH SWITCH IS UP TO YOUR RIGHT. PRESS IT AND THE DOOR WILL BE OPENED." I yelled "HE'S UNARMED" over and over to ensure they didn't enter in guns blazing. Their adrenalin was pumping as was mine. The police officer in the hind position was calling in the situation. The main fellow continued yelling his orders to the door while Vernon fucking Wreath relentlessly called out my name.

After what seemed like a lifetime everyone stopped yelling to focus on the fact that Liam had ceased his rant. The police officer in the lead position signaled he was going to release the latch. Just as his arm reached over there was a crashing sound of glass being broken.

The door was released and flung open, "GO, GO, GO." The first officer stepped forward as Liam's bloody hand glided effortlessly across the entire length of his throat with a jagged shard of mirror. Blood spurted from his artery as his body went limp like a rag doll falling in slow motion to the floor. Liam's head smashed on the tiles with a bounce until his naked body settled to stillness. His eyes were open, staring at me watching him. A smile ventured the expanse of his face before the light was dulled from his gaze.

"No, no, no, no, no, no LIAM," I screamed as I tried to shift forward. The officer who was closest to the body spun to catch me. His arms wrapped around me, pushing with force to encourage me back out the door. He stood with me in the clearing and continued to hold me as I released a howl of tears.

"Shh, its okay Ma'am, you're safe now."

The sound of the sirens echoed through the air as the police back up and ambulance scrambled through the traffic. I continued to silently chant the word, "no" over and over through my tears while the officer held my head to his chest rocking me.

* * * * *

I watched as stranger upon stranger entered my home, all with the same expression of amazement at the size and unique design of the apartment. The forensic photographer asked if he could take a few snaps to which I declined, while other less considerate officers tried to sneak candid's with their phones. It was the two law enforcement officers who were first on the scene that seemed guarded about the behavior and forced the crew to delete anything that had been taken.

There was no favored role for me in this somewhat silent scurried pantomime I witnessed before me. The police tape was whipped into place in no time. The flash from the camera pulsed ironically to the set of a heart beat that no longer functioned. I couldn't process it all.

The reality of what I had to face was far greater than my capacity to do so. I simply wasn't strong enough.

"Ma'am, we will be finished up here in a few. We're just waiting for the coroner to arrive before we can remove the body. I'm going to have to ask you to co-operate and allow us to escort you to the station for questioning."

I looked up at him through swollen, blurred vision eyes, "Ok. Can I put some clothes on? I'm still in my pyjamas."

"Sure, I'll just have officer Bradlyn escort you to your room and wait outside your door."

The officer stepped forward, nodded his head at the request and then looked at me.

"My bedroom is the mezzanine up there. I have no door and the only access in or out is that staircase."

They both turned to look at where I was pointing.

Officer Bradlyn followed me up the stairs, searched the walk in wardrobe and bathroom before returning downstairs satisfied that there was no other exit available to me. When I heard his footsteps fade I sat on the edge of the bed, placed my face in my hands and quietly cried.

Once I completed my shower, I put on some jeans, a skivvy and a windcheater. It didn't look overly cold outside but my body was shivering from the influx of adrenalin. I was aware my system was experiencing shock, so I had to try to maintain my temperature until my body readjusted back to normal. I knew there was no time to dry my hair. I flipped my head upside down giving it a thorough scrub with the towel.

In my bedroom I looked up at the blue-sky day and felt a tear roll down my cheek. As I turned toward the stairs, I noticed something jutting out from underneath the dress cushion on my bed. I pulled at it and realized it was a folded piece of paper.

If I can reach you, they can reach you.
Learn your lesson well.
Vern

"Steady .... Steady .... Okay you're clear."

I walked to the edge of the balcony and looked over in time to catch the tail end of the black bag leaving my apartment on a gurney. The officer who had held me earlier while I cried, glanced up gesturing for me to join them. I nodded, placed the note Vernon had written into the front left pocket of my jeans and proceeded down the stairs.

* * * * *

"So that's it, that's what happened?"
"Yes."

The interview room was bleak, just a table, two chairs made from a thin metal that held the chill deep enough to travel through my flesh to settle on my bones. The coffee I had my hands wrapped around tasted, bitter and burnt. This place was miserable, I was tired, and I really needed to go home. Three hours of nothing but talking to a fellow whose waist was suffocated by a belt tightened beyond any sense nor reason, which held the cause to accentuate his over sized gut to spill onto the table like a trophy of excessive consumption.

"I'm still trying to understand why you had him locked in the bathroom."

"I told you, he arrived unannounced, and in the beginning everything seemed fine. I made us a pot of tea while he looked around the apartment, then we both settled at the dining table to catch up. It was at this point he mentioned that he had been having blackouts. He said he was ashamed to admit that his roommates were accusing him of sexually depraved acts. This came as a complete surprise to me. He then said he needed to use the toilet. I left him to it. When I heard some strange shuffling noises, I called out to seek confirmation that he was okay. It was at this point he opened the door, and I saw he had undressed himself. My reaction was to push the door shut using the external latch to lock him in. It wasn't more then ten minutes before the two officers were at my door and the rest is witnessed by them, along with the others who later attended the scene."

"Why didn't you call the police?"

"I was in shock. My first reaction was to call my friends to get an insight from them on what is happening. When both of their cells went to voice mail, I hung up, then sat on the sofa to think through what I should do."

"Most people would call the police."

"There wasn't a crime. I welcomed him into my home. He is a friend, a newly acquired one but a friend none the less. I had spent time with him at length in his home, so I was familiar with his habits, behaviors, hopes and dreams. Liam never displayed any inconsistencies in his cognitive reasoning in the past, so I held no feeling of being threatened. He genuinely seemed like he was confused and needed help."

"So you locked him in the bathroom, what did you plan to do next?"

"I tried to talk to him to understand what was happening. Honestly, I didn't have much time between it occurring to when the officers arrived. I wanted to establish an insight into what was happening. He did appear dry in the mouth, so I initially wondered if this was a drug related issue. When I saw him last he was dating a fellow who was known for his recreational indulgences."

I watched as he jotted down notes, singular words that he would underline three times, poise his pen and then make a noise, either hmm or a sigh. The whole discussion was being recorded so in actuality, there was no reason for him to take anything down.

"Can I ask you a question?"

He sat up and looked at me, "I'm the one who asks the questions and you're the one who answers."

I chose to hold my tongue. "Ok."

We sat there in silence while he stared at his page of random words, while he alternated tapping on the edge of the table with his index finger then thumb. After a few minutes, he got up and left the room without saying a word. The moment the door closed I placed my arms on the table to cradle my head. The thumping of my pulse was thundering in my brain. I wanted this to be a nightmare, I could wake from.

"Harper, excuse me Harper are you okay?"

I raised my head to see officer Bradlyn holding out a bottle of water. "You need to keep hydrated, I know this has been a long day for you but there are more questions we need to ask. Detective Scanlon will be back in a few minutes to continue the interview along with a victim trauma specialist."

"I just want to go home." I said as I accepted the water. "Thank you."

"I know. We will do our best not to keep you here any longer than we need to."

"I really need to get home, I'm exhausted, freezing and I can't think straight."

The door opened without warning and in came Scanlon and another person.

"Thanks you may go," said Scanlon to Bradlyn.

"Harper this is Dr Dubawnt, she is our trauma specialist who assists with cases like these. I'm going to leave you in her capable hands for the remainder of the questioning and then I'll arrange for officer Bradlyn to escort you home or another officer if he isn't on duty. I'd like to thank you for your cooperation thus far toward the investigation." With this he walked out closing the door behind him.

"Hi Harper, I have been briefed on the situation and understand that you must be feeling overwhelmed at the moment."

My lips pursed as I did a slight nod. "What's in the file?" I asked.

"We will get to that in a minute. First, I just want to understand how you are feeling. Is there anything you want to talk about before we proceed with the remaining questions?"

Her tone was silken along with her calming disposition. It provided me with a sense of comfort that she had my best interests as a heightened priority.

"No, I just want to finish this so I can go home. Can we do that please?"

She took the brown case file, which had been tucked under her arm and placed it on the table.

"Sure, lets proceed then."

Her hand slipped into the file removing five photos which she carefully placed in what I could glean was her idea of what the sequence of association would be. I automatically reshuffled the order by right side association, left by chance and then began.

"These two are my college roommates Ted Sarouche and Brandon Zolawski." I paused for a moment to look at the image of them laughing into the camera. "They are my best friends." A tear rolled down my cheek.

Dubawnt passed me a tissue.

"Thanks," I whispered.

"Can I ask you why you are crying?"

I looked at her, "I took that picture."

She looked down at it for a moment, "They seem happy but looking at it seems to have made you sad. I would like to understand why it evoked that response from you."

I sat upright, placed both my hands flat on the cold tables surface and stared at the image of my boys, "The only reason you are showing me these photo's is because they are dead, all of them. You know my background, you are aware that I specialize in cognitive reasoning and that my field is criminology, so it can't be a surprise to you that I am conscious of more than what I am officially told. At my house, the two police officers had stated Liam was wanted for questioning in regard to a murder investigation. They described the message written on the crime scene wall in blood. Liam confessed to me, he had been experiencing black outs and mentioned being caught by my friend Ted executing an uninvited sexual act on his sleeping date. To watch Liam, take his own life to me means he felt there was no other alternative. I've assumed by reasoning that you were introduced as a trauma specialist rather than a psychological assessor / criminal profiler to deter me from gaining paranoia around the intent of the questioning. It tells me that to some degree I'm being assessed to determine whether I was a participant in the crimes that took place or can be ruled out of involvement as anything other than a victim. There are components that by your assessment thus far don't make sense and what you're hoping is for my responses to provide you the insight to confirm a pathway to a plausible explanation."

I raised my eyes to connect with hers. "You can't possibly imagine what I am feeling right now, nor could I begin to quantify it in words. I'll tell you everything I know and leave the rest to you, the expert."

She shifted in her chair and cleared her throat. I dropped my eyes to look at her neck as I watched her gulp before returning my gaze to the pictures on the table. I relaxed my posture and tapped on the next image, "This is Dwayne Cowet. We met in college and cross over in social circles from time to time. During my recent visit, I had the boys introduce Liam to him. They hit it off and from what I understand became lovers. Just before I left they had been on a few dates, Liam seemed very keen so I am assuming they progressed to a sexual relationship casual or otherwise post my departure."

I gazed upon the next two images where a single woman was captured in each frame. "I don't know who these two people are but I can make an assumption based on knowing my friends that this one was Ted's love interest and the other is Brandon's. They never accepted that they have a type, but they have a type."

"You are assuming that these women whom you have never met are romantically connected to your friends? Is that correct?"

"No, I know they would be sexually connected to my friends and trust me when I say there is no romance intended. They are still frat boys at heart. Neither of them had social interactions with the opposite sex unless it resulted in rewards of the flesh. I was the only exception to the rule. If these women are connected to either of them, then it is a sexual thread that binds."

"Okay."

"Liam." I held the picture in my hands and stared at his image. It must have been retrieved from his home. Tears poured down my face.

Dubawnt reached across touched my arm and said, "Take your time."

"I flew across to L.A for Colombo's day long weekend. Up until then, I had been working non-stop so I used the opportunity to get away for a well-earned rest. I tend to gravitate to the national park, there is something about the majesty of the forest and the enormity of the redwoods that help to re-instill a view for me of beauty and the possibility of peace in the world."

I paused to take a sip of my water.

"On the second day after a storm had passed I decided to leave my hotel room for a nice walk. I entered the botanical gardens to stretch my legs with the plans to find a place to eventually settle to read."

"What were you reading at the time?"

I looked at her, "Ah, that's right Doctor, interject requesting random specific details to watch for cues that would assist in establishing the subject's cognitive reality. The average human mind has a tendency to cloud or embellish experiences as presentable facts. The book I red was written by Simeon Gershwald, titled Light Spectrum Theory of an Inarticulate World. If there is a need I will voluntarily provide you with all the receipts of anything relevant to the corroboration of the events that I am currently conveying."

I watched as her smile revealed a nervous twitch. The Doctor readjusted her posture in her seat then consciously relaxed her body, no doubt to prevent me from reading her physical cues.

"Ok, moving right along. I came upon a lake, saw a man who was sitting on the bench feeding the local birds. I walked across and sat beside him to watch for a while. It was Liam. Post our first greet, I left to find a quiet place to read. I eventually settled under a monkey puzzle tree. I cannot recall precisely how much time had passed before I was interrupted by Liam, who saw me as he was passing by. He asked me if I would like to join him for a coffee. I accepted. That's when we went to Guilty Pleasures Café. The conversation was broad and very light hearted. We laughed, shared cake and at the end of it were ready to part ways. Outside the café he unexpectedly broke down crying, confessing that he knew who I was. He revealed that his wife and daughter were one of the victims in the Vernon Wreath case file that I had been assigned to."

"Didn't you find this strange?"

"I was surprised at the time but at no point felt that there was any level of premeditation to our meeting given that mostly all of it was driven by choices I had made. I flew to L.A, I chose to walk in the park, I chose to sit next to him on the park bench. It all came from me."

"So you are sure, absolutely positive that you had never met him before?"

"No, never. Anyway, we exchanged numbers and agreed to catch up and I left. The next day he invited me to his home for lunch, we once again enjoyed one another's company. Liam told me of his guilt about leaving his wife because he no longer could sustain pretending to be heterosexual. As he explained it to me, his wife felt betrayed by this secret he revealed which resulted in her ostracizing him. She had lost a husband whom she loved and he had lost access to her as his best friend and their daughter, both of which he professed to love very much. I held a deep compassion for his struggle. I spent some time at his place and eventually suggested that he join me on a road trip to see my old college roommates Ted and Brandon. At the time I held inkling that he and Dwayne may hit it off. I knew Liam was lonely and truly wanted a chance at love. I saw no harm in bringing him with me. The few days I was there everything went swimmingly. They all got along. I was due to return home, Liam wanted to remain a little longer to explore where things may go with Dwayne and the boys confirmed they were happy to have him stay with them. Today was the first time I had seen Liam since I left San Francisco."

"Did you talk on the phone?"

"No. I haven't taken any calls since I've been back."

"What do you think has happened?"

"Are you asking me to hypothesize or are you still searching for threads to establish whether I know more than what I am telling you?"

"A little of both."

"Thank you for your honest response." I tapped my finger twice on the metal table and released the breath I had been holding. "I know from what Liam had told me that he had demonstrated a deep obsession in regard to all things related to Vernon Wreath. I understand that he had paid a detective to surface everything that could be rummaged on him, which included me. He had not sought any psychiatric aid to assist in counseling him toward acceptance of the unfortunate circumstances. I do understand he walked a pathway of slow self-destruction using alcohol as his choice of execution. When we met he had already made a decision to stop drinking and was putting in support mechanisms to ensure he maintained the right focus on healing or at least, that is the way he consistently presented himself to me."

"Do you think Liam had a relapse?"

"I'm not sure. In retrospect I can see that he didn't present as completely stable when he arrived today but once again I saw no reason to be alarmed for my own safety. The comments he made to me in regard to experiencing black outs peaked my interest and certainly once he mentioned the reference to masturbating over a sleeping woman I recognized there was a potentially serious mental issue surfacing for him. This had me wonder whether there was an underlying guilt of enjoying his new found love interest in Dwayne that forced the psychotic episodes to develop into subconsciously acting out against his personal struggle with homosexuality. In saying this I am not suggesting he was ashamed of being homosexual, no. The struggle had been associated with his family and the fact that in his view, they paid the price with their lives for him choosing to be his authentic self. To qualify further, one of the standout comments he made at the café on the first day we met was that he couldn't move past the fact that if he weren't so selfish he would still be married and his wife and daughter wouldn't have been home alone the night Vernon attacked them. He felt he failed his duty to protect them. Honestly, I am just surmising given what little I know. Everything happened all too fast. When I found him in the bathroom naked, I knew he was not in a stable mindset, which resulted in me locking him in. There is nothing more I can tell you."

"You said you had never seen him before, yet you were both present for Vernon Wreath's execution."

"Careful with your choice of words and assumptions Doctor. You asked me had I ever met him before. To this, I answered no, never. Liam was present yes, but I did not know of him nor do I recall seeing him, and I most certainly never spoke to him. I was preoccupied with Vernon Wreath that day. The only reason I am aware that Liam was present is because he told me he had seen me on that day."

She looked down at the closed brown file and pursed her lips.

"Show me," I said.

"I'd advise against it. There is nothing here that would serve you to know or see."

"Show me."

"Harper you know as well as I do that there is nothing you can do to reverse what is seen. I honestly would advise against you looking at the remaining images."

I nodded my head, "If you believed that you wouldn't have brought them into the interview with you, nor would you have confirmed that there is more to look at. The truth is you want me to see them, you just don't want to be accountable for doing so which is why you are giving me this orchestrated prattle. Please, let's just cut to the chase. Pass me the file or open it and show me."

Dr Dubawnt shifted her seat across to hold her body on a diagonal to mine as a gesture of support before sliding the file across the table to have it settle in front of me. She watched as I stared at the cover of the cardboard file. I placed my hand inside rather than flipping it open. When my fingers grasped the contents, I pulled them out spreading them across the table in front of me. Unlike the 5x6 snaps I had already viewed, these were all full size blown up detailed images of the crime scenes. My elbows were on the table with my hands in a praying position leaning against my nose. I visually jutted between images looking for something, anything that would help me understand 'the lesson' I was supposed to learn. I could hardly discern between the victims. It was a bloody mess. Their faces slashed, beaten to a mashed pulp. The rage unleashed upon them was unlike anything I had the misfortune to witness before.

The Dr leaned forward in order to get my attention, "Harper, how are you doing?"

I shook my head from left to right, unable to speak.

"Harper, talk to me."

Just as she reached across to touch my arm, I reefed my chair back, leaned forward so my head was positioned between my legs to vomit on the floor. I found myself gasping for air, dry reaching then puking while listening to the noise of people entering and exiting the room. The Dr patted my back. Tears free fell into the expanding pool of digestive extracts as I kept visualizing the images, the word consequences pristinely carved in their skin, forced me to dry retch some more. There was bitterness in my heart for the lives that had been stolen with a fire roaring in my belly fueled by a hatred for Vernon Wreath and the lesson he delivered on behalf of the Interferon's.

Purgatory

Weeks had gone by since I had ventured out of my apartment. I couldn't bring myself to attend any of the funerals let alone answer the phone which was still running off the hook with messages left requesting interviews, comments, anything to assist in sustaining the promotion of local news horror. I was unable to encourage myself to breathe deep anymore. I hated people; I hated this world and everything about it. I was broken, no longer wishing to find a reason to wake of a morning and cursing each day that I did.

Huckleberry remained by my side the whole time. At night, I would take him to bed as he left me with no alternate choice. If I tried to leave him down stairs to sleep in his own bedding, he would whimper and eventually howl through the night until I collected him. He knew I wasn't feeling my usual self and refused to allow me a moment's peace. In bed, he slept on my chest or nuzzled into a ball near my neck. The only time I had reprieve from his contact was when I could no longer withstand my own stench so was forced to shower. Even then he would be in the bathroom waiting for me to come out from behind the frosted glass panels. In the waves of emotion where I was caught in an outburst of overwhelming pain I curled into a ball, rocking with madness, manically crying. The dear soul would frantically lap up the tears and whimper as he attempted to nuzzle and console me. I had never experienced this level of grief and didn't know how to get out from the plummet. In truth even if I did, I wasn't sure that I wanted to. I felt dead inside.

Although my mind was flattened, still a portion of it insisted that I review the details of every aspect of the situation. Completely exhausted I wanted it to stop but not even the heaviest dose of sedation set to tranquilize a horse was able to prevent my mind from its mission. I ached to temper my gnawing need to analyze the situation. My energy was low with no fight remaining, on the entry of the fourth week of my malignant state, I chose to yield to the analysis portion of my psych's relentless call.

On my writing desk was a charcoal stick. I took this and an A3 sheet of the art paper downstairs to the lounge. Once I removed everything from the coffee table, I placed the paper on it before sitting on the floor.

"Show me." I whispered.

Huckleberry climbed into my lap, spun like a cat three times clockwise before nesting in a comfortable position. I quietly stroked him with my left hand while I stared at the blank piece of paper. My mind rechanneled its thoughts to align with a series of selected critical events. I patiently endured the underlying sorrow while remaining on point for what I was being shown by my conscience. The only way through this gauntlet is to be removed from the reality of what I had to assess.

When Zivah manifested in Liam's body she confirmed that I had cordoned the way into this realm for the five I had selected to guide. As the soul key of wills it was my choice to narrow the connection to spiritual possession. Vernon's note said if he could reach me than so could they. At this point I am making the assumption that 'they' represent the interferons. If this is true than it begs the question, why he would hold a concern about this? After all, he is a slave to their bidding, one of two remaining attempters who are designated to hunt the seven soul keys. It therefore, leads me to what is deemed as an accurate assumption that Vernon was instructed by the Interferons to enter Liam. The extent of his destructive evil force was destined to mark my psych and leave me in a welt of pain whereby I would reactively scurry to find a way to close the channel so no others could be harmed. If I closed it, then no one would have access. The remaining three chosen to reach me at the point I required further guidance would no longer have a mechanism to do so. To close the channel is not just about forcing me to continue on my journey completely blind, it's to more importantly instil fear within in me about their capabilities. It would be a silent acknowledgement of their perceived power. To yield would leave me feeding the belly of the beast with a false prophecy that they are able to win, gain favor and control me. The interferons are acting out as a response to my recent play to expose their existence. Unleashing Vernon was their message to me that they hold no hesitation in ruling with an iron fist by harming people I love to force my hand to comply.

Liam was a clear choice given, he had been used as a channel prior by Bahrain and Zivah. I wonder if the essence leaves a marked trail in which others may follow?

No, no, I have to raise my thoughts above this, it's too deep down a warren. I can't assume the interferons knew that Liam was the vessel used. In saying this, I wonder why Vernon chose to remove Liam's clothes and then ended his life before the police could capture him. It's as though he wanted them to conclude that Liam had lost his sanity. This has to mean something. Vernon devotes his energies to torment. It would make more sense to allow Liam to live with the consequences bestowed upon him, so I was forced to watch him being persecuted, jailed and then eventually walked down the green mile. Why, oh why would he take Liam's life? What greater purpose did this action serve than the alternative?

My right hand picked up the charcoal and started to draw. Frantically I created lines, squiggles and shapes, my fingers smudged in areas and blackened others. I allowed myself to be guided to the strokes I felt compelled to make. It was close to thirty minutes of drawing before I shifted my position to kneel over the paper. Huckleberry now sat by my side while I used both hands to manifest this piece. Upon its completion, I looked at the length of both my arms covered in the ash. Only a small stump of the charcoal remained in my hand. I stood above the table to gaze upon it. My eyes widened as I saw the image of a person within a person depicted. Dual eyes, one set normal the other of a snake. Twin sets of teeth, with the first looking regular and the second set behind with razor edges. One tongue flat with another jutting outward split like a fork. This image depicted duality of residence in a singular host. Good and evil present, neither can escape. Perhaps this was it- once entered with mal intent, Vernon became entrenched leaving the only option of release by death of the flesh.

I released a sigh of relief as the voices in my mind dissipated to silence. This was the pathway it needed to take before it rested, and now I was completely spent. Partially delirious I wondered whether I should retire to my room or venture out to get some much needed supplies. Little Huckleberry was reduced to eating dry biscuits as I exhausted the meat supplies that were in my freezer for him a few days prior. I glanced down at him, while he peered up at me. He released a yawn and placed a single paw across a couple of my bare toes.

"You're right little man. Let's get some rest and when we wake we can work on mustering the energy to tackle what lays beyond the door."

I gently lifted him up to plant a kiss on the top of his head then went to the bedroom to get us both settled for what I was hoping would be a peaceful sleep.

* * * * *

The weighted fog from my mind lifted enough to allow me to feel the brightness of the new day warming the exposed areas of my skin. Huckleberry was still fast asleep. I looked up to the sky, finding myself hypnotized by the speed of the clouds whizzing by. It was set to be a windy day.

My only dream, of which I could recall, was related to the feather from the raven. My mom's voice could be heard in the distance suggesting that it is a gift given to acknowledge the sacrifices made on my quest. I kept looking at the bird bowing and leaving the feather. There had to be more to it than the obvious. My instincts were attuned to interpreting signs, yet this one was still somewhat a mystery. I know having a raven present meant a message was being delivered, and the feather may have been a gift but the purpose of the gift was yet to be understood by me. It held a function.

Quietly, I shifted my body to reach into my bedside table draw. The feather lay there perfectly intact. I pulled it out and twirled it between my fingers. Huckleberry stirred before opening his eyes, released a big yawn followed by a delightful stretch then shifted his torso so his muzzle was facing away from the breeze I was creating with the spin of the feather. I laughed, scratched his hind quarters and whispered, "Good morning sleepy bum." He remained still while I gave him a light scratch all over. It was clear by his disposition that he was very tired. I held no doubt the last few weeks had affected him greatly too.

After a quick shower to freshen myself up, I scooped Huckleberry off the bed cradling him in my arms like a baby as I headed down the stairs and out the door. He lay still staring at me, licked his lips and placed a single paw under my chin. I kissed the pad on his foot before strapping him into the car harness.

Our first priority stop was at the local butchers. I organized some fresh meaty bones to be cut into Huckleberry portions and then went next door to order a latte to have outside while he chewed on his well earned bone. The foot traffic was no busier than usual; people seemed to be going about their day, some with ravers on, others with headphones. Interestingly a large majority of the people listening to music were using the oversized earmuff sound systems. I wonder if the trend was favored post the discovery of the mark held within a person's ear. Its stands to reason that some would profit as a by product of war. I know there was a continued issue meeting the current demands for ravers and that plenty of new businesses had sprung up in an attempt to get a slice of the pie. I guess hats, headphones and any other products, which allowed for discrete covering of a people's ears in public was also going to receive an increased flux in sales.

"You have a cute doggy."

I turned to see a little girl standing over Huckleberry.

"Thank you. Where are your parents?" I said looking about for an adult that may be searching for a child.

"My mom is in the flower shop. I don't have a daddy."

She was very sweetly and gentle in her demeanor. "Oh, well I'm glad that you have a mom. She may be worried about you sneaking away like this. You need to go back to your momma now."

"Do you miss your daddy too?"

I smiled, "You must have me confused with someone else sweetie."

"Persephone, Persephone," called out a woman from the entrance of the flower shop. I waved my hand to gain her attention as I pointed to the little girl in front of me. The woman smiled placing her hand on her chest to show relief that she had found her.

Persephone rocked from side to side undeterred by her moms calling, "No, I'm not confused."

"Excuse me?" I said looking a little closer at her. "What do you mean?"

Her face contorted as she leaned in with a voice that sent a chill up my spine, "You're too late. The devils got his tongue."

I immediately sat upright, feeling my body tense as I curbed my desire to pick her up and shake her, "What did you just say?"

She lurched forward as though to challenge me to

fight, "Consequences." With this she bent down, gave Huckleberry a pat and turned to head toward her mom skipping along the way as though nothing had just transpired.

I projected an air of calm as I took a sip of my latte while observing the mom and daughter head down the street walking hand in hand. I knew that there were watchers everywhere subconsciously observing me. Huckleberry's reaction to the situation provided me with confidence that my interpretation of what just happened was indeed an indirect communiqué from the Interferons. If there was a presence of true evil within this girl, he would I suspect react, yet his demeanor did not alter. He was not perturbed in the slightest. This, based on what I knew so far could only mean that she is a watcher who was subconsciously charged to pass on a message. The Interferon's want me to attend my parent's home, and with such a compelling reason, how could I not comply.

Once Huckleberry completed his meal, I calmly headed to the car, loaded him in and began to drive. On my way to my folk's house, I dialed the home number.

"Hello."

"Hi Mom, I just wanted to let you know that I'm on my way over. Is there anything you need me to pick up?"

"Harper where have you been? Your father and I are worried sick about you. I'm so glad to hear your voice, don't worry about running silly errands just get here as quick as you can."

"Why is there a problem?"

"We saw on the news what that horrid monster did to your friends. I know that you needed some time to grieve, but you could have at least left a single response to one of our messages to let us know that you were okay."

I detected her hesitation and there was a distinct strain in the tone of her voice.

"I'll be there in less than an hour. I don't want to talk about it, there is nothing to say that will change what happened, so it's put to bed. I just want to have a nice afternoon with the both of you. Not a word please mom, try okay? Is dad home?"

"Yes," She paused, holding her breath.

"Mom, is everything alright?"

"Yes, he's in the garden, he will be so relieved. I'll go tell him now. Drive carefully and we will see you soon."

She hung up the phone without making a commitment to put a lid on any discussion pertaining to the incident. I knew it was impossible for her not to, but I really needed for her to make an exceptional effort this time. My head was weighted under the pressure of knowing that I may be entering into another environment where I am immobilized.

When I turned into their street Huckleberry sat up and began to wag his tail. He knew where we were and was excited to be here. I couldn't help but smile. I decided to reverse park into the drive. At the point that I turned the engine off, I saw from the corner of my eye that the front door to my parent's house was opened by someone. My eyes remained fixated, waiting to see who would come out. Nobody did. Unleashing Huckleberry from his restraint, I grabbed him and my valuables and then headed to the door. Prior to walking in I turned to survey the area. The curtain in the window of the double story house across the way moved erratically, watchers I thought to myself. I had no idea of what I was about to face but knew there were copious witnesses activated to capture everything that transpired. It appeared the puppet masters cornered me once again, or at least it was beginning to feel this way.

"Mom, Dad, I'm here."

"I know Harps I opened the door when I heard your car. Come in I'm cooking, sorry I don't want it to burn."

There was a wave of relief felt by me as I closed the door and proceeded down the hall.

I placed wriggling Huckleberry on the ground in the kitchen. No sooner did his paws make contact with the floorboards he scurried straight out the back door. I laughed, "Hey mom, can I assume by Huckleberry's charge into the yard that his bestie Dad is out there?"

"You can," she said with a glint in her eye. "You look awful Harps. The color has been drained from you, and those clothes are falling off. I understand you have been through a lot lately but it looks like you haven't been eating at all."

I took a deep breath and then released it. In truth I couldn't recall the last time I had eaten nor what it was. I leant in to give her a kiss on the cheek as she continued stirring the pot.

"I'm sorry for your loss Harper. I know those boys meant the world to you."

"Mom stop, seriously if you don't I'II leave. I just can't do this. Put it to bed."

She took pause for a moment to look into my eyes, before nodding. "Okay," she pushed the hair veiling my left eye and tucked it behind my ear, "Okay."

The worry lines across her brow presented as her eyes moistened on the edges. I could tell when she pursed her lips that she was doing her utmost not to cry. I held no strength to console her. "I'm going outside to say hello to dad. Whatever you're cooking smells nice."

"Let him know lunch will be ready in five minutes. He needs to come in to set the table."

"Will do," I said as I walked outside to the welcome sound of my dad and Huckleberry playing in the distance. I followed the path around and found dad on his back rolling on the patch of grass with Huckleberry jumping on him.

"Hey Beanie Bear, I wanted to give you and your mother a chance to catch up." He said as he stood to greet me with a hug. "How are you?" He whispered as he squeezed me tight. "God damn it kiddo, you had me worried."

"Sorry dad, it's been tough but I'm doing okay."

He continued to hold me in a tight embrace while rocking me from side to side.

After a while I gently pulled back to look at him, "Mom told me to let you know she is expecting you to set the table for lunch."

He shook his head, "Of course she did. Okay, let's head inside. You look like you could use a proper feed."

I poked him in the stomach, "and you look like you could skip a few. What's up with the midriff podgy coating?"

"I think it's endearing," he said wrapping his arms around himself.

I laughed.

When we entered the dining area mom had already set the table and was in the middle of bringing over the food.

"Wow look at all this fanfare," I said truly amazed at the selection she had laid out.

Dad laughed, "I'm thinking mom plans to have you back in a normal weight range before you leave."

I smiled and nodded my head. The smell of the food did get my gastric juices engaged to flow, but it also gave me nausea. It had been far too long since I had eaten a meal. I'd have to consume slowly to prevent indigestion.

"Come sit now and start before it cools down too much. This is spiced pumpkin and squash pie. Over here we have the rice noodle pasta. The Asian spicy greens are contained in this bowl. These are the complimentary relishes to go with it. Oh, and here, I almost forgot the sweet potato mash."

"You prepared Asian food and pumpkin pie? What an odd mixture of flavors. Since when do you dabble in cooking Asian cuisine?"

"I'll have you know I've been attending gastronomy of the world. It's a group of people teaching each other home recipes. We set the calendar for the year in advance allocating a month to each country represented. The people who have recipes for the region they want to share provide it to the rest of us to select which of them we wish to learn. We then get together to shop, cook and eat what we made. Its fabulous."

"I can see it's had an effect on dad's waistline too."

She slapped him on the back across his left shoulder; "You know your father is the weakest when it comes to food and moderation."

Dad just shrugged before lifting his plate in readiness to be served.

The banter was nice. Mom managed to honor my request not to reference what happened. In actuality, she seemed to be in reasonably good spirits. Dad mostly listened while hoeing into his meal. After lunch, he retired to the lounge for a rest while mom flittered about in the kitchen. I offered to help, but she insisted I relax too.

"Mom, when did you get this piece?"

"I had it for years and only recently thought it might be nice to display it on the wall. Your father says it doesn't fit the décor but I like the colors."

The frame must have been over a meter in length containing a high quality print of an Egyptian scene involving Ma'at. "What does it represent?"

Mom walked across to me, "Its an excerpt from the 'Book of the Dead' depicting the weighing of the heart using the ostrich feather of Ma'at as the measure of purity. If the heart is without burden of sin than it will be proven on the scales to be lighter than her feather of truth. If it is not, then Ammut is unleashed to devour the heart thus thrusting the soul into purgatory, in theory never to be released."

"It seems to be a more elaborate depiction of what is on the anon birthday cards I received each year."

"Yes. My curiosity stemmed from the cards initially and then held a life of its own. Egyptology is vast and extraordinarily fascinating. There is so much to learn."

"Did you ever hold a theory around why Ma'at and Ammut were chosen for me?"

"The obvious conclusion would be pertaining to obtaining the truth. Seeing things for what they are rather than what people want you to see."

I watched her eyes flicker for a moment before she bit her bottom lip.

"There, right there, whatever that is may be exactly what I need to know. You're hesitating, to protect me. What is it mom?"

She looked at me, "I hate it when you do that."

"I dislike it when you insist on withholding information under some guise that you are protecting

116

me when in actuality you may be a hindrance in my progression. Please mom, you don't know what is best for me because you are not me. It pisses me off that you think hiding shit from me is going to prevent me from getting hurt. Enough, just tell me."

I never meant for my words to sound as harsh as they were delivered, but I was feeling the pressure of everything, and my mind ached from having to be constantly on guard.

She shook her head, "I've only ever had your best interests at heart. I worry about you Harper but you're right. I am not you." After a moment she released a sigh, "Come with me."

I followed her down the hall and up the attic stairs. I stood back and watched as she manoeuvred between the tightly packed boxes to weave her way across to the far right corner. She disappeared from my view when she bent down. All I heard were sounds of things sliding on the ground and her grunting. When she stood up, she was holding a metal container that was a hybrid between a tall hatbox and suitcase. Mom placed it on top of the box closest to her and then proceeded to slide it along as she shimmied her way back to me.

"You really need to consider offloading some of this stuff you have up here. Its like you are an undetected hoarder because you have the fortitude to be organized about it."

Mom laughed, "It is starting to become a little overwhelming up here."

"What's in the odd box?"

"Take a look for yourself. I don't know what it all means but the part I had hidden from you and your father actually, was that each year for the first nine years you received a gift along with the birthday card. I opened them, naturally out of concern but everything is in here including the wrapping paper."

I placed my hand on the lid to feel its vibration.

"Harper, some of the presents are rare, perhaps even priceless."

"Are you referring to literal value?"

"Yes. An item in here is one of two that exist in the world. It is so rare that the last publicly known one in auction was promoted to reach higher than two hundred and fifty thousand dollars. The bid was silent with the final figure not publicly disclosed. I understand it stirred significant interest from collectors around the globe, some of whom confirmed they pulled out once it reached a certain figure. One person interviewed by the media said they were unsuccessful with their submission of five hundred and seventy-five thousand dollars, so I know it went well over half a million."

"What is it?"

"A single feather from an Ostrich."

"What am I missing here? Why would a feather from the common Ostrich be considered rare?"

"The only known recorded reference to this particular plumage was found in Egypt, which told of an albino ostrich that was born the purest of white with the exception of two tail plumes that held a unique golden to fading peach hue. This was only discovered in the current century by the Egyptian archaeologist Mahalid Quatoum. Mahalid and his team uncovered a whole new vein of tombs that are interconnected to all of the pyramids found thus far. Every entrance of significance depicts a picture of Ma'at similar to the one I have on my wall downstairs with the exception of a few key things.

Firstly, the hieroglyphs above and below it indicate that the entrance is only granted through the weighting of the soul rather than the heart. This judgement is made against the soul depicted by using this unique ostrich feather. There are no scales, just Ma'at holding the feather in her left hand. It was a revelation, a secret revealed, not even the book of the dead held reference to it. The hieroglyphs state that only pure of soul coupled with good intent can hold the feather to enact the mode of judgement and summon Ammut to devour an evil essence. Any who dare to hold the feather to judgement will first be judged."

"Wow, that just sent a shiver up my spine."

"Do you recall the time we all went on a family vacation to Egypt for a tour of the pyramids?"

"Sure, I was eight I think or close to it. I kept sitting on the sand fascinated by the way it felt to have it sift and fall between my fingers" I said with a smile. It had been a long time since I thought of that.

"Do you recall the man who gave us a tour of the tombs?"

"Hmm, not particularly."

"It was Mahalid Quatoum himself."

"Really? An archaeologist gave tours?"

"No, I had written to him before we left to go across to Egypt explaining I was a student of Egyptology and was keen to learn more about his discoveries. At the time there wasn't much literature on it and obviously I was motivated to learn all I can given my daughter seemed to be in possession of one of these feathers. I made the assumption it was authentic because other items that had been gifted to you were confirmed as the genuine articles so I held no reason to believe otherwise."

"Did you tell him about the feather?"

"No. That's the thing that was odd, I didn't need to. Your father had taken your brother off to explore the markets, and for some reason, he was fixated on riding the camels. I had an appointment to meet with Mahalid and I brought you along."

"I don't recall this," I said trying to search my mind for anything that could confirm what I was hearing.

"When we met he seemed immediately fixated on you. He insisted on speaking to you in a language that I didn't understand yet you were responding to him answering all his questions as though he was speaking English."

"Wait, what? Was I responding in whatever the language was or in English? I'm confused."

"He spoke in a strange dialect, you listened, then responded in English."

"I don't remember any of this. I recall sitting on the ground near the edge of one of the tombs playing with the sand, but not much else."

"Yes, well we can get to that in a minute. I obviously found this situation a little unnerving to say the least and wanted to get you out of there. As I stood up to gather my things he said, "do not fear what is not known by you and should not be known. Your daughter is in possession of the feather, yes?" I looked at him without being able to speak. I just nodded, to which he said "good tell no one of it." Then he became insistent that he be allowed the honor of hosting us for the duration of the stay. He made arrangements to get private access to visit the tombs then joined us to become our guide. You stood by his side the whole time while he explained the history, what the hieroglyphs meant and on occasion he would point to specific things while speaking to you in that language."

"Mom, all those adventures you and dad took Dylan and I on, were they driven by a need to find answers to the contents of this box?"

She looked across at it for a moment, "Mostly, yes."

I could feel a flood of emotion well from the pit of my stomach. "Thank you," I whispered.

"For what Harper, I wasn't able to figure out a damn thing? It all became one puzzle on top of another. Nothing seemed interconnected. It scared me and fascinated me. At one point it started to feel like I was on a quest but each time I would be proven wrong."

"What do you mean?"

"Do you recall the time we trekked through the Kyosan Mountains in Japan? I think you were only five or six at the time."

"Vaguely, an image of a forest, containing some huge trees, there were statues and gravestones which come to mind, but that's all."

"Yes, the forest was filled with extraordinarily large trees. There are a lot of people buried up there in marked and unmarked graves. When we got to the monastery, it seemed to be deserted, not a soul in sight. The waft of the incense greeted my nose as I crossed the threshold in bare feet to look inside. Your father and Dylan followed, but you wanted to stay outside. You sat on the ground with your legs crossed, picked up handfuls of the nutrient rich earth and let if fall through your fingers. We let you be while we explored the temple. Your father and I took turns in checking to make sure you were okay."

There was a sense of familiarity to what my mom was describing but it didn't quite feel like a memory I owned. It made me wonder why such moments of significance were not etched in the forefront of my mind.

"The interior of this massive open plan room we entered was truly spectacular. Scriptures along the walls with detailed illustrations in inks possibly thousands of years old, cracked and worn in places but still managing to hold its vibrancy of hues on whole sections, which only stimulated my mind to the potential wonder of what it would have been like in its original form. Everything in there was labored by hand using techniques all but lost these days. There was a sense of preservation of purpose to what was contained within these walls. It stood as a reminder of what is possible to be achieved with very little."

"You make me feel the need to visit this place again."

"You should if not for simple curiosity's sake. Let me finish so you can understand why I'm telling you this. Your father ushered Dylan and I to return to the edge of the monastery door quietly. As we got closer, I could hear you giggling. When we peered from the side there you were in the same position except now a circle was forming around you by a group of monks in orange robes. They approached you, bowed to the ground in front of you placing their forehead on your feet, they then rose, found a spot in the circle and sat in the lotus position before closing their eyes. Each of them did this while you giggled holding the earth in your hands, that was teaming with wriggling worms."

"Seriously, I don't recall this at all."

"They chanted for a solid thirty or so minutes with you seemingly oblivious to what was happening. You kept giggling at the worms tickling your palms. Dylan was getting restless and needed to go to the bathroom so your father took him to find one while I waited for you. When the chanting stopped you gently placed the worms back on the ground and covered them. I watched you shift your posture to sit on your knees with your bottom on your heels. One by one the monks entered the circle to sit in the same position in front of you. They placed their hands in a praying position with the long edge of their hands touching their forehead. With your soil covered tiny hands you placed them on the outside of theirs, leaned in to connect the other side of their hands to your forehead whispering the word baransu."

"Baransu, balance. It's the Japanese word for balance."

My mom nodded, "Yes."

"The whole experience sounds amazing. It would have been nice to remember it, but I simply don't."

"I doubt that you have forgotten, its nestled in that mind of yours somewhere. I have a theory that we recall the things we need to when we need them. I believed this more and more while watching you across the years do some pretty unexplainable things. Its like you have the capacity to retrieve knowledge acquired across lifetimes to utilize at will."

I smiled, "That would make for a good story."

"Yes, but there is always truth in fiction and your truth seems to be one with the potential to trump them all."

"Thank you for telling me all of this, mom." I leaned in and gave her a cuddle.

"You're welcome. There comes a time when a person has to accept their role. All these years I held onto this perhaps not just because I wanted to protect you, but also because I enjoyed the elements of the fantastical about it all. There is definitely an indefinable sense of magic in what is occurring around you. Its high time I accept that it is in actuality about you, not me."

I squeezed her tight.

"Its just hard to let go of the very thing that I have secretly allowed to rule my life."

"I know, baransu." I whispered.

I could feel her release the tension from her body as I continued to hold her.

"Okay Harper, I'll leave you to have a look at the contents while I make us a pot of tea. I made some scones we can have some of them as well."

"Sure mom," I said as I stepped back to allow her free passage to pass by me.

She paused for a moment, placed her hand on the lid of the box nodded her head, "It's the right thing to do." Then she left the room.

I wasn't sure whether she was speaking to herself or to the contents of the box as though it was an old friend. I knew her attachment to it was strong. It did strike a thought in me about the role she is destined to play in all of what is happening.

The latch was worn making it hard to leverage open. When it released, the top sprung open with the sound of the rusted springs stretching. There were so many interesting items enchanting my eyes, I didn't know where to start. My hands were drawn to the pile of pictures. Images of places and faces that didn't seem familiar to me yet there I was frozen in time suggesting otherwise. It truly had been such a long while since I last saw myself as a small child. Mom was obsessed with photography and even had her own darkroom set up in the basement. She, no doubt hand processed these grainy pixelated black and white images.

Carefully curled around the edging of the box I could see the ostrich feather partially protected by a silk wrap. The color was almost luminescent, gleaming with a radiance that seemed to call to me to touch it.

"Hey Beanie Bear."

I spun around and held my heart, "Jesus you scared the shit out of me."

"I'm sorry I called out to you from the bottom of the stairs but you didn't seem to hear me. It looks like you were lost in thought."

"Really you called out to me? I didn't hear you at all."

"Your mom sent me to get you. She has a pot of tea ready and some yummy scones." He said licking his lips.

"Ok dad I'll be down in just a minute."

"Sure, hey it's really nice to have you home." He said placing his arms around me for a cuddle.

"Thanks, I'm glad I'm here too."

He squeezed me tight as I felt his right hand run down my back to my ass pulling my torso closer to his body.

"Dad," I said trying to pull away.

"I missed you Harpuuurrrr." He said as he used his tongue to lick the side of my face.

"NO!" I yelled as I struggled to get out of his vice embrace. He released a laugh then flipped me around securing my hands behind me forcing a bend in my back so he could push his ridged penis against the cleft of my ass.

"Oh Harpuurr you don't know how long I've waited for thisssssss. Fucking you as daddy is a far sweeter reward I will gladly continue to rot in hell for." He pushed harder against me, "Oooo can you feel my cock? Ooooo."

My mind was racing through options on freeing myself from his grip while he continued his obsessive rant.

"When I FFFUUCK you and you're about to

cuuuummmm call me DADDY. AH HA HA HA HA ha ha ha ha, AH HA HA ha ha ha ha, AH HA HA ha ha ha ha ha"

He laughed like the insane mad man, he was then paused to take a deep breath before leaning over my back to whisper in my ear. "Cause if you don't I'll kill your mommy, I'll kill your brother, I'll hunt down, fuck and kill everyone you ever loved." He kissed me on the side of my cheek, as I remained still, "You Harpuuurrrr are going to make sweet love to me while I fuck you like a rabid beast."

I shifted my foot position to buck him off me, trying my best not to allow myself to be consumed by hatred for him. I knew this is what he wanted, needed from me to feed his unsavory hunger for pain.

"Vernon, let my father go or I will hurt you in ways that will make you realize your time in hell was a picnic."

"Oh Harpuurrrr, you can't hurt me cause you would be hurting your dad dad too." He said as his shifted to allow his free hand to glide across my stomach up to squeeze my left breast above the bra hard enough to make me gasp from the rush of pain.

I bit my bottom lip. "Okay, you need to let me go or mom will be suspicious and come up here."

"No, no Harper, no she won't."

I tried to contain the surge of panic that overcame my senses, "What did you do to her?"

"Relax, she's sleeping, it's only a small bump on the head. Pfft."

I shifted my body left to right trying to wiggle out of his grip. "Vernon LET ME GO."

He wasn't remotely fazed by me and was clearly enjoying a level of comfort that he held me in a position of checkmate. If I didn't comply he would harm everyone, if I did comply I knew him well enough to understand that he would still harm everyone. I couldn't physically hurt him without hurting my dad. It was clear to me now that Vernon would continue to be sent through open channels. The only leverage I held at this point was to use his weakness of insatiable need to feed off my rage, fear and fight. Using this against him was my only option. I couldn't bear the thought of what I might have to do to gain an advantage. I tried not to gag at the flood of thoughts racing through my mind.

"I'm going to taste you now my little Princess. Call me daddddddy, I want to hear you puuuurrrr."

I had no idea if he was telling the truth about my mom only having a bump on her head but knew that if he was lying than there was nothing I could do about it. I relaxed my breath and allowed my body to soften. This is not dad, this is not incest was all I chanted over and over as I tried not to cringe when I gently pushed up against him, inviting him to connect to my flesh. "Okay. You win Vernon, don't hurt anyone else, I can't have you hurt anymore people. I'II try and do as you wish. Fuck me. I want you to fuck me Vernon."

"NO," he said immediately recoiling then thrusting his groin into me while tightening his grip. "You don't get to call the shots now Harpuuur, aint no guards to watch out for you, chains to hold me down, no-one knows you need to be rescued. I'm gonna use this daddy dick to rape you over and over and over again. Maybe even have you make a daddy baby. Then when I'm tired of raping your sorry ass, I'II still kill everyone you ever loved."

"I know." I said calmly.

"Do you?" He said smugly as he pulled my hair back

to encourage me to become upright. I closed my eyes as I felt his hand force its way between my loose jeans, past my panties and into my crotch region. I wanted to flinch, fight, scream but my senses told me to still. I released a gasp as he mercilessly inserted his fingers into me. He pushed so hard upward that I could feel my feet lifting from the ground. I wanted to cry, I wanted to kill him, but I mustered all my strength to curb my rage from sight.

In frustration Vernon momentarily loosened his grip on my hands as he yelled, "ARGHHHHHHH, FIGHT ME YOU CUNT."

I quickly reclaimed my arms freedom, braced my hands on the boxes in front of me and used it to bridge the force of my right leg as I lifted it to disperse a thrust to my father's right patella hard enough to hear the crack as it shattered under the weight of my fierce blow.

As he released a scream falling to the floor holding his leg, I spun around, "LOOK AT MEEEeeee.' I seethed. "WHO AM I?" I said placing one hand in the box and the other on my dads forehead pushing down hard to maintain a connection as my arms jolted outward from my body being held upright by a force scurrying around my veins.

"AHHHHHhhhhhhhhhhhh," I released a call of agony as my left hand lifted the feather of truth above my head. The pulse of the entity occupying my core blurred my vision to only see partial distortion of shadows. I felt the vibration of energy beaming from the golden hues of the plume. My body cooled while my right hand seared hot channeling outward to my father's skull.

No longer able to command my limbs my head twisted to gaze upon him, "VERTUM AKBAH LOC

TAHE. AKIM NAYET TOHOR AKBAH. AMMUT TAHE NE VERTUM." My eyes felt like they were blistering from a fire arising from within. There were sounds of a distant chant growing increasingly louder. The sheer power of energy pulsing through my veins seemed to emanate from a surge through my feet upward into my body. It was as though in any moment my skin could peel to reveal this raging ball of sunlight.

Vernon tried to use his arms to disconnect my hand, then frantically felt about to look for something. In a clear panic, his hands searched for anything he could use as a weapon. The moment he was successful in grasping the end of a broken wooden handle from an old broomstick he immediately started to repeatedly hit my dad on the side of the head.

"TOROOM DAK MAR KEE."

As my right hand rose so did Dad's body. The levitational hold placed Vernon in a state of limp flux. Dad's hand dropped releasing the piece of wood. There would be no escape this time. Judgement had been passed and now the executioner was on its way riding on the coat tails of an evocative chant growing in strength as its presence drew near. The definitive beat held a different energy wave rising through the boards of the floor in what I could only describe as the vibrations of sound. It was a gnarling noise holding a melody, which seemed to be drawn to the call toward negative life force energy.

My right hand disconnected from my fathers forehead, allowing him to collapse unconscious on the floor. The sound waves pulsed as it grew in size to cocoon my father's body. There was tension felt in unvoiced screams depicted by the way the waves shifted, jumped and swirled around. It lifted the torso up toward the ceiling then dropped it down, this happened several times. Vernon was clearly not surrendering without a fight. Perhaps that made the devouring of the soul taste more rewarding for Ammut. It didn't take long before a pulse of light jolted from my father's solar plexus upward to a hover. The vibration around the body increased to a frantic rhythm for several seconds before dissipating back through the floor. The light from above dropped back through my father's chest causing his body to shift as his mouth opened wide to draw in a deep unconscious breath.

In the silence, I could feel my body being left in peace. I fell to my knees on the ground while focused on father who lay there still. As my eyesight returned with clarity, I could see his pants were soaked in a patch from the release of what I hoped was pee. His breath was shallow, but he seemed calm. I looked at the feather held tightly in my trembling hand. "Thank you." I whispered, then tilted my head to the side and promptly threw up.

* * * * *

"Wake up mom." I said stroking her hair. "Come on, you need to wake up now." The cold press lay across her brow. The knock on her head was nasty but didn't look like it would need stitches. I just couldn't afford to get other people involved, no neighbors, no ambulance. This was too odd to be explainable. I needed her to wake.

"Harper ..." she whispered. "You're safe."

"Yes, can you open your eyes please? I need to see your pupils to check how badly you are concussed."

"In a minute, my head hurts," she whispered. "What happened?"

"I think you must have slipped and hit your head." I responded.

"No, no, no that thing did this to me," she said slowly raising her hand to support her head as she lifted it off the table.

"What thing?"

"Harper where's your father. Is he okay?" She squinted with one eye looking around. "Where is he, tell me he's okay. Is that thing gone?"

"Mom, relax yes its gone okay. It won't come back and it can't hurt anyone anymore. You're safe."

She looked at me then burst into tears, releasing a whaling sound while sobbing. "Are you sure that monster is gone?" she asked between gasps.

I wrapped my arms around her, "Yes."

"It's been here on and off for days, taunting, switching, looking for you. I was scared Harper, so scared but I didn't know what to do." She gulped as continued to force her words through the tears, "I knew it wasn't your father, he felt different, had a smell about him that made me want to be ill whenever he touched my skin."

I closed my eyes not wanting to imagine how it must have felt for her to experience this with no context to understand what was happening.

"I didn't know what to do, I didn't know what to do, he could hear everything, was always watching, I'm so sorry I couldn't warn you. I couldn't take the chance. The feather, I kept dreaming about Ma'at and the feather. I realized it was the only way but I wasn't the one, it had to be you. I knew it had to be you."

Her crying wrenched at my heart like a vice, "Hey, shhhh." I rocked her gently trying not to engage the need to shed my own tears. She never needed to know what happened in the attic. I was barely able to acknowledge it myself.

"You did great mom but I need you to continue to be strong right now."

Suddenly there was a look of panic across her face, "Where's your father?"

"In the attic unconscious. He has a broken kneecap coupled with some minor contusions to his head. He is going to be in an awful lot of pain when he wakes. We need to call for an ambulance but first you we should carry him down the stairs."

"What happened?"

"Mom, keep focused, there is no time for details. I'm going to get you to help me carry him down the stairs, where we can place him face down at the bottom. I'll load up the car and head off before you call for help. Tell emergency services that you both lost your footing and fell down the stairs, then lost consciousness. This will explain the bumps on your heads and his fractured knee. Don't try to embellish anything or it will make you come undone. Keep your answers short and sweet. Dad will have a sensation of a black out because he won't recall anything that had occurred while V, while that thing was present."

She paused for a moment as she glanced down at the table, "It's attacking everybody around you to hurt you, isn't it? That's why Brandon, Ted and the others were murdered. It was going to kill us too."

I lifted her chin, so she could meet my gaze. Slowly I nodded my head and blinked.

Mom began to cry again, "Then it's my fault. If I gave you, the box with the things that belonged to you earlier, you would have been able to use the contents to stop this evil maniac sooner. Why is it after you Harps? I don't understand, I simply don't understand. What is happening? Who is doing this?"

I had tears beginning to form in the corner of my eyes, "No, that's not true. There wasn't anything that was set to save them from the fate that was bestowed. I won't explain it further, you just need to know that it is not your fault, none of this is your fault. The opposite, however, is true. The information you told me upstairs, the life long pursuit for answers drove you, but the importance of the journey in actuality was having me reconnected with key people around the globe. Without realizing, what you provided was the right connections to fuel hope."

She tried to use my words to console her tears but was naturally struggling to do so.

"Lets move dad into position, we need to get his knee addressed ideally before he wakes and has to endure any of the pain. Can you stand up?"

She used her hands to brace her as she rose from the table. "I can."

It was a struggle to get him down the narrow attic stairs. He was no lightweight coupled with his body being limp, it proved hard not to give him extra bumps and bruises along the way. I reasoned in my mind this would only support the story.

"Okay, swing him around, now place him down, there like that." I fetched a cushion to put under his head. "I'll be back in a minute. I just have to load up the car with my things. Can you find Huckleberry for me please? I suspect he's in the yard."

"Sure." Mom went outside while I ran up the attic stairs, placed the feather back inside the box, fastened the clasp and carefully lifted it to carry to the car. It was heavier than it looked, something in there held some weight to it. Once I returned I checked on dad before tucking my bag under my arm and heading out the back.

"Mom, did you find him?"

"No, I'm still looking."

I followed the sound of her voice doing my best not to feed the thoughts swilling in my mind. I hadn't noticed Huckleberry was missing, I was so preoccupied with what was going on around me I never thought to check on him.

"Huckleberry, come here boy." I called somehow knowing he wouldn't be able to answer. My instincts guided me to return to the house. The closer I was to the back entry the more my sense of urgency was felt as I ran inside to the lounge where dad had retired after lunch. On bended knees, I looked under the sofa, between the cushions, in the TV cabinets. He was in here I knew it.

"Did you find him?" asked mom scanning the room.

"No, but I know he's here somewhere." I said with a shaky voice. "I've checked the sofa, the TV cabinet, under the cushions, help me find him."

Mom got straight to work searching the curtains, looking behind the cabinet; I removed all the cushions from the sofa and started patting them down.

"Is there a way to get into that fake fireplace or is it completely sealed?"

"No it's sealed." She said shaking her head.

I started checking around her pot plants and in them to see if the soil had been disturbed. We were quickly running out of options.

"Maybe he is outside." She said with her hands placed on her hip still scanning the room for possible areas to check.

"No, he's here. I know it."

I saw a thought flash across my moms face as she leapt toward the coffee table. She swiped off the items it had on it, "This lid lifts to store things. Help me."

I bent over and grabbed either end to lift the top. There he was lying still with my dad's dirty sock stuffed down his mouth. I pulled it out and lifted him up to bury him into my face as the tears came streaming down. "No, no, no, no, no."

"Oh God Harper I'm so sorry," said mom covering her face with her hands.

"I have to go, call the ambulance, get yourselves to the hospital. I love you mom. Please, don't utter a word of any of this to anyone. You have to trust me, please." I said with tears streaming down my face. I didn't wait for a response, "I have to go. I have to go." I ran out the front door, placed Huckleberry in my lap as I sat in the driver seat while simultaneously switching on the ignition. My seatbelt was barely fastened before I sped off down the road. His heart was beating faintly if there was a chance he could be saved. I had to try.

Checkmate

The door to the building swung open as my car screeched to a halt outside the Veterinary clinic. Victor ran to my window. Looking in he saw Huckleberry was on my lap. I scooped him up, passing him through to Victor's waiting hands. The moment he had him securely in his care Victor disappeared back inside. I followed suit, when I entered, the receptionist pointed to her right. Room three was all I heard her say before I burst through the door. Victor had Huckleberry positioned on a heating pad and was shaving the side of his leg to prep the area for an IV drip.

"It was smart of you to call ahead. His heart is faint, he's awfully dehydrated and from what you have told me may be hypoxic from lack of oxygen. I'll do what I can to stabilize him and then look at running some tests. Wash your hands over there then put some gloves on. I have the other nurses covering for me by attending the basic appointments so I'm short staffed."

I turned and immediately did as he asked.

"Hold his leg still while I insert this into his vein. When I tell you, let go and get that tape placing it here,

here and here to ensure its secure okay? It needs to be firm enough to hold it in place but not so tight that it restricts the blood flow."

"Sure."

Once the IV was in, Victor used his hands to check him all over. He paused when he felt around his neck, he then inspected Huckleberry some more in the same region before placing his stethoscope on his throat to listen.

"Harper you said you found him unconscious with a sock down his throat."

"Yes," I said tears in my eyes looking down at him.

Victor reached across to his left to grab the clippers. Carefully he began to remove the fur from around Huckleberry's neck. Then he used a razor to get the skin to be completely revealed. "It seems like whoever did this also crushed his throat. His airways are constricted. All this is significant tissue damage, and the darkening discoloration confirms internal bleeding. Harper I'm sorry, he's too weak to operate on."

"No, there has to be a way to help him recover, make him better, you can't give up on him. Please, you don't understand, he's not allowed to leave me."

"I know this is difficult to hear and I'm sorry that this is happening but I feel I have to prepare you for the worst. He's only a baby and he's been through a lot. It's amazing that his heart is even beating."

I was beside myself, crying with my head lightly hovering above his little torso. My body convulsed with a profound sadness that would never be consoled if he died. It wasn't over; there is no way that this was it. With no shame I howled as snot came out of my nose, shaking my head repeatedly saying, "No, no, no, this can't be it for us, no, no, no."

Victor placed an oxygen mask on him. "I'll try a few things but there is no promise I can make greater than this. I'll try."

I nodded as I continued to cry. Images of the first time he looked up at me, waving his little paw only fueled my anguish. I watched as Victor added an electrolyte booster to his IV to assist with rehydrating his system. Then he injected him with a mild dose of cortisone to see if this could aid in the reduction of the inflammation, thus giving his airways a chance to reopen. The whole time he kept intermittently checking his heart, each time he would look at me with pursed lips partially shaking his head to indicate there appeared to be no change.

After a couple of hours of the same no improvement, no response Victor slumped over the table. "I've exhausted everything I can think of that would offer him a fighting chance and he still hasn't shown deviation toward getting any better. The only other thing I can think of doing would be to give him a shot of adrenalin."

"What good would that do?"

"I would have to be careful to administer just the right dose with the aim to speed up his heart to beat at a normal pace. Hopefully as it wears off his heart will maintain its natural rhythm. I don't know Harper, I'm just thinking out loud right now."

"If his heart beats faster than he will need more oxygen. If his throat is still closed he won't be able to sustain the demand placed on his body, which would cause increased pressure on his heart and place him in high risk of cardiac arrest. Even if you incubated him to assist with the supply of oxygen you would need to have the tube travel down his damaged throat. The probability of causing a perforation or just adding to the inflammation is more likely than not. It doesn't seem to be an option to me."

"You're right. It does appear to hold greater risk than a proposed value. That being said I'm not able to do much more than what's been done. I can keep him here connected to the IV, administer painkillers, so he is comfortable and give it time. I will need you to sign an instructional waiver to allow the on duty vet to do what is required in the instance he wakes and is in breathing distress or significant pain. We have to be allowed to do what is right for the animal."

"I can't leave him. I'm never going to leave him. If he is destined to die it won't be alone. How much more fluid is left to drain from the bag?"

Victor turned to inspect the IV. It's almost done. Harper I would strongly recommend you leave him here with us. We can keep him comfortable, it's his best option."

I looked down at Huckleberry and stroked the length of his tiny body. "Unhook him. I'm taking him home."

Victor clamped the drip, removed the tape and finally the needle. Once he placed a small bandage across the entry wound I bent over and collected Huckleberry off the table. Carefully I tucked him under the crook of my neck and whispered in a broken voice, "We're going home little fella. Everything is going to be okay, were going home." Victor opened the door for me. I looked into his tear filled eyes as I too was crying and could only muster the will to mouth the word, thank you. He nodded his head and let me go.

At home, I positioned Huckleberry vertically on my chest tucked under my singlet top with his head poking out between my breasts. I placed the lighter blanket over the top and then the duvet. I wanted to ensure he maintained a decent body temperature as his was struggling to do this on its own. I lay in the dark looking at the shadows from the moon lit sky dancing on the edge of clouds. The world continued to go on yet my whole world was dying.

There was a part of my psych that felt like it was a rag doll trapped in a front loader machine on wash cycle. Tossing, tumbling, being pushed and pulled in all directions while gaining glimpses of a distorted view of the world through the soap stained window. It was my way of guiding me to recognize my current state was tainted by the invested emotions I held to the experiences.

Eventually, I closed my eyes to refocus on channeling toward positive thoughts of healing energy. My body hummed with a vibration that seemed to covet us, perhaps exhaustion made me feel there was a pulse to my surrounds, whatever it was aided me on my course to slumber. It didn't take long before I was drifting weightlessly on tranquil waters.

* * * * *

The morning came quicker than I anticipated with my eyes heavy coupled by my head shrouded in a mottle of thoughts. Instantly my heart skipped a beat as I felt the rough of a tongue lick the underside of my nose. The light breeze on my skin told of the presence of a wagging tail. Displaying a drowsy smile across my face I patted Huckleberry with my right hand to check I wasn't dreaming. As my fingers stroked him, he reciprocated with kisses all over my face. My eyes still closed, tears streamed down the sides like waterfalls. I never wanted this moment between us to end. The extent of the relief, the joy, the love I felt was inexplicable yet sublime.

I laughed as he migrated to lick my left ear. When I turned my head to open my eyes to see him, his entire body wiggled from excitement.

"Hello you." I whispered.

All he wanted to do was keep licking me. It seemed a thousand kisses would not be set to satisfy him today. I couldn't stop the tears from falling; I was so thankful that he was alive. He still looked like he had been in the wars but there was a gleam in his eyes that told me he was feeling better.

I picked him up raising him high, so I could inspect the underside of his wriggling torso. Huckleberry used his little legs to propel forward in the air, signaling he wanted to be placed down. The moment I lay him on my chest, I could feel his little heart thundering with strength. He lay there for a minute staring at me. When I closed my eyes, he began to crawl forward, ever so slowly, one paw shimmy, then the next. I looked at him, which resulted in him freezing. Smiling at the idea of the game, I closed my eyes to feel his immense cuteness when he began again, one paw shimmy, next paw shimmy, each time I looked at him, he froze. I burst out laughing when he eventually got to my neck and was licking frantically at the underside of my chin. God, I love him so much.

After a quick shower, I collected the box from the boot of my car and placed it under my bed. As much as my curiosity would have me rummaging through it I knew more questions would surface compelling me to investigate and I couldn't afford to be side tracked. I was already behind schedule on executing my strategy against the interferons, which is precisely what they wanted.

Huckleberry joined me on the sofa once he had his fill of the meat I freshly puréed so he could easily consume it. The poor fellow was so hungry he barely lifted his head from the bowl, not leaving until he licked it clean. Curled in a little ball near my armpit, he closed his eyes and released a sigh.

My first point of call was leaving a message for Victor to let him know that Huckleberry was on the mend. The second was to my parents.

"Hello."

"Hi Mom."

"Oh, Harper I've been waiting for you to call me back how is he?"

"Huckleberry, he's getting better. How are you and dad?"

I could hear her exhale the breath she had been holding, "I'm so relieved to know he is okay."

"He is, I'm relieved too. Tell me what's happening. Is dad okay?"

"He's doing fine, we both are."

Click, the line was silent preceded by a strange crackling noise. We were disconnected. I tapped the end of the phone on my forehead while I felt a hesitation in calling back deciding to wait for a few minutes to see if my mom would dial me instead. She didn't.

I gently moved Huckleberry, who was sound asleep down toward the end of the sofa, on the top of a blanket bundle before heading into the kitchen to rummage around in my third draw to find my spare pay as you go mobile unit. While it was charging I got online to activate one of the many prepaid sim cards I held as spares in case of emergencies. Once the unit was partially charged, I dialed the home line rather than my mom's cell.

It rang for a while before I heard the receiver engaged. "Hello."

"Mom."

"Harper, thank God, I didn't recognize the number. How is Huckleberry? I've been so worried."

"He's pulling through mom. Can you answer a question for me please? It's important and I need you to trust me and to answer it quickly without trying to understand why. Okay?"

"Sure," She sounded hesitant.

"What was the name of the Egyptian archaeologist you spoke of yesterday?"

"Do you mean Mahalid Quatoum?"

"Yes, thanks. How is dad?"

"You were right, his patella was cracked, in three places actually. After the operation the surgeon told me, it was a positive result. He said judging by the injury if your father is diligent with his post surgical rehabilitation he will have a full recovery with the possibility of a slight limp, maybe some limitations in his range of motion but that's all."

I closed my eyes and silently cringed, "Poor dad, it's awful. He must be a little confused about the series of events."

"He is. All your father remembers is you coming to visit, having his fill at lunch and retiring to the living room to watch television."

"I guess it's a small blessing. There is nothing about what happened that's worth remembering." I said still repressing any need to deal with the experience.

"Its hard to watch him in so much pain, feeling confused. He told me he's concerned he may have a brain tumor. I know I can't tell him the truth so I'm just consoling him and hoping his fixation on trying to remember what happened subsides. The last thing I want is for him to recall hitting me on the head, let alone what happened in the attic with you."

"Mom, don't."

"You broke his knee and hit him across the side of his head several times Harper. I know you have your reasons but I can't help but think about what that thing must have been trying to do to you. The surgeon said the force it would have taken to make the break was...."

"MOM, DON'T" I gritted my teeth.

She gasped as she began to sob.

I leaned into the phone wishing I could console her. Closing my eyes, I shook my head knowing the enormity of pain the experience had stimulated for her, "I'm sorry for yelling, I'll never discuss what happened between that thing and I. You need to find a way to let it go."

I heard her cup the phone to blow her nose. In a feeble voice she said, "You're right, I'm sorry. I know better, I'm sorry."

"Talk to me mom. How are you?" I asked.

"I'm fine."

"Mom, how are you? I know this is tough and mentally exhausting."

"What if."

"Go on, what if ..."

"What if it comes back?"

"It won't- not in this lifetime, I can promise you. That dance card is spent."

"How do you know for sure?"

"Nothing is ever a certainty but I trust my instincts. He is gone to a place where he is not able to readily return."

"Why does it want to hurt you?"

"I can't mom. Its best if no one knows anything."

She whimpered as she struggled to say the words that gave her the most sorrow, "You're all alone Harper."

I paused, listening to her cry.

"Harper, are you still there?"

"Yes, I'm here. I need to be on my own. It's how it has to be. It is how it is meant to be."

"Isn't there anything I can do?"

"Sure, live your life, be happy. Know that love will one day heal the world. Participate in the vibrations of healing by staying true to who you are."

"I'm terrified for you," she whispered.

"Don't be, nothing can harm me, only I can harm myself. I'm stronger and more resilient than you probably realize."

"I know you are. I was blessed with the privilege of watching you grow. I'm really proud of you Harps."

"Thanks mom. Tell me, how is your head?"

"Oh, that bump, no its fine. I have a headache, but the doctors cleared me of any concerns. It's your dad that has a way to go before he is steady on his feet."

"I know. Focus on helping him to get to a quick recovery point and please don't ever share what you know with him, or anyone else for that matter. It wouldn't aid me to have the two of you worrying. I need positive, healing, loving energy generated."

"Harper, I promise you I won't ever tell a soul." She paused to take a deep breath, "I'm sorry this is happening to you but I know if anyone has the ability to rise to the challenge, it will be you."

"Thanks for the vote of confidence." I said with a forced laughed. "I should have asked earlier is dad home or still in hospital?"

"They kept him there overnight for observation because of the bumps on his head and his inability to recall what had happened. I think they may release him this afternoon. I'm just waiting for the call to confirm the verdict once the orthopaedic surgeon does his final rounds for the day."

"You should probably try to encourage them to keep him in for a few days. They can manage his pain better while it gives you an opportunity to organize yourself in readiness, perhaps even provide you with a chance to rest before he comes home. Initially he will require a lot of care."

"It all sounds good in theory but your father has already texted me three times today saying he wants to get out of there. I'm exhausted but I would rather have him home."

"Then go get him mom. Here, take down this number. Call me from your home line not your cell if you need anything, Okay?"

"Is your other cell broken?" She asked.

"No, I'm just being cautious that's all."

"Okay, I have the number. Please take care Harper."

"I will mom, I love you. Give dad a cuddle from me. Let him know that I love him."

"I love you Harper. Come visit when you can."

"When I can, I will. Bye mom."

"Bye."

I could hear the sadness in her voice; she found it hard to mask the intense worry she felt. How frightened she must have been when she detected Vernon's presence occupying dad's body. There were things, which possibly occurred that I would never discuss unless she raised the topic herself because she needed to speak about it. The look mom's eyes held yesterday when referencing how she recoiled from his touch made me cringe. I took a deep breath and shook my head as I released it. Nothing positive was going to come from dwelling on this. I have work to do. The assholes clearly had a phone redirection set from my main cell. The charlatan on the line certainly sounded like my mom. It was mindboggling to think they needed to go to such an extent to stay informed to try to keep me in check.

I had a hankering for a strong brew of coffee but absolutely no desire to leave to get it. I smiled as I recalled on the inside freezer door panel I still had one unopened packet of the finest Turkish coffee known to man, called Gul, left. I set up the water to boil on the stovetop; added several heaped teaspoons of the rich blend and waited for the magic to happen. The aroma quickly filled the air. There was something undeniably delicious about the smell of a quality coffee brewing. Heck, in truth, even crap coffee smelt good on a bad day.

On my way to the back room where my office was located, I checked on Huckleberry. He was still fast asleep, hopefully having sweet dreams. The dear soul had been through so much. Careful not to spill my coffee, I bent down and gave him a kiss on the head then left him to continue his slumber in peace. I was set on focusing my energy to getting some overdue wheels of strategic play in motion. The interferon's made it quite clear that they can mercilessly go to any lengths to tame me. It was time to return the favor.

Switching on my laptop, I placed the IP multizone

re-router on. Once the network was signaled as secure I opened a private browser window to log into my virtual mail server. There were a few emails I needed to send. The first message went to the head of the Sanctorum Avow news crew to provide the instructions for the next viral article launch. The second was to my stockbroker to ask him to confirm he had secured the shares I requested six weeks ago. He had sent me an email to acknowledge the request but not one that communicated, he had completed it. The final note I issued was a request to the hackers who had been helping me thus far to give them the details of the spy drone along with some images, so they could track down the owner, with explicit instructions to break into their network to find the surveillance photo's that were taken of my apartment. I wanted to sight the copies to understand what they saw. The boys would feed a hook to bait his network with a silent tracer and key logger to see where it would lead. As much as I wished to delete the images from their server, it would only lead to possible suspicion. A far better approach was to maintain an undetectable connection so that I can have my hackers watch the watchers. Finally, I requested they find a way to tag my cell phone, so I could see how and where it was being redirected. I'm determined to regain some privacy and there had to be a clever way to punish those who would deny me this right. I was no longer in the mood to be nice.

Sipping on my coffee, I flipped through the previous week's news to see what had been listed as the highlights. The lobbyists were still organizing protests in the major cities across the states in the US calling out demands to have an independent inquiry take place around exposing the governing bodies who participated in the authorization of the drug anathema to be leached into vaccinations. Article coverage around the globe showed that people of influence were banding together demanding a cure.

A message popped up on my screen stating that emails had come through. I switched across to my mail account. The first one was my broker confirming he had bought the stocks, and it provided me with a link to the purchase note against my account. The other message was from the Sanctorum Avow office stating they will arrange for the article to be launched on Friday. It indicated it would be live by no later than 3pm, with an estimate of viral response across the globe by 5pm. These guys certainly had some impressive media influence and networking nous. There wasn't much more I could do for now. My strategy had very precise steps I felt needed to be executed in sequential order. It is an intentional maze of combined direct hits and misleads, with the aim of blindsiding the interferons into a dead end. This is the only way I can think to lock them into a corner and to force their hand to choose to either become exposed or to retreat. Unlike the strikes they made at me, when I call checkmate, it will be set to place an end to their invisibility in this masked war.

Patience

Huckleberry was in a deep sleep when I returned to the living room and settled back down on the sofa. I picked him up along with a blanket for us to share. Gently I rubbed my nose against his. Ever so slowly, his tail began wagging as he lifted his head to look at me through sleepy eyes.

"Its okay, go back to sleep." I kissed him on the forehead and then positioned him on my lap so he could continue his slumber. I knew allowing him to rest was the quickest way to assist his body with healing, so I let him be.

Using my right hand, I flipped the floorboard under the coffee table to reveal the letters I had stashed for safekeeping. Although I was exhausted on all fronts, I knew I needed to press forward. The interferons set their wheels of influence in perpetual motion to distract me, slow me down and perhaps even deter me from wanting to proceed. It worked, to a degree, but mostly it educated me on who they were and, more importantly, who I was in light of the heinous circumstances I was forced to face. There was no room for failure and most certainly no option to stop. Nevertheless, there are moments where I find myself wishing for my life to be the one, which ends. I recognized this was gaining strength by presenting at a frequency not experienced before. The thought birthed a silent singular tear to my right eye.

Acknowledging my need to clear my thoughts I repeated the word 'Baransu' slowly, methodically until I felt the tension from my body dissipate. I was emotionally tired and feeling extremely vulnerable. I had nowhere to hide and no one to confide in. I knew I was alone, but I had never felt so alone in my life.

Rather than leaving the letters unopened until I was ready to read them, I felt the need to release them all. With the letter opener in hand I set to the task, unfolding each of the letters carefully to ensure I maintained the order by placing them face down on top of one another. The pile was not as large as I expected. Some of the envelopes contained a single A5 page covered on one side where others were multiple.

There it was, my small bundle of letters representing components of a life someone else led who saw it fit to impart their tale on to me. At present, with all the distractions demanding my attention, I was yet to feel invested in Patience and her story. Still, I looked at the pile and knew by the end of the last word on the last page when all was said and done, I would be left wanting.

I couldn't imagine it would take me long to read it all. It was crucial that I absorbed an overall understanding of the story, but I knew I needed to keep a vigilant focus on the details. There were secrets hidden in the realm of her words, I could feel it in my bones.

My nights felt cursed, as I had been robbed of my ability to greet it with restful slumber. Awoken to the presence of footsteps in the halls, hinges on doors telling of entry and exit, the convent held itself to be a hive of activity from dusk to dawn. I wanted to approach Sister Lydia to request insight regarding the favor she provided the cardinal to retain me, but Nathaniel held insistence on my sworn word not to echo a skerrick of what had been exchanged between us. Instead, I was forced to lay in wonder about the elements, which eluded my understanding.

Several nights passed as I remained attuned to listening to the noises. I tried to imagine who was the cause of each noise and what they were doing. It was hard to delineate between the steps; sometimes there were several while other times I could only hear one pair. Mostly, it was the occasional whispers intermixed with muffled laughter and then the scurry post this, which made me yearn to know what had transpired to instigate such late night folly.

During the day, I watched the Sisters in execution of their duties, listening to the shuffle of their feet as they went about the day. Sister Maud was heavy set in her motion while Sister Gertrude held a levitation capability to her swift pace. Nathaniel refused to ever speak of what had been already told stating it was knowledge, I held no business to acquire detail of, further to which he exclaimed he held regrets in instigating its surface. My curiosity surrounding this intrigue became insatiable. I simply had to know more.

On the eve of the Sabbath, I told the Sisters, I was set to retire early feigning exhaustion as my reason. Instead of resigning to my bedchambers as expected, I chose to skulk down the halls with the intent to hide in the closet of one of the vacant rooms. My recent narrowed observations held to note the nine rooms with no occupancy seemed to hath the bedding laundered every day, yet mine was laundered with infrequency. I was determined to acquire an insight into why.

The room I chose had an oversized poster bed, a single wooden stool and some tapestries on the wall. The candlesticks were laden with remnants of wax in a pile surrounding the base. My eyes glanced across the setting to find a place to hide. The wooden chest at the end of the bed could be fit for purpose but limited my senses to the proposed experience. I required an undetectable space where neither sight, nor sound was inhibited.

The underside of the bed was my chosen position. It held vacancy enough to allow for my movement to be undetected while giving me access to the reverse of the mirrors lengthy reflection. In preparation for the eve I collected some bedding from the wooden chest, coating the ground to protect me from the chill and nestled in to wait.

Hours had passed as I felt myself drift to slumber then retrieved to the call of footsteps and whispers. It was certain this night began like any other I had heard in the darkness with the exception of the clarity retrieved by the proximity providing allowance to recognize the voice's whispering in the halls.

"Sister Agnes your presence has been requested in the farthest vacant chamber. Sister Margery, Sister Elizabeth and Sister Katherine, thou art requested to all be present in the chamber aside Sister Agnes. Sister Phillippa, ensure preparation for your chamber this eve as he is reputed to possess a heavy hand and insists to request thee to charm. Sip the elderberry wine prior to ease the burden beholden to thee this night. Sister Anne, prepare the rooms, stay vigilant to keep watch across the halls ensuring swiftness of entry and exit of our guests. Lastly, Sister Gertrude thou hath managed to once more retain the one who insists upon the night's entirety. Careful he may feign the intent of a suitor, but he uses his gilded rights for access rather than pursuing thee in the light *of day and asking for thine hand as with a proper gentleman toward a lady. Go now Sisters and prepare. May our hearts remain in the protection of God while your bodies sin."*

I heard the murmurs of the others as they repeated, "May our hearts remain in the protection of God."

'Twas Sister Maud, who was speaking to them. Post the deliverance of instruction her heavyset footsteps left the vicinity with others shortly to follow suit. My heart pounded when the door swung wide. I watched as the feet entered the room, first there was a clanking of something being placed down, then a scurry to the bed where a fuss of plumping cushions with several whacks could be heard before turning down the sheets. Fresh candles were placed in the holders, lit and positioned on the available shelving around the room for heightened ambience prior to it being vacated. This must hath been Sister Anne, who was charged with preparing the chambers. I was too frightened to confirm by reflection but knew from the instructions that it could be no other.

Thoughts of the conversation with Nathaniel and the intense expression across his brow, all became prominent imagery. I recoiled when I began to hear a stir, in the distance, breaking the silence. Anxious, I felt a surge of desperation to revoke my decision to be present. As the steps grew nearer, my heart pulsed loudly within my head.

"In here sir, please make yourself acquainted with the room. There are refreshments to quench thy thirst while you wait. Sister Gertrude will be in attendance shortly."

There was no response from the person wearing the pointed leather polished boots. No sooner had Sister Beatrice closed the door than I could hear the person help himself to a beverage. I watched as portions of the liquid escaped the chalice marking the ground where the shoes paced the floor. Whoever this was clearly displayed no regard for the quarters.

The door squeaked open slowly as dainty bare feet entered the room. It was forbidden to walk the floors without coverage. I had never seen feet other than my own. There was a heat rising within me. It seemed a sin to be skulking in the shadows to witness this. I felt torn and immediately closed my eye's tight.

When the polished boots without a word sat on the edge of the bed, my curiosity drove my face forward to gaze upon the mirror. Sister Gertrude stood presently with no habit just a white bed gown so light in fabric it barely veiled the outline of her body from view. Her hair of gingered auburn fell free in curls to touch the edges of her bare shoulders. This beauty to my eyes had gone unnoticed prior to this witness. The candlelight's flicker played upon the material creating a dance among the shadows. She reached up to the ties holding the garment's position. Slowly, Sister Gertrude crossed one foot forward as she pulled the string, loosening the gown. She licked her lips, smiled in the direction of the man on the bed then shook her torso until the gown was draped around her ankles.

I cupped my hands to my mouth to muffle the gasp I'd released from seeing her naked skin revealed. The man leapt from the bed; sliding to his knees before her, immediately separating her legs to bury his head into her upper thighs as his right hand faltered to her bosom. Sister Gertrude raised a leg across his shoulder as she moaned. This only set the man's face to plunge deeper with vigor to which Sister Gertrude responded with more of the same. My heart was a flutter feeling my face flushed with heat. I knew nothing of this behavior to exist and clearly felt that I did not hold business to. Yet, I was so compelled by the scene that I could not look away.

My attentions were drawn to the distorted sound of whacks preceded by yelps quickly escalating to screams occurring down the way. It only set Sister Gertrude to moan *louder again. My assessment concluded her synchronization seemed to align to mask the sounds carried through the walls rather than what the man engaged between her thighs was doing. It was undeniably clear the presence of another, in the distance, could be heard sobbing. It made me wonder if Sister Phillippa had drunk the elderberry wine as instructed or whether she braved the entry to the chambers with just her wits to guide.*

Sister Gertrude released a squeal when the man took her other leg upon his shoulder grunting while exerting effort to stand. He then spun, tossing her on the bed. Slowly, he walked forward released his belt, unclasped his trousers allowing it to fall to the floor. With a shuffle his draws were down exposing the fullness of his rose colored buttocks in the mirror. I watched him jut his hips forward then pull back over and over while holding Sister Gertrude's legs in the air. It seemed to transition them to expel a range of noises. Hers was light, softly released, while his had a guttural pitch similar to that of a wilder beast courting a mate in the distance. It was menacing to say the least.

After they bounced together, in earnest, he fell forward to lay his head on her chest releasing her legs from his grasp. His torso heaved as he panted while Sister Gertrude stilled. It was not long after she was on bended knee carefully removing his boots, socks and remainder of his attire. He then positioned himself on the bed propped up by pillows while she neatly folded his clothes, fetched him a fresh beverage and finally joined along side him. Her ability to comfortably walk about unclothed in the presence of another fascinated me.

"T'will thee ever make an honest woman of me? Sister Maud warns against wishing so, but it has been nearly two winters passed since thee first stabbed me with thine pendulum sire, and thou art yet to attempt a proper courting."

"Hush with thy nonsense. 'Tis known by thee I am already betrothed. I find it a challenge to remove myself of my duties to be here with regularity let alone be absent from my quarters all night. Can thee not see the extension of my efforts as a sign that I hath thee as often as I can afford?"

"Perhaps my willingness to please you in ways your bride deems a sin stands as a reminder that without me you will remain lacking, lest thee lay with diseased whores."

He flipped to his side grabbing her face, "And need I remind you in the absence of my generosity you would be subjected to the countless whom would hath thine skin tainted with lashings of pain as with the other maiden heard crying this eve. Be present and thankful for what thou art granted. 'Tis all I can provide. Enough now, I grow tired of your ungrateful whining."

"I'm sorry I hath allowed my mouth to run free of expression. I know thou hath been exceedingly generous with thine efforts."

His thumb ran across her bottom lip, which she kissed. He repositioned himself on the pillows, so he was propped upright.

"'Tis high time I gave occupancy to that mouth of yours. If thou insist upon deliverance of a tongue lashing, let it be toward glory."

With this, she smiled, placed herself on her knees and bent over to greet the fleshed staff he was gripping. It reminded me of the portion of flaccid member found on a stag's underbelly near his hind quarters. It was always tossed into the woods during dissection. Sister Gertrude's head readily bobbed up and down on his protruding flesh as he threw his head back to gasp. Occasionally she employed the use of her hand to pull at it before bowing down once more to leverage the use of her tongue. At the point that his *face became flush, he placed both his hands into her hair wrapping it in a knotted bundle then pushed her head direct while he thrust to greet her open mouth. Each time releasing a guttural noise that once again held me compelled to a desire to stab him. This continued until it eventuated into an overspill of liquid spurting from his faulty stem. To which Sister Gertrude seemed to lavish by spreading it across her chest while he watched.*

The night was long with continual stints of rest and repetition of acts that would see them seemingly reel in spurts of pleasure. My initial curiosity had been sated. By the early hours of the morning, the escapades of the two became mundane to witness. There was nothing more I was to learn from this venture between Sister Gertrude and her would be suitor.

* * * * *

The following two nights compelled by exhaustion I retired to my chambers early to catch a gain on the absence of rest I was lacking from the night prior. My head was filled with dreams of beasts courting. Their motive to impale fueled my desire to repel them. Feverish heat rose in my body as I felt the sweat drip from my brow. The intensity of their uninvited touches to my exposed nether regions set a blinding wave of light causing my physique to shudder as I wriggled to resist the delights that coveted me. I woke to feel my chest pounding while I panted to catch my breath. Each time an occurrence presented, I would make a quick assessment of my bedchambers to reassure myself I was in complete solitude. Something was happening to me. I began to feel the rise of a hunger for more.

* * * * *

Weeks passed where I would alternate between the rooms to peer from the darkness at the favors exchanged. The variants of position and spoils with some held intrigue while most were leaving just as quickly as they had entered. It appeared that certain gentlemen callers had little stamina to proceed past a thrice thrust. This seemed to be the common stimulus for the shared laughter between the Sisters in the halls upon their exit. There were eves when one of the Sisters could be subjected to hosting as many as twelve such men. The effort one must achieve to venture to the convent for such a feeble reward made me wonder why they chose to attend at all. My witness to the night callers had me learned by observation of their ways. I assumed their own hand might better serve then to travel the unruly roads for a poorly adept thrust in a Sister's nether region. 'Twas a certainty to be far less effort, coupled with saving their precious coin. Still, they wandered into the convent in countless drove's night upon night to receive their spoils.

* * * * *

There was silence between us as we walked the forest on the hunt. I watched Nathaniel pace forward. He had not done this on any of our prior escapades. 'Twas more usual for his stride to be tempered to match mine or hold a step behind to shield my hindquarters. This day I struggled to maintain alignment with his widened stride.

"Nathaniel what drives thee forward so?"

He surprised me as he swung around, "Why hath thee not ventured out beyond the walls?"

"Oh" My hand rose to my chest. "That was simply child's

159

folly. I've reached the mastery required thus no further need compelled me to practice."

"Did thou not fair to tell me this? Night upon night I wait beyond the rivers like a fool."

I looked down at my hands, "I'm sorry. It did not occur to me. On occasion of late I had been retiring early due to exhaustion."

"How could it not? No sooner had I confessed my presence, thou ceased to attend. T'would be an idiot who could not see why thou chose to no longer venture beyond the walls. There can be no denial of this. The actions hold clear evidence of the truth."

"Come now, knowledge of thou watchful presence held no bearing on my stimulus for absence." I considered whether I should tell him what occupied my time so fully that I had not since thought to venture out.

"Then what?" He said with his hands on his waist.

"Then nothing, if it please thee ask the Sisters, I hold no cause to lie in regard to retiring early from experience of exhaustion. I at times seek solace before the sun has even held opportunity to set to dusk. None of my actions are related to what thee suggest."

He glanced at me, "You don't appear unwell."

"I am not unwell. I only felt exhaustion and thus retired accordingly to rest. I am refreshed now."

Nathaniel's posture straightened, "Doth this mean on the coming Sabbath when the moon is at its brightest you will join me here?"

I took a moment to ponder his request. The Sabbath was the busiest and most visually rewarding of the nights in the nine chambers.

"FINE." He said interrupting my thoughts as he stormed ahead.

"No wait Nathaniel, yes, yes I will join you here, but could it not be the day prior? The Sabbath seems so far away and the slight dimness of the light is charmed as with that of a candle."

A smile birthed across his otherwise sullen expression, "By the riverbed?"

"Aye, by the riverbed at the stroke of midnight."

He nodded his head.

"Then let us hath no more talk of this and focus on the hunt."

To this, we walked side by side through the forest in search of wild boar for our plates.

* * * * *

At the stroke of midnight, I arrived at the riverbed as agreed.

"Nathaniel."

Only the noises of the creatures of the night seemed present. I sat by the edge on a smoothed rock to wait. The cool of the air carried a blanket of mist across the waters down the length of its belly. I imagined it would feel mystical to float upon its waters with such a whimsical covet.

My body held still as I felt something glide across my right shoulder. I closed my eyes to protect from venom spray if it were a snake I could easily become blinded. As I quietly readied my knife, I heard Nathaniel breathing.

"Patience," he whispered.

I turned to see he was holding a single ruby red rose in his hand. With a slight click in his heals, a bow and rise with a smile he passed it across to me.

"My apologies for keeping you waiting."

"No matter," I said reshuffling to face him. "What is this?"

"I would hath thought it quite obvious, tis a rose," he said with a smirk.

"I can see that, but why are you presenting it to me?"

"I thought you might like it."

"I do, thank you, but still it holds me curious as to why you chose to give me a rose. Thou hath never done this before."

"Aye, well 'twas a moment of whimsy which had me compelled to present thee with a rose. If you like I can take it back, here give it to me. I can easily find another who is appreciative of such a thought." He stepped forward with his hand out.

I twisted my torso cupping the rose, "No. Tis mine now." I brought it to my nose to inhale its intoxicating scent. "Delicious."

"There is a bush by the way to my house where the seeds hath run rogue. The perfume they release as a bushel is quite extraordinary. Perhaps I will get to show thee one day."

"Perhaps," I said still delighting in the scent of the one he presented.

"Would you care to walk with me somewhere?"

"Of course," I said rising to a stand before he was able to offer his hand.

"It seems thou hath given much thought to our hunt this eve," I said beginning to step toward the path.

"I may hath placed mild forethought toward the matter."

I glanced at him and smiled as my comment was made in light jest yet his reply stood to tell me he held unannounced ideals pertaining to this evening.

After a short walk, we arrived at a clearing where I saw the pre-laid blanket in the meadow accompanied by a carafe, two chalices and some fruits with an assortment of cheese.

"Why these are the spoils of the rich?" I exclaimed looking around to see whom else may be present.

Nathaniel released a laugh, "Father has been taking to assist the blacksmith with his mending of the King's soldier's armory. There is little coin involved, but many of the soldiers hath become accustomed to rewarding the blacksmith on his good craft by providing wine and such. He has ample in his pantry so he passes some to father as compensation for service."

"Oh, may I?" I asked bending down to take a grape.

"You may, 'tis here for us to consume."

I looked at him in amazement, "All of it?"

"If it please thee to, yes, all of it. Mind the wine though, it may seem light to taste, but its trickery can cause thee to fall about with no ability to command thine legs if over consumed."

I bent down to sit on the edge of the blanket. "I've never been afforded the chance to taste wine although I confess to succumbing once to the temptation of portioning a small sip of the Sister's elderberry."

"Thou art a deviant one indeed," said Nathaniel reaching across to pour me a cup. "Here, drink it slowly, savor the taste. 'Tis not for quenching a thirst."

"Thank you." I took the cup to my lips as he watched me take my first sip.

Suddenly Nathaniel turned to walk away stating, "I almost forgot, I hath something for thee."

I watched as he fumbled about the base of an old oak tree quickly returning with a bundle wrapped in cloth under his arm. "Here, 'tis a gift for thee."

I readjusted my position as I placed it on the blanket in front of me. "What is it?"

"Open and you will see."

I took one more grape into my mouth, wiped my hands on my filthy trousers and began to unwrap. The shimmer of a deep green material caught my eye. I ran my fingers on the seam as I pulled it up from the remainder of its binds. "'Tis beautiful." I said holding the gown.

"Put it on," he whispered.

I looked at him, and shook my head to decline then returned to witness its glisten in the light of the moon.

"It holds a portion of the color within thine eyes. I knew when I saw it I had to gift this to thee. I would dearly like to see it on."

"I don't know what to say, 'tis a glorious color chosen, the detail in design, fabric, it all holds together with visual splendor. 'Tis my first witness to such a garment. It never occurred to me there was anything other than a Sister's habit to be worn by a woman."

Nathaniel released a laugh, "Indeed."

I stood up to place it against my body then looked down the length of the gown. The noise it made was a wondrous swish. I glanced at Nathaniel and smiled, "The sound of the fabric pleases me."

"Go beyond the shadow cast by the tree and exchange those tatters for the gown."

I shook my head, "'Tis a dress befitting for a proper lady of which I am not. My comfort is placed in the attire I currently possess. I hold no need for such opulence, nor find myself wishing to obtain it. Here, offer it to another who is worthy."

I crumpled it into a loose fold to pass it across.

Nathaniel took a step back, "Apologies for placing my eagerness ahead of your desire to do as thee please. Patience, 'tis a gift and thus yours to keep."

I looked upon it once more, "I shall never wear it."

"Then place it somewhere that allows thee to witness its glory with regularity. The look upon thine face when thou first laid eyes upon it, is reward enough for me, for now."

With this I carefully returned it to the packaging using the original twine to tie it in a bundle.

"Let us eat shall we," He said finally settling into a position on the blanket.

I partook in another grape while he poured himself a serving of wine.

"Hath thee sampled the cheese?"

"No," I said shaking my head.

"Here, try this with a portion of the fresh fig." He leant across to place it directly into my mouth. I opened wide enough to accept the offering while feeling my face flush as I noted his eyes fixated on my lips.

I raised the chalice to cover my mouth from view as I completed my morsel. The flavors combined I could hath sworn were divined from the Gods themselves. The tart of the cheese and sweet of the overripe fig could not hath melded better to my taste buds.

"Is it to thine liking?"

"Aye," washing down the delights with a sip of wine.

"Patience, do you not grow restless within the confines of the walls and want for more?"

"Secretly, everyday."

He leaned forward to engage my eyes as he spoke, "Then would thee consider a proposal of courtship from me as an offer to leave the grounds with permanency? I hath saved enough to afford a wife. My father and I hath spent three seasons felling the trees from the forest to build my own dwelling on his plot. The foundations are laid and come this summer t'will be finished in readiness for occupancy."

I diverted my eyes to the blanket beneath me. "I hold no need to be bound by marriage, I see no value in it." I said, knowing full well a hefty majority of the men who frequented the convent for the Sister's favors were self confessed as unhappily betrothed.

"How else doth thee imagine thou art eligible to leave the premises? Thou hath no riches to sustain thee other than your unlawful ability to hunt and thy unnatural beauty. You

will be bound to the walls or bound to a man. There is no other way."

"There must be more and I shall set forth when I am ready to find it. I will not accept a proposal of marriage from thee or any other, this is a certainty."

Nathaniel's expression quickly altered to disdain, "Thou art still a foolish child, filled with ideals held steadfast by thine naivety. Had thee more sense you would be grateful, for my offer is generous. I need not even ask thee direct or court thee in the manner you find yourself in this eve. I could just seek permission from Sister Lucinda and hath thine hand forced. Is this what you would hath me do?"

"Why doth thee persist in speaking of this when I hath made myself abundantly clear that I will not partake in any such commitment? I may fail to hold an expanse of knowledge, but this can be acquired. The very essence of what thee ask of me Nathaniel is something which cannot be acquired."

"Enough! You set to spoil this night with thine idiotic, tempestuous, narrow minded view. Drink the wine and grace me with silence as thanks for the bounty before thee."

"Pray tell of how you differ from the Cardinal or the King for that matter who would demand me for themselves. Art thou not displaying equal commands on my virtue?"

"Do not profess to mention my name akin to those who would hath thee as no more than their whore. I seek to make an honest life with thee and, God willing, be blessed with children. My intentions are to wed thee not simply bed thee. Thou art infuriating."

We sat in awkward silence as we both mulled over what had transpired. There was a sense of stupidity I felt toward the carrying of my bow and arrow; making assumption our meet was associated to an eve of sportsmanship.

* * * * *

"Hurry along now Child we must be clear of the region before sunrise. There is much ground to cover between here and where we are due," called out Sister Lydia.

"I'm gathering my final things, Sister Maud please come and assist." I yelled as I scurried back and forth around my room.

"Oh, Child I am going to miss you so." She said as she entered the chambers.

"And I thee, but I must make haste or be beholden to Sister Lydia's temper for the duration of the journey. No sin warrants such exposure." I said with a smile folding down my bedding.

Sister Maud released a hearty laugh, "Indeed. Come now, I will help thee." She set off to pack the remainder of my things in the wooden chest.

Outside, the Sisters gathered to bid me farewell on my travels. There was little time left for emotion before I was ushered into the carriage and found myself leaning on the door, waving goodbye as the horseman set the pace for the journey. The fresh breeze of the eve coupled with the sound of the horse's hooves gave a feel of enchantment. I smiled as I allowed myself to wonder what exciting fate was to be bestowed upon me.

"You must try to rest. T'will take four nights to cross all the lands. The days will be set for the horses to regain their strength, which affords plenty of time to gaze outward and explore. Sleep, Child."

"I'm excited to finally be on an adventure and with thee no less. I can hardly contain myself to sit still, but I will try." I said tucking my hands between my thighs.

"The twitch in thine toes confirms thy truth of the matter." She took a moment to watch them moving about.

"As an infant in the crib, when you were being entertained by the Sister's the same would occur. It didn't matter how tightly I wrapped thee in a swaddle thine toes would find their way free to wriggle when you were the happiest."

"Did they?"

"Indeed they did and clearly they still do." She said pointing to my toes.

I looked down, "They do seem to hath a life of their own."

We both laughed.

Not more than twenty minutes into our travels I caught a waft of perfume, which filled the air. I threw my weight at the door unwittingly thrusting it open as we passed a large cluster of wild roses.

"Goodness Child," said Sister Lydia as she pulled me in and latched the door securely. "What are you thinking to lunge forward in such a manner?"

"I'm sorry, I was compelled by the bushels of roses, I smelt the lure of their perfume and felt certain 'twas the roses spawn from wild seeds that Nathaniel had so charmingly spoke of. His father's house must be near."

"Hath thee been to his lodgings?"

I shook my head. "No."

"No?"

"Never, I swear upon my own life I hath never ventured this way."

"Did thee tell him of thine departure, bid him good tidings?"

"No Sister Lydia, I hath not seen nor heard of him in the longest time. At one point during a hunt he bantered of ideas of courtship with an intent to speak with you to seek permission to grant my hand."

She readjusted her position to sit upright, "Thou art aware of his intentions then?"

"Aye, I was. Did he speak of this with thee?"

She seemed reluctant to tell.

"I know he was very pressing on the matter with me so I thought he would most assuredly request your audience to present his position."

She released a sigh, "Aye Child, he did."

"What came of it?"

"He requested blessing for receipt of thine hand as thee hath suggested, but I, due to circumstances, saw it best to decline his interest."

I leant forward, "No. You declined?"

"Aye Child, 'twas not a match without great risk. There is reason why we travel in the cloak of darkness and there was reason for my insistence you be hidden all these years. To allow thee to venture beyond the walls, betrothed to a commoner who is not skilled enough in the art of war to protect, nor rich enough to retain thee as his own would be ludicrous."

"Why would he require skills of war and riches to retain me?"

"Child, you possess the uniqueness of beauty that could set feuds among men. I saw it begin when you were but a true child and know for certain it would exist now. The first nobleman who sought to claim thee as his own would, undoubtedly kill Nathaniel."

"Did Nathaniel concede to this?" I asked in the hope that he was not left pining unrequited.

"He begged me to reconsider vowing to take you far across the lands where none would recognize thee. I held steadfast. He was clearly besotted and speaking out of mind rather than application of rationale. He could not leave the district, as an only child, he holds responsibilities to look after his father when he reaches the age where he can no

longer sustain himself. The winters are harsh if there is no coal to warm the hearth."

I was sad for Nathaniel. It seemed I caused much trouble and heartache by my mere existence.

"Here, let me wrap this around thee. 'Tis time for thee to retire."

I let her make fuss, tucking the blanket around me, so I was trapped within its warmth. "Goodnight Sister Lydia."

She shifted into a more relaxed posture in preparation to rest. "Goodnight Child." She whispered.

I put the page on the completed pile before grabbing both lots and placing them back in the cavity for safekeeping. Releasing a yawn while I stretched my arms and legs I realized little Huckleberry was awake quietly watching me.

"Hey, you." I whispered as he lifted his head. I picked him up to place him on my chest so we could look directly into one another's eyes. He licked his lips while wagging his tail.

"You must be hungry. Come, I'll fix you some supper." Carefully I took him across to the kitchen bench. This seemed to provide a little bounce in his step as he walked over to the basin. I turned the cold tap on slow enough to prove a stream of water that he could lick. Initially, he used his paw to tap at it before extending his neck to allow his tongue to lap up the water. The whole while his little bottom swayed with his tail wag. Visually, it was too cute for words.

He waited patiently as I chopped his dinner into cubes, placed it through a mincer and then the blender transforming it into a disgusting pulped puree. He didn't seem to mind that his meal was liquefied, his head once again remained buried in the bowl until the last of it was consumed. I waited until he was finished before taking him upstairs to my room. All this reading and talk of sleep had me desiring to get some myself. I placed Huckleberry on the bed while I went into the bathroom to have a quick shower.

My body welcomed the warmth of the water. As I shampooed my hair, I wondered about the concept of unrequited love. There seemed to be cross over parallels between experiences in the story of Illuminarium and here with Patience. I admitted to myself that I could feel an underlying nagging ache of sadness associated to the idea of someone wanting, hoping, waiting for another person to return their affections. I'd never personally been in a position where I wanted more from someone who wasn't willing to participate. I know there is a pattern I'm not seeing which I feel I need to understand, but what it is alludes me.

I finished up briskly towel drying my skin and placed my hair in a high bun before proceeding to brush my teeth. All the while, I was present to the fact that I really felt sorry for Nathaniel. It was like he was destined to love the wrong person, thereby never allowing himself the chance to be open to meeting the right one. I wanted to reach into the pages and shake him into a state of awareness. The dear soul was lost and he didn't even know it.

Snuggled under the duvet I made a little nest for Huckleberry to join me as I was settled into the centre of the bed laying on my right side. He immediately took position, spun in three clockwise circles before curling into a perfect ball of sweetness. I leaned in to kiss him on his head.

"I love you." I whispered as I closed my eyes to rest.

Secrets

The basement was just as I had left it. Ol' Yella, my garishly vibrant yellow beanbag still in the same position, the pool table, my college studies map of cognitive extremes, all of it was in order. I walked around the room compelled by a sense of comfort yet overwhelmed with a feeling of emptiness. I knew there was something missing. The smoke from the incense pot rising caught my eye as it released the fragrance of rose, frangipani and frankincense. It wasn't my usual choice of aroma. There was something different about the place, I just couldn't identify what it was.

"Hey Fluffy."

I spun around placing my left hand on my chest to contain the thumping of my heart as I looked at him. "Peppy." I yelled. "Oh my God, Peppy." I leapt forward wrapping my arms around him while squeezing him tight. "You scared the shit out of me." I whispered. "Jesus, I've missed you so much."

He laughed as he placed his arms around me, released a breath and said in a calm tone, "I've missed you more."

I buried my face into his chest. "Don't let go of me

Peppy. I want to tell you something so I need you to hold me okay?"

His arms became like a vice securing me tight, "I won't ever let you go."

The tears streamed down my face as I tightened my grip allowing myself to howl with sorrow. "I'm sorry, I'm so God damned sorry Pep." I shook my head as I continued to cry, "I'm sorry for everything. I simply can't …" overwhelmed by my body heaving for breath as I continued sobbing I couldn't release the words. A million thoughts jumbled my mind with the things I wish I had conveyed and hoped he, and Sam knew. All those years, the laughter, the friendship, the acceptance of me meant the world, and now they were gone, robbed of their lives. This was the price they paid for loving me, being present in my life. My sadness was overwhelming. In all my days, I would struggle to forgive myself and would never feel worthy of their forgiveness.

It seemed as though hours had passed as we held each other while I selfishly cried intermittently whispering the words, "I'm sorry." Peppy continued to hold me as he led our body's to rock to a rhythmical sway from side to side.

"Fluffy, you have to let go of the pain. It's not your fault, none of us blame you. We all love you so much."

I burst into tears wanting to reject his kindness. I simply didn't deserve it. I was in pain. I felt so much sorrow and guilt over their fate. I couldn't bear to relinquish my duty to suffer, for their loss of life was mine to carry.

"You know when I crossed over there was this flash of my life that presented. Things I had forgotten, life experiences that seemed insignificant at the time they occurred but in the final moments held more weight than I had ever imagined."

My body calmed as I meld into feeling the vibration resonating from his voice.

"I only have one regret." He whispered.

He loosened his arms and stepped back while lifting my chin so my tear-drenched eyes could look into his. I mustered a half smile, "Tell me, what it is?"

"That I never kissed you when I had the chance."

"Then kiss me now so you hold no regrets." The tears rolled down my cheeks as he leant in for our lips to touch for the first time. He shifted his body, tilting my torso in his embrace as he kissed me so deeply I could feel his love for me penetrate my core.

When we parted to stand he smiled with a glint in his eye that I recognized and dearly loved.

"Now I realize I have one more regret."

I couldn't help but return the smile suspecting I knew where this was leading, "What is it?"

"That we didn't make wild uninhibited passionate love when we had the chance."

I burst out laughing as I poked him. "Really?"

He stepped forward and placed me within his embrace again. "You can't fault me for trying." He said as he chuckled.

I squeezed him tight, as I felt us being drawn away from each other.

"I'll love you forever Fluffy."

"Oh God," I gasped crying, "I love you too, I always have, you are my best friend, don't ever forget that. I love you, Pep. I love you."

"I know," he said. A single tear fell from his right eye as his presence faded to translucent before dissipating into thin air.

There I was, alone once more, standing in that

wretched blood stained room. Vernon's laughter echoed loudly above the curdling, anguished screams. I fell to my knees as I cupped my ears to stop the sound from piercing my ear drums.

I woke up to a pillow soaked with tears and Huckleberry manically trying to lick every inch of my face as he whimpered. My eyes were so swollen I could hardly see as I fumbled to put him in my arms in an attempt to settle him while I once again burst into tears.

If I was not charged with the responsibility of caring for Huckleberry, I could have lost days, perhaps weeks, in my bed staring at the skies wishing for something to remove the pain I felt about practically everything. It made sense to me now why Liam and countless others held the impetus to drink, snort, do anything to hold a moment's reprieve from needing to feel. I was tired of having to be strong, the better person, my resolve to proceed was being tested by my own psych. The next few days I would need to be careful as I could see I was teetering on the edge of rejecting the world and shutting down. I knew myself well enough to appreciate that at times such as these, I was my own true worst enemy.

I tried to muster some enthusiasm in my voice to help settle my little guy who had trails of wet strips of his own from his eyes telling me that he too had been crying. "Come Huckleberry, let's get you some food."

He sat up and placed his paw out waving it in the air toward my face but not touching. His head tilted slowly from side to side inspecting me before releasing a little whimper. It was hard not to burst into tears again as I leaned in and kissed his raised paw. "I'm okay baby boy, I'll be okay. I promise."

In the kitchen I prepared Huckleberry's meal first and

then something for myself. A roaring grumble within my belly reminded me that I had not eaten since I had lunch with my folks. There weren't any fresh groceries available in the fridge. My choices were to venture out or remain in and settle for a bowl of muesli. I chose the latter.

Once I was done eating, I washed it down with a piping hot cup of tea. Huckleberry finished his meal then sauntered off to the bathroom to relieve himself in his litter box. I watched the door for his return. When he poked his head out I smiled, "Come here. Come on." His spirits immediately lifted when he heard the raised pitch in my voice. He ran as fast as his little legs could carry him toward the sofa where I was sitting. He barked and twirled at the edge of my feet then raised himself up on his hindquarters. I snuffled him into my arms for a cuddle. He lay so adorably on his back, cradled in my arm like a baby staring up at me as I rocked him, "You are simply too cute."

With my belly full, I felt torn between taking a nap or continuing to read the story. I was close to a third of the way through from what I could gather. Her life seemed to hold a destiny for punishment stimulated by peoples draw to her unparalleled beauty. There was no freedom granted to her in a world filled with narcissistic righteous people who felt entitled to simply take. It seemed that she had been shielded while living within the convent, but also to a large degree by her own naivety. I wondered if her perpetual oblivion once unveiled to highlight the world that truly surrounds her, when she obtained this knowledge would she understand it to be a blessing or a curse. I personally think a little of both.

Huckleberry was already drifting off to sleep. His little exposed rotund tummy rose and fell, to the demands of his breath. He too has been subjected to so much as a result of me. It would be a sacrificial kindness to find him a new home where he is loved and safe from further harm. I just couldn't bring myself to imagine living without him. I leant forward slowly to retrieve the pile of unread letters, mindful not to squash Huckleberry who was still cradled in the crook of my arm. I didn't have the heart to shift him in case he woke. He sleeps more soundly when we are connected by touch, we both do.

"Wake Child we hath arrived."

I opened my eyes slowly to look across at where I expected to see Sister Lydia, but only her crumpled blanket lay present. I turned my head finding her standing outside the carriage with her hand extended. Pushing the blanket aside, I shifted to place my feet on the carriage step and took up her offer to assist with alighting.

"Where are we?"

Sister Lydia's arms extended out while she twirled in a full circle and smiled, "We are safe within the walls of the Sister of the Sacred Light convent. Come, our things are already inside. Let us freshen up before we eat."

I looked around at the expanse of stone wall encasing the yard where we stood. There were armed guards walking on the top of its edges. Two of the men I noted, were positioned closely to a mechanism, which functioned to haul the main gates open and closed via the use of a lever.

"What kind of a convent requires guards to protect its contents?" I asked.

"Thine eye for observation is keen. We hath entered a portion of the lands torn by war. 'Tis not without warrant, having these soldiers stand guard ensures the safety of the people."

"The people?" I said looking once more at the vacancy of the space we were occupying.

"Aye, Child, here is where we house the ones who need protecting the most. Farmers and their families who held the sad fortune to be subjected to the atrocities of war. The homeless and the injured seek refuge here to heal and regain their strength."

"Excuse me Sister, shall I tend to the horses now if you hold no further requirement for the use of the carriage?"

"Aye, of course. Head to the stables and then upon your return join us in receiving nourishment. The Sisters hath a room set for thee to retire. We must be prepared to leave once more upon the greet of darkness."

"Thank you Sister." He nodded his head and went on his way.

"Come, remain close." She said to me as she walked toward the door of the convent. Sister Lydia knocked twice, then paused. A lady in commoner's clothes swiftly arrived at the helm of the door. She smiled and curtsied as she stepped aside for us to enter. My eyes widened when I witnessed a flurry of activity providing stark contrast to the baron yard. People seemed to go about their day, carrying items, shifting things about, there was laughter and minstrels creating harmonious music. It was wondrous.

As we walked past, people acknowledged our presence with a bow or courtesy, *"Sisters."*

Sister Lydia smiled as her head bowed to return the sentiment and I followed suit. When we entered the archway, a Sister of the Sacred Light immediately embraced Sister Lydia.

"I am glad you held safe passage to us."

"'Twas charmed with little than an occasional bump to disturb my slumber."

I watched as the Sister glanced at me then back over to Sister Lydia.

"Hello Child I am Sister Beatriz."

"Hello." I said with a smile.

She stepped forward placing her left hand gently on my cheek. "The last time I saw thee was when thou were nine. My, how thou hath grown."

I looked at Sister Lydia with an expression of confusion before looking back at Sister Beatriz. "My apologies, my mind must be hazed as I do not find thee at all familiar."

She smiled, "Tis no matter. I remember thee enough for the both of us."

"Come Child, enter the bed chambers through here. Find the bowl set on the table, use the cloth to freshen prior to changing. There is a need from this point to adorn commoner's attire. Tis laid out on the bed. Place them on in the order that you see, beginning with the corset. We must try them to ensure a good fit, else we hath this day to get them mended. Go now."

My mind was filled with curiosities as I nodded my head then proceeded down the hall to the room.

* * * * *

Sister Beatriz entered my room shortly after to help me to dress. I had never worn a corset before, nor had I felt the tightness of breath she insisted was required to ensure a lady of proper standing held all her possessions in securely. Once she completed adding the layers of garments onto my feeble frame, she spun me around so make inspection as I glanced in the mirror.

Gasping for breath I asked, "Can I not wear commoners attire like that to which I am accustomed when I am charged to attend a hunt?"

She covered her mouth as she released a laugh, "Sister Lydia allowed thee to venture beyond the walls to hunt?"

"Aye, each time the King's men arrived to make claim of the taxes she ushered me off the grounds with Nathaniel as my charge."

"Oh," she said now glancing at the ground.

"Do you know something of it?" I said trying to gain her attention.

"No more than the Sister has told me. Come we must get thee to the dining room so you may eat. Surely thou must be famished."

"I am indeed famished, but I fear I may not hath room enough to consume a single morsel with this corset strangling me so." I said, trying to make adjustments to seek relief.

She laughed, "Come now stop fussing, and follow me." Off she went down the hall returning us to the main foyer where there was still such wondrous bustle.

Sister Lydia was already seated at the table with a portion of cheese, some bread on her plate and soup on her spoon. "You wear thy garment well child," she said as she glanced over before placing the spoon in her mouth.

"Are thee not required to wear the same?" I asked.

"I am but the corsets are too restricting for my liking. I will place it on prior to our departure."

Sister Beatriz once again covered her mouth to muffle the sounds of her amusement.

I stepped forward, "Can I not do the same or better still be provided the equivalent of the hunting garments I hath worn all these years. This corset is simply madness."

Sister Lydia ushered me to sit beside her.

"You must wear this and no longer make reference to the hunting garments nor thine capacity to hunt. 'Tis time to ensure you hold the posture and etiquette of a lady."

"What if I do not wish to be a lady?" I asked in a whisper.

"Wishes hath little to do with it. Thou must embrace these new ways to ensure thy safe passage. I'll hear no more of it. Eat now while the soup holds heat enough to warm thy belly."

I quietly ate my meal as instructed. The previous excitement of the adventure before us waned. I was now feeling a sense of melancholy in regard to the journey ahead.

* * * * *

Sister Lydia was absent for the remainder of the morning. She insisted I stay within the confines of my quarters. I did so begrudgingly. The lure of the melodies floating through the convent held me captive to a desire to be present to witness its creation.

Midday felt as slow as a day's entirety to arrive. I was fetched by one of the Sisters who took me to the dining area once more where this time the expansive table was held in full occupancy by the Sisters of the Sacred Light.

"Come Child, we wait to say Grace."

I scurried to my seat and grabbed the hand of Sister Lydia and Sister Beatriz before bowing my head to partake in the Lord's prayer of thanks.

The richness of bounty spread across the length of the table called on my mouth to salivate with anticipation of its taste. Our convent's pantry faired rather poorly in comparison. It made me wonder how they were able to achieve such richness.

Sister Lydia leaned in to quietly speak to me. "Hath thy fill, then return back to the quarters. We leave at the point the darkness greets the horizon."

I rolled my eyes, "Why art thou so insistent upon my confinement? I hold no desire to venture beyond the walls of one convent only to be restricted to the bedchambers of another. Please, I beg of thee to allow me to hold free reign within the walls of the grounds. I wish to see the minstrels play."

"It can not be afforded. There are too many present who bear witness."

"Then provide an alternative other than solitude. Allow me to tend to the worst of chores. T'will be done with willing execution. I can assure thee any task would be chosen in favor over being confined to wait in a room."

"Tempestuous child," she muttered. Sister Lydia paused for a moment as her lips pursed. "Upon completion of our meals you will come with me to aid me in my duties. Now eat in silence."

I smiled feeling triumphant. The thought of having to return to the room while there was so much to witness here was sending my mind into madness. I gratefully ate what had been served on my plate then ever so patiently waited for Sister Lydia to complete her meal.

We walked through the convent halls turning this way and that until we reached the entrance to stone steps that cascaded down. Only the flicker of the flames of light dancing on the walls, in the distance, gave glimpse to the uneven surface. No sooner had my feet completed the descent, I began to hear a disturbing cacophony of sounds. I turned to look at Sister Lydia, my hands were shaking as I demonstrated hesitation to venture any further.

"Thou hath expressed a wish to witness the mistrals, to partake in the joys, unhappy with thy lot. 'Tis the folly of naivety which still commands thine senses."

Sister Lydia, continued down the length of the poorly lit

arched tunnel. The ground was moist from water trickling through cracks in the stone work. The deeper we ventured the worse the stench of rot invaded my nostrils. I knew by the sounds of men now heard loudly wailing in pain, that we were arriving upon the resulting war's gateway of life and death.

We entered a room with rows of beds, a man in each covered by singular white sheet. All of them were unwell. Countless shamelessly crying from the pain of injuries so gruesome to witness, I could not fathom how their hearts continued to hold the will to beat. It held my own heart wrenched with sadness.

"This is the result of rich men's pursuant greed for more land, titles and riches."

"Are these men soldiers?"

"No, all are common folk, farmers, men of trade forced to defend invasion of their lands with no more than their tools of trade and bare hands. Those who were not slain were set to endure the witness of rape of their wives, rape of their daughters, death of their sons and loss of their homes. These are the ones who hath been blessed with the fortune to still hold their wits about them and are destined to mend. There are rooms still beyond the door, that of women, another filled with their injured children, many of which are orphaned, then there are the ones who are riddled with madness unable to recover from the atrocities, they hath succumbed to an illness of the mind and thus require containment."

Overwhelmed with sadness I asked, "What do you require me to do?"

"Come." Sister Lydia ventured deeper into the room as I closely followed.

The other Sisters scurried about feeding, making beds while some tended to wounds. They all glanced at me and smiled in a way that seemed to tell of a knowing. We *walked through the sector containing the women and pressed forward to the space that held the children.*

"Sister Aleyn the Child will assist in here, but first I will hath her work to tear the pile of sheets into lengths. Can you please demonstrate?"

"Aye, Sister Lydia."

Sister Aleyn immediately set to demonstrating while I made close watch. There was no utterance of another word, just a brief glance between the two before Sister Lydia pressed ahead to speak with the others in the room. She then proceeded forward disappearing beyond the next door. I was pleased she held the kindness to hath me remain in the presence of the children.

"Do the same with all the sheets, then hath them folded and stacked neatly into the baskets. They will be used to freshly dress wounds."

I nodded my head.

"Thou hath no recollection of me, doth thee Child?"

I looked at her as I shook my head, "My apologies I hath none."

"'Tis a curiosity."

"How is it possible that Sister Beatriz and yourself profess to hath met me when I hath never ventured beyond the walls of the convent with such distance 'til this day?"

In a gentle tone she stated, "'Twas I who placed thee in the basket. From the time you were an infant until you were a grown child 'twas I who was charged to care for thee."

"You were? I had been led to believe it was Sister Maud who had first laid eyes upon me."

Sister Aleyn held a wry grin, "So doth Sister Maud but it is a fable made none the less."

"Doth thee hath certainty of this?"

"I do."

"Then what of Sister Beatriz?"

"Sister Beatriz held origins to the convent of the Holy Heart. Indeed, all the elder Sisters present here originated from the Holy Heart."

A thought clouded my mind, "Pray tell when did the Sisters venture to this region?"

"You were nine." She said with an air of sadness to her tone.

I looked at the cloth between my fingers, "Was I a child of the orchard?"

Her lips pursed as she shook her head slowly, "No, as exclaimed this is a fable told."

"Oh," I said as I recommenced tearing the sheet into strips and folding them neatly into small squares to add to the pile.

"I was in the forest collecting wild mushrooms and fallen seeds for our pantry when I heard the cries of an infant in the distance. There, near the waters were two who were set upon an argument. I peered from a distance sheltered from view by the thicket."

"What was the argument regarding?"

She bowed her head slightly in pause, "They deliberated in regard to who would be set to the task of drowning the infant."

"Me?" I asked as I felt my body stiffen, bracing myself with folded arms.

"Aye, child. They were both men of superstition so neither wanted to be cursed by the infant who possessed skin of taint and the eyes of the devil."

"Is this another fable to be told for my purchase and thine amusement?" I said feeling angered.

"No, this is the truth I swear to thee." She said stepping forward. "The reason you stand before me this day *flourishing in beauty is attributed to my quick wit. For it was I who saved thee by causing a raucous, instilling fear that there was a beast approaching. They chose to leave thee to be its supper thus absolving their need for execution by their own hand."*

"If this is thine truth why did thee see fit to create a fable of my origins, which withheld thy glory as savior?"

"Sweet child, if those who sought to see thee harmed heard even a whisper of thine salvation they may hath returned to attempt the same. 'Twas no other way to ensure thy safety, the fable held purpose, a masked necessity. 'Twas told to all. 'Tis believed by all still. Sister Lydia and I were the keepers of thy secret."

I looked into her eyes and held no reason to claim falsity to her words, "I hath nothing that affords me a way to reward you for your bravery and dedication toward my safekeeping."

She reached across and touched my hand. "'Tis by the grace of God that I was made present and drawn to your call. I am merely a servant of his desires. You were saved by my hand only through his guidance to do so."

I nodded my head, "Thank you."

"Blessed be, thou art a miracle to behold standing before me." She touched the side of my face and smiled. "I must tend to the children now, perhaps we can speak more once I am done."

"I would very much like that." I said as I watched her walk away.

My mind, coveted by a swill of untruths revealed, held me silent. When Sister Aleyn had stated 'twas she who had placed me in the basket, I thought it to be confessions of motherhood. 'Twas no relief to hear otherwise. I pondered on how I would be able to delineate between fables and truth if so many are equally misled by the same. 'Twas made apparent now that my oddity had set me on a path of challenge from the moment, I held breath. Why would a creator make me so, knowing the nature of man? How strange it was that all seemed to glance upon me to claim witness to extraordinary beauty when in actuality, I felt as though I was somewhat bland.

* * * * *

Upon the hour, when light traded for dark, I was ushered in secrecy into the carriage to once more be on the road to venture farther beyond the common regions.

"What is the matter Child, you seem somber in thy disposition? Did witness to the atrocities of war take hold upon thine heart?"

"Many things hath taken hold since I entered this journey."

Sister Lydia placed her hand upon my knee to hath me look toward her rather than the passing landscape. "Tell me, Child."

When I remained silent I saw her hand grasp the end of the curtain partially drawing the fabric across to obscure my view.

"Silence only sets to rot the insides. Speak of what ails you?"

"Sister Aleyn confessed that my origins of the orchard were a mere fable and told a variant where I was set to be killed by the riverbed. She said she saved me."

"Aye, it is as she says."

"In all these years why did thee not tell me thineself?"

"I felt it her place to express when the time came to do so."

I peered beyond the side where the curtain had not

reached, to glance upon the landscape once more. "How did it come to pass that all the elder Sisters now reside within the Sacred Light convent in lieu of the Holy Heart?"

"There is much to tell and thou art yet to take rest. Perhaps in the morrow we shall speak more of this."

I turned to glance at her, "Sister with all respect intended, to fair in knowledge of the tidings I hath acquired this day my preference would be to receive the answers to questions that cloud my mind. I can assure thee the enlightenment would be doing me a service of kindness."

She released a sigh, "Then let it be so said this night and never more."

"Agreed." I said readjusting my posture to face forward so I could look into her eyes.

"Oh Child I fear the knowledge acquired may overwhelm thee."

"Please Sister Lydia, I feel the urgency in knowing all thee can spare the time to tell."

She released a sigh, "Very well. Many moons ago there was a Cardinal who came to visit the convent."

"I know of this, Nathaniel told me how the Cardinal wanted to claim me as a prize and you had made arrangements for him to return to which he did only to be greeted with ill tidings of a fable regarding my passing. This set him to disbelief and anger. He implored the King for two days to hath his soldiers search the grounds for me and this was the beginning of the King's demands for taxes to be paid."

Sister Lydia carried an expression of astonishment as she listened to me convey my understanding of events.

"Nathaniel held no business in the telling of such things. Is there more?" She asked with a frown.

I tempered my eagerness to speak knowing the remainder

of my telling's would need to be done so with caution. "Nathaniel told me he bore witness to my folly of venturing into the forest to practice my archery on eves where the light was the brightest. 'Twas his father who charged him upon his eighteenth to guard me from a distance."

Her eyes narrowed, "You left the grounds?"

"With regularity Sister. I held a desire to master the craft so my hunts could be rewarded with an abundance for our pantry."

"Oh dear Child 'tis a wonder you manage to still live. Hath thee no sense of the dangers which lurk in the forest at night, beasts so quick with skin so thick an arrow could not penetrate?"

"I know of none. Any I hath placed aim to hath swiftly fallen by my hand."

She shook her head with a laugh, "Thou art indeed an oddity."

I looked down at my hands, "Is it true the taxes were imposed by the King as punishment?"

She nodded her head, "Aye."

"Was the Sister's departure from our convent driven by the fear of being slain for refusal of demands of favors as payment?"

Sister Lydia gasped, "I thought thee naïve, but it seems I am the one shadowed from witness to your wisdom."

"'Tis merely knowledge acquired, nights observed, which holds me to my thoughts. I hath secretly held much guilt for the regularity of demand on the Sisters to deliver such favors."

"Child, all is not what it seems. Thou hath reached beyond my expectations of thine blessings upon the convent and the Sisters within. Pay no regard to those chosen to execute favors, this is but another fable intended and sustained."

"How can this be when I hath been witness with my own eyes the coming and goings of countless men."

"The occurrence is a certainty to this there is no denial. Grant me thy silence from banter to afford me the chance to tell in the absence of interruption."

I pursed my lips and nodded my head eager to know more.

"Thou art likely aware a favor was given to the Cardinal to persuade him of need to hath thee remain to learn the ways of pleasure, yes?"

"Aye, tis how it has been told to me."

"The Cardinal presented post the expiration of the agreed annum eager to receive thee. He was, as you might imagine, reluctant to accept the fable told of thine untimely call to God due to fever. This infuriated him, so he sought the aid of the King to deploy the soldiers to find thee. They searched the village; throughout the convent, and even neighboring lands were scrutinized. There were rewards issued to entice the greedy to confess to the knowledge of thy whereabouts. Once the news was received that their efforts held no lead, the King was infuriated, as he had now become obsessed at the thought of possessing thee. The Cardinal retreated back to his lands and all seemed settled until I received informal word from sources that there were whispers the King intended to lay claim on the convent and with this apply taxes. I had further heard he intended the payment to be made by pleasurable servitude as punishment. I made haste to seek the assistance of Nathaniel's father to make arrangements for the Sisters to be granted silent passage to the Sacred Light convent. They traveled in pairs while we gathered selected whores from far regions to be positioned in place of each who left. Careful planning gave assurance we would not be seen to dwindle in numbers. None could afford suspicion to be drawn while the trade took place. We enticed the women with guarantees safe housing, enough food to make their plates overflow so they may never feel the taunt of hunger in their swollen malnourished bellies again and finally a hefty portion of their charges for service to be retained by them. Nathaniel's father, under sworn secrecy, hand selected each and brought them to us. The few Sisters remaining set to work grooming these women in the ways of God, teaching them the Lord's prayers and assigning them their daily chores. On the night the King's men arrived unannounced to make claim of payment for said taxes, they were being served by willing whores dressed in Sister's habits who feigned resistance before succumbing to their barbaric demands."

I cupped my mouth, "No, all these years the Sisters that I hath grown to love are nothing more than whores of service?"

"Child, hold your tongue, we are all from God possessing place as well as purpose in his heart. These whores willingly serve God in fated ways to protect the virtue of the Sisters who otherwise would hath been beaten, raped and slain. I hold much gratitude toward them."

"Thou art right Sister Lydia, I care for them dearly, 'twas insensitive of me to allude to anything other than this. Still it shames me to know all of it attributes to me. Perhaps I am cursed. I can see nothing but grief imparted to those who hath known me."

"Consider all which has transpired coupled with its resulting inspiration. If not for thee my dear there would be no way for the convent to amass coin in secret to aid those we assist at the Sacred Light. We hath healed countless across the years, rebuilt villages and strengthened the commoner's faith in God. Those women who are now occupants of the Holy Heart are provided a far greater life than previously bestowed to them in their lot. They are thankful. We are all grateful *for the challenges presented by thine existence. Our numbers secretly grow in strength Child, and it all stems from thee."*

"I am uncertain what to say."

"Then sleep, we hath a way to travel and you must maintain thine strength across the journey."

"Sister Lydia, where doth this journey end?"

"In the morrow Child, we shall speak of it. In the morrow."

With this, she closed her eyes to rest.

* * * * *

There was no passage to a sound slumber for me this night. I lay awake 'til the break of dawn in contemplation of my life. The birds, in the distance, could be heard, their voices mildly lifting the spirits of my heavy heart. There was a rise of fear I nurtured in regard to the looming journeys end. I could not fathom what Sister Lydia held in store given my existence seemed to present challenge to those nearest. Where could I possibly reside with safety?

The carriage halted post a dip then a thud prompting Sister Lydia to wake as her body thrust forward causing us to collide.

The door immediately opened, "Sisters are you safe?"

"Sister Lydia collected herself to stand, "What has happened? Are we under siege?"

"No Sister the wheel has been compromised by a hole I had not seen on the path. We will hath to make stop while I attempt to repair it. I need to offload all the luggage and such prior. Bear no concern, it will be remedied post haste. If all else fails, the next township 'tis not far should I require assistance."

"We will assist in any measure possible. Come Child, I do not wish us to be here any longer than necessary."

It took a significant portion of the morning before our efforts were rewarded with a satisfactory mend. I was pleased to be in motion once more, for my throat was parched and my body craved to receive nourishment.

I patted my midriff, "I hold a hunger in my belly."

"When we arrive thou shall hath your fill, 'tis a while longer I suspect."

"Can thee indulge the need for distraction from my hunger with nourishing my mind in regard to this journey's end?"

"Perhaps 'tis best spoke of post our arrival."

I shook my head, "I suspect what you hath in store will not be to my liking. The insistence upon my adorning of a gown, reference to my need to behave as a lady ought to, all of it places me in fear that I will be burdened with a life I do not seek."

She touched my knee, "I hold nothing but the best of intentions and hath puzzled for a solution to thine continued safe passage in a world where men hold obsession to claim thee. You bear the burden of beauty my child. There are sacrifices to be made and holding resistance to this will only place risk on all those who sought to save thee. Can thee fathom the rage of a King who shan't be denied his demands, if he learnt of thine existence? In the absence of sighting thee, just from the mere description provided from the Cardinal, he was driven to madness enough to concoct the enforcement of new laws that would see all convent's who were once free to now be ruled by his command. This very same King so enraged that his efforts to find thee were unsuccessful that he in bitterness imposed taxes that must be serviced by favors from Sisters who are sworn to vows of chastity."

"Could I not remain at the Sacred Light with the Sisters to spend my life in servitude aiding the wounded like the others?"

"The risk is too great. Any of the commoners whom we mend could venture out and speak of the witness of thine presence. This given your uniqueness of beauty would be a certainty, which thereby places all that has been built from the hardships endured at risk. 'Tis no small measure of sadness for us to bid thee goodbye but it must be done now that thou art of age."

I felt faint, "Coming of age for what precisely?"

"Oh child, your insistence upon knowing in advance will only set thy mind on fire with unnecessary fear."

"This may be so, still I insist upon knowing prior to our arrival."

Sister Lydia adjusted her posture briefly glancing out the window before releasing a deep sigh, "Thou art set to be betrothed to Prince René. He is the only son of a great King who resides in foreign lands."

Upon hearing this, I held no tongue to speak.

Sister Lydia gave momentary pause then proceeded to fill the silence. "When the wars were at their worst, the King of France had his only son and the Queen seek passage across the oceans to hold refuge within our convent in complete secrecy. She adorned a habit, tended to chores and executed prayers at service for nearly four years remaining undetected. When the wars were regained in advantage, King Édouard's soldiers sent word it was safe for them to return."

"Did I meet him as a child? I do not recall any other than myself within the confines of the walls."

"No, ye arrived later within the same year, they had already departed for France."

"How is it possible that I, an orphan child of no worth can be considered worthy of marriage to royalty? Doth they hath no laws governing the strict requirements of birth entitlements as they do here? What hath thou not told me?"

"At the time Queen Marguerite was in the convent I

had become her confidant and trusted advisor on matters which concerned her heart. Prior to her departure, she had made arrangements for avenues in which we could remain in contact, and thus our friendship extended beyond the time we had shared together. I wrote to her at times expressing concern about thee. The Queen is well aware of the atrocities bestowed upon the convent stemming from the time of the Cardinal to this day. In the strictest of confidence, I sought her wisdom on how to maintain thy anonymity across the years, while also giving consideration to the safety of those who sought to protect thee. 'Twas Queen Marguerite who proposed a solution."

I placed my hand up to request a cease of the discussion, "It seems preposterous that a mother with an only child of such importance would present her own blood as a solution to save an unknown orphan. I feel it to be a trap of some kind."

"No Child. There are no ill tidings conceived. This good fortune is granted due to thy insurmountable beauty, and a knowing that thee must hold greater purpose than life has presented, 'til now, for thee to oblige."

I shook my head, "I am simply, me."

"Thou art extraordinary. One-day child you will know it to be true."

"I am not suitable for marriage. I know only the ways of prayer and how to sustain a full belly with the use of my hunting skills. I am well groomed for a life of chastity and servitude not to be served upon like royalty."

"Queen Marguerite has had her most trusted of scribes create a lineage traceable by nine generations to provide the papers required to entitle thee for expressions of royal interest and courtship. There will be no question of it."

"I still fail to see why a Queen would go to such lengths

to present me sight unseen to her only son. It seems a farce." I said feeling agitated.

Sister Lydia smiled, "Doth thee recall the gentleman I had thee greet. The one who stayed within the village but visited every day and spoke to thee for the better part of a month?"

I sat upright as the image of this elderly man with a prominent wisped pure white beard surfaced to my mind. "I do. He had been the only guest at the convent whom you had granted me unfettered access to. He vividly conveyed the most fantastical stories of adventures beyond these lands. Day, upon day we spoke for many hours. I told him how I favored hunting to which he seemed amused. I cannot recall his name, but I remember still, how he possessed such kindness in his eyes. What of him?"

"He was the Queens artist in residence, issued by the Queen herself to hath thee assessed. At the time, I held no knowledge of her intentions, only an order to grant him access to thee. Upon his return, he had drawn hundreds upon hundreds of images of you. This was presented to the Queen along with his account of the interactions. 'Twas his opinion after meeting you, that you are undoubtedly of royal origins, placed in the secret keeping of the convent to prevent those who would seek to harm you from doing so."

"But that is an untruth. I wasn't placed in the convent; I was set to be drowned and by fate's hand was saved by Sister Aleyn." I said in a whisper.

Sister Lydia dipped her head to seek mine to be raised so she may engage my eyes, "You must never speak of this. It doth not bode ye well to tell the truth in regard to thy origins."

"So my life is set to be a multitude of masks and lies to sustain my presence in a space I do not wish to occupy. I am indeed a cursed child."

"Stop now, countless people risked their lives to assist you. There is a reason for it; many hold faith that thou art destined for great purpose. Thy true origins hold no weight in the matter. 'Tis of paramount importance that you apply reason and embrace this as nothing other than immeasurable good fortune."

I nodded in acknowledgement but felt heavy of heart causing me to remain silent for the rest of our journey.

* * * * *

Thankful for the meal I retired to my chambers to seek refuge from further banter on the looming matters at hand. 'Twas only yesterday I felt the struggles of confinement wishing for access to be granted so I may be thrust upon the world with free reign to witness its joys. This day holds me to the desire for sanctuary from all, which is proposed. Nathaniel's words echoing the realities of freedom from the convent would only be achieved by binds, held true. A prophecy it seems destined to be fulfilled.

"Wake Child I need to prepare you," said Sister Lydia unraveling me from my slumber.

"Has the dark emerged?"

"Within the hour it will be set. Rise, wash, then come consume some supper." With this she left the room bantering to herself. "There is much to do, much to do."

I prepared myself as requested then set to join Sister Lydia in the innkeeper's kitchen as that is where we had eaten prior. The precise moment I walked in the room the voices from those who were gathered became silent. On my count, there were five men, Sister Lydia and another woman who was dressed in a garment of sheer opulence.

She stepped forward to make closer inspection of me, "I

197

see reason now why Marcel to this day draws you still. He is yet to master the essence of your beauty for he has captured some fine imagery, but none do justice to having you stand before me. You are captivating."

Sister Lydia stepped forward, "This is Odette who the Queen issued to be thy chaperone and these gentlemen are the King's men who will protect thee on thou journey to new lands."

"Hello." I said feeling my heart pound at my chest.

"Lady Jocelin 'tis an honor to finally make your acquaintance."

I mustered up a partial smile with a bow to my head in response, "I thought the French only spoke French," I stated in an attempt to feign composure.

Odette laughed, "I speak many languages, of which English is one of them."

"Forgive us, Lady Jocelin has just awoken hence I held no time to inform her of your arrival. The journey has been extensive from the convent. Please allow me to hath a final word before departure," requested Sister Lydia.

"Of course, we shall wait outside and ensure the carriages are ready." They all left through the back door leading them directly outside without another utterance.

Sister Lydia stepped in grabbing both my arms, "I'm sorry child they were not due until the morrow. Bide thy tongue not to resist Odette's teachings. There is much to master prior to reaching the ports of your new home to ensure you are ready for immediate presentation to the royal family."

"Why doth she address me as Lady Jocelin?"

"'Tis thy name, the scribe required details for the creation of the lineage. 'Twas Marcel as I understand it who chose this for thee. Secrecy must be sworn in regard to all. Do not make an assumption those who present with smiles are

by default thy friend. There are many who want the position of Princess. Odette holds to the fable of Lady Jocelin being secretly raised in a convent and understands her charge is to ensure you are groomed in the French ideals of the proper ways of a lady."

"Will she not grow suspicious of my lack of known etiquette?"

"She will question nothing for Odette is the primary entrusted servant to the Queen herself. She has been instructed to teach, and thus she shall. Do not concern thy mind with such things."

I shifted my hands to hold Sister Lydia's within mine, "Am I ever to see thee again?"

Her eyes dropped for a moment before looking at me once more. "No Child, 'tis here in this place that we must bid our farewells. I cradled thee in my arms as a child and I will carry thee in my heart forever."

"And thee in mine."

With this, she touched my face and smiled. "Go now. I cannot bear to watch, so I shall remain, there can be no fuss while others take witness, 'tis for the best. The men hath shifted thine trunk to the carriage. Time is of the essence. The moment you leave this room you can never think of us again, thou art Lady Jocelin, God willing soon to be Princess Jocelin. Safe journey, Child."

Neither of us imparted tears. Sister Lydia remained in the kitchen as I walked out the back door. The first draw of crisp air burnt my lungs as I fought to resist my desire to run. I understood now the life I thought I knew never really existed, and the life I was to hath, would hold to origins of a new fable.

I placed the page down, shaking my head in amazement.

Lady Jocelin didn't seem to fit her as nicely as the name Nathaniel gave her, Patience. The way everyone continued to emphasize her beauty had me compelled to imagine what someone with such impact could look like. In actuality, I only knew of one mythological figure holding relatable reverence regarding beauty, and that is articulated in the story of Helen of Troy. It stems from Greek mythology. She was known as the face that launched a thousand ships. Patience and Helen's experiences differed but they shared an underlying truth, their presence triggered people's obsession to possess them. Its like their beauty stimulates that human weakness prevalent even in society today where it's still seen as acceptable for a bird to be caged for its song or wild animals captured for containment in a zoo or to have them trained for display in a circus for entertainment, it goes on and on. They are deemed a trophy to be collected, paraded, nothing more. How implicitly sad this would be as a reality for Patience if she is to succumb to being forced to a life of stifle by presenting what is expected rather than being celebrated for who she is. I wondered if in hind sight Patience will end up regretting her lack of consideration to Nathaniel's offer. Her whole world has been turned back to front and upside down.

I stretched out my arms while releasing a yawn. My eyes were still partially swollen from crying in my sleep. They felt like sand paper as I blinked. It was time for me to rest. I knew I should possibly place a call to my parents to see how things were going but I simply couldn't muster up the energy to connect with the outside world today. There were only a few more days before Sanctorum Avow was set to release the third article. I had to find a way to maintain a sense of calm in preparation. Internally I was aware of the presence of a rising fear in me that the punishment the interferon's dished out as 'consequences' may be my absolute demise. I've already lost the dearest friends of my life in the most heinous way and been molested by my possessed father. The interferon's reaction to my next article will be a certainty to stimulate their retaliation. The fact that they target the people I care for, terrifies me. I know there isn't a damn thing I can do to protect them.

Patience's story was a welcome distraction for my mind.

Virtue

Sitting with my legs crossed on the floor in my bedroom, I peered inside the trunk my mom had given me. This collection of artefacts was so diverse in their origins and yet they all seemed from what I knew to be interconnected by one common element, mythological magic. My knowledge was limited in the minute historical details but mom's talent for research coupled with her years of obsession compelled her to search for answers was set to assist me. She had a file overflowing with information on each of the items. Origins, use, everything I could possibly need to know about an item from an observer's perspective. The true curiosity for me was the unique vibration I felt when I held each item in my hand. It was as though we were exchanging secrets with our touch.

Huckleberry sat quietly on the edge of the bed peering down. Each time I looked at him his body would shake due to his tail wagging. The bruising on his neck was finally showing clear signs of healing. I could see tiny hairs beginning to break through the surface of his skin where he had been shaved. I'm so grateful he is set toward a full recovery. I knew he still wasn't one hundred percent himself but then again, neither was I.

There was a temptation to begin delving into the research mom had made on all of them, but my instinct told me this wasn't the time nor the reason I found myself drawn to looking inside this trunk of collective wonders. My compulsion was set to hold within my grasp one item, in particular, a stone. It was a subsection of rock with elements of the most glorious partially exposed gem that I had ever seen. The saturation of colors in deep greens and aqua marine blues with flecks of black held me mesmerized not just for its majestic beauty but more so for the way it made me feel as I held it.

Satisfied in my choice, I returned the other items into the trunk before opening the file mom had dedicated to researching the stone. I wanted to have a quick glance at what she had discovered to sate my curiosity. The first page was a series of photos of the item from all angles with the name Cintamani written and underlined three times. The word Cintamani was unfamiliar to me. On the following pages, there were cut outs of foreign Asian newspaper articles glued to a board. Once again, there were some hand written notes which I assumed were a subset transcript of the article contents. It mentioned the Cintamani stone was believed to be a relic of Buddha. The legend of the stone suggests the owner can be granted a multitude of wishes. It didn't mention how this was to be achieved but it did go on to state the stone itself held its power by representing the Buddha's beliefs and associated teachings. The Cintamani is a stone of universal healing.

I rolled the rock in my left palm before closing my eyes to feel its vibration. There was no doubt that it made me feel better when I remained in contact. The file had a good sixty or so additional pages of information. I knew enough for now to accept there was a definite reason why I was drawn to finding it within the box. I returned the file, then latched it closed as I simultaneously pushed it back under the bed.

Only a few minutes had passed and already my body vibrated with a gentle hum. It felt as though it was resonating from all around me. The air seemed to pulse with a cushioned comfort as how I could imagine a caterpillar may feel nested within the safety of an intricately weaved silk cocoon. All the concerns swelling in my mind seemed to quieten. I knew they were present but the energy I had assigned to give them a voice had been muted, for now.

It was time once more to read Patience's story. There was hope in me that she would disclose that she was able to fall in love and live happily with the Prince, but I was wise enough to know this only ever seemed to exist within fairy tales.

The passage across the oceans was arduous. I did not fare well being placed upon the rough seas for months. My mind was unable to still from the motion of the vessel fighting through the regular storms that danced with the hull. Odette also frequented the need to release the contents of her stomach, all the while assuring me it would pass, but it never did. The entire journey challenged my constitution, and compromised my capacity to retain all that was being taught to me.

Upon the day of arrival, I held such relief to see the shores ahead I never thought to be fearful of what was in store. I all but leapt off the vessel the moment the plank was secured. Grateful to feel the strength of steadied ground below, I vowed never again to set foot upon a vessel.

Odette caught up with me presenting her pursed lip coupled with a slight headshake, which I had seen frequently and had now grown to enjoy.

"I gather that was not the proper demonstration of how a Lady should alight?" I said in jest.

She laughed, "Come now, the carriage over yonder awaits. T'will take three days to arrive after which you must rest and then hath thine final preparations in readiness to be presented to the Queen."

"Odette."

"Aye, Lady Jocelin."

"What about my possessions?"

"T'will arrive on another carriage. The King's men will see to this."

"Then I am set to remain in these garments until we enter the castle?"

She smiled, "You concern thyself with such trivial matters when there is no need to hold consideration. 'Tis taken care of. Thine new garments and other necessities are stored on the carriage over yonder. I can assure thee all matters hath been thought of and pre-arranged to provide comfort for the journey ahead."

"Oh."

As we arrived upon the carriage, a man stepped forward to open the door. I turned and looked at Odette who gestured with her hands that I must alight. No sooner was I in, she followed suit, the door was closed, and we were in motion. The sheer beauty of the carriage held my eye's captive.

"This carriage is glorious however I do wish we could hold the speed of the journey so we may reacquaint ourselves to the joy of stillness."

"'Tis best we arrive so we can take proper rest."

"Odette, may I ask thee something and receive an honest insight?"

"You may, I shan't lie to thee."

"What if the Prince doth not like me?"

Odette leaned forward patting my knee as she spoke, "Dear sweet Lady Jocelin, I hath only known of thee for the past months and I already understand my heart nurtures thee as my own. You are one who enchants onlooker's eyes to distraction with thine unparalleled beauty, but those who are blessed to know thee, cannot help but truly love thee. 'Tis by this reasoning I am certain the Prince will too."

I nodded my head. "Thank you."

She reclined in her seat and gave a gentle smile, "Let us both take rest." With this she closed her eyes.

After all of the sacrifices made, I did not want to disappoint them or worse hath elements unravel, which may place them in harm's way. I held steadfast to embrace my fate and would endure the restraint of being betrothed.

The three days were filled with Odette's insistence of my practice of her teachings. 'Twas repetition of madness from the moment we woke until the night, she maintained relentless pursuit of my attention. I feared I might die of boredom before we made our first step on to the castle grounds. Still, I knew I must pay heed and execute my utmost performance of the countless ways imposed on one in order to be deemed 'a lady.'

The comforts within the carriage made the travel along the roads feel as though we were floating on clouds in comparison to the one Sister Lydia, and I had used. The magnificence of the horses was unlike any, I had ever laid eyes upon. The convent did not possess horses so the only ones, I held a cause to meet were when a carriage was borrowed or people of nobility arrived. Mostly on these occasions I was either confined to my room or in the case of the King's soldiers, I was ushered out to the forests with Nathaniel to hunt.

When the carriage finally arrived at the drawbridge, we received entry without the standard fanfare given to guests of significance. Odette had said it was the Queen's wish to hold a private audience with me first before she brought my existence to the attention of all others. It made me wonder with the allocation of soldiers to guard, Odette to teach me, how was their absence across these many months accounted for? People, from my understanding always shared whispers. Perhaps they loved the Queen so greatly they dare not betray their loyalties to her. 'Tis a curiosity to know one could hold such a command over many from the simple utterance of a request.

My mind could hardly fathom the sheer size of the castle. It looked to be more than thrice the size of the convent. 'Twas impossible to imagine all of this being assigned to the occupancy of a King, Queen and their son. The furnishings inside caused my mouth to gape in awe of their beauty. Walls filled with vibrant colored tapestries, such detail in the paintings of landscapes, the oversized portraits of ancestry looked so real I felt them judging my presence.

"Hurry Lady Jocelin, we must get thee to thy room so you may take rest."

I quickened my pace to follow as she manoeuvred her way through the maze of corridors and stairwells.

She released a sigh as she opened a large door and entered the room, "We hath arrived at your chambers. All that you require is here to freshen before bed. Do not venture the halls. The King's castle guards patrol the grounds and are yet to be aware of thy presence. They will surely kill thee *within an instant for trespassing. Remain until I return to assist thee with dressing in the morrow."*

"I shall. My mind is so weary I most assuredly will take rest. I yearn for stillness."

"As do I." She quickly made inspection of the room, "Everything seems in order. I bid thee goodnight Lady Jocelin."

"Rest well Odette," I said as she closed her door on the way out.

My first night at the castle presented me with the best sleep I had never imagined was possible to achieve. 'Twas perhaps exhaustion which caused the depth of my slumber, but the comfort of the bed had me drifting off so sweetly I held amazement that such comforts exist.

* * * * *

Odette opened the arched doors to the chapel signaling for me to walk inside. As I stepped across the threshold, she closed the door leaving me to stand there at the tip of the aisle. The wonder of the stories depicted by the stained glass allowed for my mind to be distracted from why I was placed here. The light falling from the skies danced upon the colored panes.

"Do you not acknowledge thy Queen when she arrives?"

I gasped as I stepped back in fright, then bowed to courtesy, "I'm sorry your majesty I did not see thee."

"Look upon me child, I wish to make closer inspection."

I stood still as she made an assessment of my every detail.

"'Tis incredible, thou art indeed all what people hath hailed thee to be, perhaps more so now that you stand before me."

I held nothing to say in reply.

"Manners would suggest at this moment that you acknowledge my words, Lady Jocelin."

I stumbled to speak, "I mean no offence, I simply do not know what to say."

She pursed her lips slightly, "A mere thank you would suffice. Great lengths hath been taken to hath thee journey to our shores with safe passage. Gratitude, loyalty and thanks should never lack in these circumstances. In deed 'tis what will keep thee alive within these walls."

"Thank you for all you hath done for me. I am forever indebted."

"Aye, indeed ye shall be," she said as she turned her back to walk down the aisle. "Follow suit."

Her words spiked the run of a chill up my spine, for I never held true heart towards being indebted yet her response told me there was a debt owed. Odette had bound the corset I wore this day impossibly tight with countless layers of fabric overheating my body. It only set to exacerbate my displeasure of being present. The novelty of the sound of the fabrics swish began to place a toll on my ears, 'twas now representative to me of nothing more than the labored sounds of conformity. I was not more than two days trapped within the walls, and already I could feel my loss of joy grow. This castle I knew could not hath been built with foundations of love. 'Twas a certainty that blood was spilt to create, to retain, to upkeep these cold stone walls, and I was now well within its royal grasp. My heart ached to go home.

"Sit here."

I sat where the Queen had directed me to do so.

"I will inform the King to make the royal announcement stating in precisely four week's time that there will be a celebration in honor of the engagement of our son. Upon the arrival of the guests, we will introduce you as Princess

Jocelin, for we will hath executed a closed ceremony to hath thee wed in secrecy here in the royal chapel prior. 'Tis best that it is done this way."

I had my hands positioned in a clasp on my lap, struggling to breathe with the corset so tight. I nodded my head to acknowledge her words.

"Do you hath anything thee wish to ask?"

I shook my head. "No, your majesty."

"Very well, remain here I will hath the guards watch the doors so no one else may enter until I return with my son. 'Tis time for you both to meet." I watched, as she seemed to glide across the floor effortlessly. The moment I was alone I stood so I could allow for my breath to be drawn deep. All I wanted to do was peel off these layers and return to the glory of my bedchambers where sleep was the only joy I seemed to revel for its afforded freedom.

A significant portion of time passed before the door was once again opened. 'Twas only when I saw his hand that my heart started to palpitate. There was no escape from this.

He entered alone with a somber expression. "My apologies for keeping thee waiting, my Lady. Thy presence here came as a complete surprise to me. T'would seem my mother has brought it upon herself to decide it was time I wed, and as it would appear by thine presence, the Queen mother has already made selection."

I nervously did a quasi bowed curtsey, "Tis an honor to make your royal acquaintance. I am Lady"

"I know who thou art Lady Jocelin. I hath been thus informed this hour. Did thee not hear me? I am infuriated by all of this, by THINE PRESENCE." He said pointing at me before dramatically glancing away.

"Oh, then I shall leave at once. I thank thee for thy time Prince René." I said turning to exit the chapel.

He quickly spun around to look upon me once more, "Pay no heed to my anger, t'will pass. Please return, take a seat I require a moment to gather my thoughts."

I released a sigh, then returned close to where he stood, "If you don't mind Prince René, I would rather stand."

His hands waved at me, "As thou please."

My eyes gazed up at the stained glass panes once more, hoping the time would pass quicker with a distraction. After a while, watching his pacing and intermittent glances across at me, he broke the silence.

"I find the idea of being told what to do insufferable. My mother insists upon her continuance of treating me like a child cursed with idiocy." He paused his speech as he adjusted his hands to be on his hips then shifted closer to tower over me. "Why by the good grace of God doth she select thee?" Shaking his head with an expression of disgust he scuffed his foot on the floors surface. "I hold no desire to be bound to the insufferable nagging of a woman. The beauty you clearly possess holds no charm on me as it undoubtedly doth for all others. I care little for such things."

He seemed so angry yet his eyes demonstrated curiosity. He watched me closely while continuing on with his rant in regard to; my limited use to him, that I held no signs of being an appropriate match and clearly the Queen had lost her mind when she decided upon me as the chosen one. I continued to listen in silence and eventually sat down.

"Are thee, are thee falling asleep?"

I lifted my head up to look at him, "I guess I was." I said lost of any desire to address him by his titles.

"Doth thee understand in this land I could hath thee beheaded or hanged for such a display of disrespect?"

"Then let it be so, perhaps peace will reign for us both." I said in annoyance.

His eyes squinted to take closer inspection of me, "Are thee insane?"

I knew I should withhold my tongue but I simply found myself unable to, "Insanity Prince René is being afforded a solution for it to be declined only to hath continued indulgence of the focus placed on the problem which to mind no longer exits."

He placed his hand on his head and swirled in a circle, "Pray tell, what doth thee speak of?"

"With all due respect, I offered to leave. 'Twas only by thy request that I returned. 'Tis been passed two hours and all thou hath done is tell me in anger how I am not suitable for thee. Nevertheless, the solution to my mind is rather obvious. I can leave, never to be seen or heard of again. Instead, of accepting my offer, thou seem to hold a preference to retain me for sport, whereby I am forced to endure listening to thine insistence on not wanting me here. What precisely would thee hath me conclude in regard to this display?"

His mouth gaped open as he stared at me for the briefest moment before he released his breath in a huff and stormed out the chapel.

It did not occur for me to leave. I simply waited. 'Twas nightfall before Odette entered the chapel to escort me back to my chambers. I dare not breathe a word of what had transpired nor did she ask. The relief felt when the corset was removed caused me to smile for the first time that day. All I required was a perfect night of slumber with hope that by the greet of the morning light, they would hath come to their senses, and I granted permission for safe passage away from here.

"Thy meal will be delivered shortly. Consume thou supper for you will need thy energy. I hath been told to hath thee prepared before day break."

"To leave?" I asked, excited at the prospect.

Odette shook her head. "The Prince requested the announcements for engagement be made sooner than planned as he intends to take thee on a tour of the lands."

I looked at her puzzled by her words, "I don't understand"

Odette smiled as she placed her weathered hand on my face, "Lady Jocelin, thou hath clearly made quite an impression. A Princess thou shalt be."

"When will this take place?" I said feeling faint.

"By the morrow all across the lands the town criers will make delivery of the good tidings. Prince René and yourself will be escorted by the King's men on horse back to the townships to allow the people to display their affection for his choice."

"I held reason to believe he disliked me."

"Such nonsense Lady Jocelin, 'tis not possible."

As the food arrived, the smell of the meal had my stomach turn nauseous. I had consumed little during the course of the day.

"Eat and then get some rest. I will return to assist you in preparations." She headed for the door.

"Odette, I've never mounted a horse before."

"Then in the morrow it shall be thy first of many times, for once thee hath felt the strength of the beast beneath thee, and the reigns within thy hands, thou shalt never be quite the same. There is much joy in it." With this she closed the door.

* * * * *

Some of the King's men were already upon their steeds. The horse's expressed impatience with their constant attempts to shift forward. Two men positioned on either side stood to hold secure a pure white magnificent horse for me, while Prince René waited by an equally majestic black beast. He watched intently as I followed Odette, who with grace navigated through the mayhem toward the mounting platform. A horseman presented to carefully guide me upon it's back positioning me astride. Once I was securely in place, Odette stepped away while Prince René swiftly mounted his steed, followed thereafter by the remaining soldiers. I glanced across to see how they held the reigns and aimed to mimic the same without falter.

My own heart could be felt pounding against my corset as the horse took its first stride. I glanced down at Odette, who smiled as my mount aligned itself to be closer to the black horse. When the gates were drawn, the soldiers held a formation around us. With no instruction required my horse matched its pace to an identical rhythm to that of Prince René's. 'Twas only once we cleared the grounds I relaxed enough to deviate from the focus of my steed to notice the Prince smiling at me.

"Art thee secure upon thy steed Lady Jocelin?"

"Aye, thank you for asking Prince René."

He glanced at my horse, "Is the beast I chose for thee to thine liking?"

I turned my head and smiled at him, "Oh yes, 'tis divined from the heavens. I've not held the cause to ride before, it doth feel like magic."

"Thou hath never ridden, how is that possible?"

"Oh, my lot did not afford me such opportunities. I was kept hidden within the convent walls, and as thee must know the Sisters hold to the vow of poverty. Horses are a luxury which could not be sustained. Any beast that was used for purpose had been borrowed and thus returned."

He rolled his eyes, "Aye of course how silly of me. Doth

thee like him then?"

I smiled as I drew my hand down the length of my horse's muscular neck. "I do."

The Prince leaned toward me as he whispered, "Then consider him thy beast."

I looked at Prince René completely astonished, "You would gift me this horse?"

"No my lady, 'tis not that I would, I already hath. He is yours."

I looked at the beast beneath me and held little ability to express in words the joy I felt toward the thought of owning him. "Thank you, but.."

"But what, come now I wish thee to possess the freedom to speak candidly in regard to thou thoughts in the absence of hesitation."

"Yesterday Prince René, you left my company in a state of anger post a lengthy berating from thee on how unsuitable I was as a choice, threatening beheadings and such. This day you exude kindness and gift me a horse. I am unsure of what the morrow shall bring."

He released a laugh upward towards the skies, "Oh that. Pay no heed to yesterday, 'tis from this day onwards that matters."

"'Tis beyond my comprehension why thou would choose to marry me after all that was expressed from thine heart."

"I doth owe thee an insight and more so an apology for I behaved rather poorly albeit with intent."

"Intent?"

"Mother has presented me with countless courtiers for my assessment. Each had been told by mother that they were chosen. Upon the greet I subjected them to the precise theatrics you too had received and all bar thee hath been sent home the same day marked as unsuitable."

"Why insist upon subjecting each to such humiliation? Doth thee not feel it to be cruel in nature?"

"'Tis a test that none hath passed with the exception of thee."

"A test?"

"The opportunity presented to be titled royalty doth illicit unsavory behavior. There are some who display greed, other's obstinacy. 'Tis an ugly course to bind and endure at length. 'Twas why the scheme was devised. The purpose held to provide a measure for circumstance to reveal thine truth. The chosen after all was set to be my betrothed, bear children and someday stand present while I hold to the arduous task of ruling the kingdom."

"My curiosity is awoken, may I be granted the insight of what others before me hath said when thou had behaved in this manner?"

"Cry mostly, some attempt to beg as if they hold no pride, however thine reaction was somewhat unique. Upon my first rant, you offered a solution, which demonstrated no hesitation on thy part to sacrifice the opportunity of receiving title and riches. 'Twas thine immediacy of response further supported by thy attempting to leave, which assured me thine intentions were pure. When I insisted upon thee remaining, so I may continue my theatrics, you listened. In lieu of interrupting with retaliation, crying, pleading for me to alter my mind, making promise of anything I desire to alter the decision, you Lady Jocelin held steadfast to silence." He paused to release a laugh, "and then upon my coaxing thy speech I was greeted with thine uninhibited tongue, which in delivery made it abundantly clear you held me in contempt for my poor display of manners. This tells of a person who holds no desire in the vast gains the position of Princess affords. 'Tis why I knew mother had chosen well this time."

"*Thy theatrics are well served, I was certain by the furrows of anger expressed across thine brow that I was either set to be sent away or drawn and quartered in the morrow.*" *I said with amusement.*

"*Alas, the portion of the eve you refer to held no theatrics. I'm afraid thy voicing of my behavior caught me somewhat unaware, coupled with the delight to be present to such pureness of heart and strength of conviction. In truth, I felt embarrassed this was our first meet. 'Tis why I arranged for this day, so I may acquaint thee with who I really am and court thee in the proper fashion you deserve, my Lady.*"

I felt myself blush.

I was smiling like a fool as I re-read the last paragraph out loud. This is the first time I have felt the presence of Patience's softer side. She likes him, I can tell. There is more to these two than I first suspected and I'm so relieved for her. Knowing I'm not destined to receive love in this lifetime finds me wanting to live vicariously through her story. I knew my silent growing ache for Patience to have a happy and fulfilling life was something I also desperately wished for myself.

It seemed to be that I was quickly settling within the best part of a life, which was grander than any dream I might hath thought to imagine. Every waking moment, which could be afforded, I was upon my stead learning the art of riding. I tried to insist on being charged with his grooming to which Odette intervened reminding me that a Lady never executes menial tasks. When I could, I would scurry to his stable undetected just to place my hands upon him. I was so happy for the first time in my existence, I felt as though I had found a place where I could belong.

Much of the Prince's time was consumed by managing the affairs of the court and other such duties in the King's absence. Each day I would note his presence attempting to hide from view as he watched me ride. Of an eve we would dine with the Queen mother who presented us with all of her plans for the upcoming wedding. On occasion, the Prince would search under the table to find my hand, so he may hold it in secret while she spoke. Each time I would feel a sense of light-headedness when he traced his fingers across my palm. I would quietly draw breath and hold to savor the feel of his touch to which he would smile. I felt I began to understand a hearts yearn to love.

The week prior to the wedding, the King was due to return to the castle. All who knew seemed to display an expression of fear when reference to his return was made. There were tales I overheard spoken by some of the kitchen hands telling of him, as though he were a monster. There was a temper within him, 'tis for certain, I thought given that all of the stories amassed held themes of violence and tragedy. I was yet to make his acquaintance to determine the truth. The Prince had previously told me his father left early on royal matters the morning we had both ventured out to ride for the first time. To this, I held no cause to believe otherwise.

Advance word made its way to the castle that the King was set to arrive ahead of schedule and indeed on this day. The sounds of voices filled the hallways with servants scurrying about in preparation for his attendance. The kitchen servants were ordered to present an evening feast, minstrels held place in the dining hall. Flowers were strewn across the table's already lavish setting. I felt nervous at the thought of meeting this man, although I knew not why it was so.

Odette bathed and prepared me in a gown of extreme

opulence. 'Twas laden with crystals and seemed thrice as heavy as any other she previously had me display. The corset was tight but I had learnt a valid lesson from my magnificent white stead, whereby I extend my belly while tightening occurred to Odette's satisfaction. I thereby release the extension of my belly only when 'tis done. This affords me a level of comfort I had previously struggled to obtain. 'Twas clear to me now that these garments were purely designed for obtainment of one's ideal depiction of beauty for it held no practicality.

Odette collected me when it was time to commence the celebratory feast. The King's return to the castle meant I was required to be escorted and formally announced. The sweat beaded across my brow upon entry to the room. The gown felt as though it weighed me down preventing my ability to move freely as I had otherwise grown accustomed to do in others.

All the formalities took place as Odette had advised, and I was promptly seated at the table with the King, Queen and Prince, shortly thereafter. He was a man of few words this night, occupied by eating and staring at me as he brutishly gulped his wine. The way he chose to chew with his mouth open for all of the content to be seen made a wild beast appear to hold a better capacity for execution of dining etiquette. I did my utmost not to glance across, for his eyes were unabashedly fixated on me. The Prince did not attempt to find my hand this night, nor did the Queen mention anything in regard to the wedding. In actuality, she never spoke a word. Once the King had eaten to his sufficiency, he remained present, drinking goblet after goblet of wine while we all sat in silence. 'Twas a most unpleasant evening.

Odette escorted me back to my room after supper. I recognized by her expression, she carried some worry across her brow. I quietly walked the halls with her, not wishing to know the realities of her concern for I could not bear to learn of anything that may cause disruption to my joys. By the time she had assisted me out of my gown, I could hear noises outside my chamber.

"Sleep now, all shall be well."

I wanted to respond with saying I never realized it wasn't well but thought better of it. As she opened the door to leave she paused to look at the two King's men who had appeared unannounced standing guard outside my chambers. She smiled at them, took two steps backwards, turned to face me while using her hands to gesture that my silence was required before arriving at my side once more.

"Lock the doors this eve, open it for no-one but me. I will return in the early morrow to assist with getting thee dressed." She whispered. "Fear not, all will be well."

I nodded my head to acknowledge her words and waited until she left the room before securing the door as she requested. Sitting on the sill of the window, I looked down into the courtyard of the castle where the flicker of the flames kept the shadow's dancing. There was a sadness looming in me as I lifted my sight to gaze out at the night stars. There would be no visiting my stead tonight.

'Twas well after the stroke of midday when Odette entered my chambers. The tearstains on her swollen face of sorrow fueled the rise of fear in me that all was not well, as she had suggested it would be.

"Whatever is the matter?" I asked.

"We must get you dressed." She said rather loudly while briefly glancing at the door. Then she stepped in and whispered, "They listen, careful not to speak."

"Thank you Odette, thy late arrival see's me famished." I said aloud feigning annoyance.

222

She smiled and nodded, "My apologies 'twas not with intent. Let us make haste so you may dine." Odette leaned in to whisper once more, "The King has ordered the Prince to tend to the King's own affairs on his behalf across the shores while he remains present."

My mouth gaped, "But we are to marry in less than a week." I said quietly. "The seas take months to navigate. I must see him. When doth he leave?"

Her head bowed down, "I'm afraid I must bear the burden of sad tidings for he hath already left this morn. The King insisted, there was nothing he could do to alter his mind."

I tried to remain composed, holding back the tears as my soul felt the need to cry.

"Then the wedding is to be postponed?"

"Announcements are yet to be made but I imagine no other way for it to be."

"I understand." I whispered sadly.

When I was dressed Odette escorted me to the dining room. As I entered I realized there was only one person present at the table, and he was already in the midst of consumption. 'Twas just set to be the King and I.

"Eat." He bellowed between mouthfuls as I sat down.

My appetite had been lost to the knowledge that my Prince had been sent away with an urgency which gave him no time to bid me farewell. I could not fathom what would warrant such need. I ached to feel his presence beside me.

The King mercilessly stared at me while he ate like a rabid beast. Anyone who took witness would assume he had failed to be serviced with a regular meal, but his rotund belly revealed the truth of his overindulgence. After he had several helpings of wine, he released a belch that made a servant jump from fright. It seemed he was pleased with himself *this day, whereas I seethed at the sight of him and felt rather lonely in his presence.*

Three days passed with much of the same. Each day I would rise, be taken to dine with the King and returned to remain under guard in my quarters until the next meal was due. The variant was the eve of this night when the Queen's own lady in waiting Esther attended my chambers. We had never spoken 'til now although she glanced across at me often.

I stood to curtsy as she entered the room.

"Doth thee know who I am?" She said upright in posture peering down her nose at me.

"I am aware." I said

She placed her clasped hands before her as she walked freely about the room making inspection, "Tell me Lady Jocelin, 'twas this always thine intention?"

"My apologies, I'm not understanding thy question posed."

She stopped to look at me, "Doth thee attempt to play me for a fool?"

"No," I said stepping back with my hand on my chest.

"'Twas it always thy plan to come forth and obtain not the title of Princess but the title of Queen?"

I gasped at the thought, "NO, what nonsense doth thou speak of? The Queen already exists, and I am irrevocably in love with her son. Indeed, I can say with ease that I am happily betrothed to my Prince. If it weren't upon the King's insistence his son tend to business on his behalf, we would be in exchange of vows forthwith. My heart has been wrenched with sadness by his unexpected departure. I hold every intention to immediately wed upon his return."

She released a muffled laugh as she turned to face me directly, "Thou art a poor naïve creature. There is no postponement of thine wedding. 'Tis set to remain for the announced time and will indeed proceed in the absence of thine Prince."

I shook my head, "You seem to be speaking in riddles. How can vows be exchanged in my Prince's absence? Surely you make jest." I said taking a step forward.

"No, the King has set forth motions with the Church to annul his marriage to the Queen so he may claim thee as his bride."

With immediacy, I leant over as the contents of my stomach released itself on the stone floor. The nausea held me captive. Lady Esther stepped back covering her nose and mouth as she watched me continue to heave.

"Odette," I stammered. "I wish to speak with Odette."

"Her services to the royal family were deemed no of use. Odette has been sent away and advised never to return."

I mustered my strength to regain a modicum of composure. "What of the Queen, where is she?"

"I'm afraid she has been banished to her quarters to remain until after the vows are exchanged and post this she will be caste aside. If she dares to resist, the King forthwith threatens to strip her of all remaining titles and offer no riches as compensation. Indeed, this is a generosity knowing his penchant for beheading."

"How is such an atrocity allowed? Why is this occurring? I fail to understand the heartlessness of it all. 'Tis not the sound actions of a King but a monster. Who else would so readily steal from his only son, and discard his beloved Queen, for what? Me? Please, I implore thee to confess to me now that what you speak of is some extended folly played, for it surely cannot be fated to occur. It simply cannot."

She stepped in and grabbed both my arms to shake me, "Listen to me carefully Lady Jocelin, the King can execute whatsoever pleases him, and thine presence has held him enchanted. He hath sworn he shall hath thee at any cost."

I looked into her eyes with tears filled in mine, "I would sooner die."

"This indeed is what the Queen wished for thee and in her jealous rage hath sent me to make arrangements to hath thy supper poisoned. I confess to thee now I shan't bear the burden of execution to one who demonstrates the purity of such innocence. If thee can be sworn to secrecy, upon the grace of this eve I shall return to aid thee in thine escape. Thou must swear never to return nor shall ye be afforded the ability to resurface across these lands whilst the King still holds breath. 'Tis a certainty he will charge his army to relentlessly find ways to seek thee out from hiding." I felt her warm breath as she leaned forward to speak directly into my ear, "Are thou'st willing to trust me with thine own life?"

"I hold no choice but to do so." I said shifting my posture so I was able to gaze into her eyes. "My only request is that I retain my horse, the white beast the Prince gave me. I shall not leave without him Lady Esther."

She took pause for a moment before nodding her head, released me, and shortly thereafter left the room.

I aimlessly paced the floors and knew I would continue to do so until her return. Countless hours passed with my mind reeling from all that had been told, trying to ascertain what held true and what could possibly fall beholden to fable. I knew with certainty my history revealed the pattern of many of those who went to great lengths to assist me, had in each instance sought to leverage off fabric from the tethering's of truth to weave a new tale to be told. If I held to believe all that Lady Esther had conveyed, then I would be doomed to an ill life if I remained and most certainly hunted for the remainder of my days if I ran away. I pondered on why Lady Esther hath proposed to go to such great lengths of risk to assist me when her life of servitude and allegiance is devoted to the Queen. I understood if I remained, the Queen would lose her position. If she held success in poisoning me as suggested by Lady Esther were the Queen's wishes, then she would surely be punished by the King regardless. To hath me escape and hold the onus on my motive alone would abolish the Queen of all responsibilities, given she could not aid me while held captive in her own chambers. So, the favor was weighted greatly toward my escape. I noted Lady Esther seemed to hold authority to make decisions, as she presented with little resistance to my insistence of the horse. Her need for me to leave in cooperation was clearly placed higher in rank of importance. There was more to this, I simply knew it.

The poor dear soul, what a nightmare this is turning out to be. It seemed after all Patience had been through, there was finally a possibility of happiness. Yet here she is again being presented with a spanner thrown in the works. She hasn't even been afforded the chance to enjoy herself for all that long before more traumatic circumstances are imposed. I don't understand why this has to happen to good people.

I gave Huckleberry a pat; there was so much pain evident in life and, at times, it honestly felt like there was far less joy in comparison. It seems as though there is always something, someone, willingly robbing the happiness from other's lives. At least, this is how it feels. It's hard for me to read this part of her story without wanting to warn her of what's to come. I felt my own impending frustration increase as I read her words. She is thinking, trying to figure things out, learning from her experiences but not quick enough for my liking. It's obvious to me that the Queen is behind Lady Esther's visit. The suggestion of poisoning is a farce to attempt to gain trust and win Patience's confidence so that she co-operates. I agree with her conclusion that the advantage for the Queen is that she is confined to her quarters which means there is no attributing her directly to any part of this ploy. Still, I can't imagine Lady Esther could gain access to Patience without being seen by the King's men standing guard. If Lady Esther is seen, then this will place the Queen in jeopardy as they are linked. I'm definitely missing something here. My instinct tells me that Patience is headed toward being murdered. If Patience disappears, then the Queen's position is once again secured, or at least this is what she is possibly hoping for. The Queen can't afford for Patience to resurface or the King will force her return and their fates will remain the same. The Queen's only move to prevent the marriage would be to have Patience killed so she can never be found. I suspect the plan to escape is simply a rouse concocted to get her off the grounds so they can have her killed while they remain in the castle with witness's to corroborate their innocence in association to the events that are yet to unfold.

I shook my head, while thinking about how crazy the world is. Nothing ever seems to change. People have been assholes throughout the course of time. Before I continued on with the story, I wanted to take a quick break to stretch my legs while I prepared a fresh batch of food for Huckleberry. Nothing was going to make me ready for what she was about to reveal, but I knew I had to press forward to read what she needed to convey about her life. I required some time to settle my own surfacing emotions. I just felt so damn sorry for her having to go through all of this. She was finally in love and now fate would see to it that she was denied access to the pleasures associated to this sacred experience. I felt devastated for her.

After pottering about for an hour, I decided there was no time, which would be a good time to recommence the story so it may as well be now. I readjusted the sofa into a recline position to elevate my feet then wrapped a blanket over my legs. Huckleberry patiently waited for me to settle before he jumped up on my lap. I moved the Cintamani stone, now positioning it between the centre straps of my bra so it was pressed against my solar plexus. I relaxed my body as I continued to feel its pleasant hum vibrate against my skin. Gently, I stroked the length of Huckleberry's back while he nestled into a comfortable position.

When I heard the door creaking, my heart quickened to a speed so great I could hardly silence my breath. Slowly, the door became ajar, Lady Esther entered adorning attire matched to the shade of complete darkness.

She looked at me with eyes of amazement. "What is this?" She whispered.

"Commoners attire, a mans to be precise. I could hardly leave the grounds in a gown. If I am to remain unseen or hold less attention than I see no alternative."

Stunned she stammered, "Why yes, of course. This is quite brilliant actually and will most certainly aid in our fable."

My curiosity peaked, "What fable doth thee speak of?"

"'Tis a certainty there will be talk of how thee vanished and all whom serve here shall be questioned on the matter."

I glanced at her, "This makes little sense. If I hath not

been seen, then how would one hath cause to speak of my attire to aid the story as thee suggest?"

Lady Esther hesitated for a moment then placed a scowl across her brow, "We must be gone before the guards return. There is no more time to folly with words. Come."

I took pause at the opening of the door, "Where are the guards?"

"I ordered the maidens of the kitchen to lure them with favors. Three consecutive nights of folly is enough to entice a man with no doubts or hesitation to a fourth. Men are driven by the fire in their loins, 'tis all you need to know."

With this, Lady Esther walked down the hall into a passageway I had not been before. She scurried through what I imagined was the heart of the castle. Eventually, we arrived at a marbled statue to which Lady Esther insisted I aid her in pushing. After several attempts at coordinated exertion, the statue made way to reveal an opening in the wall. Lady Esther panting from her efforts ushered me to press forward. My reluctance to proceed had her regain her breath before she entered first, while I followed suit. 'Twas not more than fifty lengths of stride before we found ourselves tightly wedged between the narrowed walls of the castle. Slowly, we traveled a great length sideways, as it was our only option. I held my breath when I felt our gradual descent. The deeper we ventured the ground softened, which made us intermittently lose our footing. The rushing sounds of water could be heard as we drew closer to where the passage began to widen, affording us the ability to adjust our steps to be gratefully taken face forward. When we arrived at the end of the opening, there was a sound akin to the roar of thunder as ice chilled water sprayed upward onto our faces from the particles splashing the rocks.

"What is this place?"

"'Tis the back of the castle. This fall rushes to be freed upon the river below which escapes the grounds. The narrowed passage thus traveled was built to provide safe passage for the King and his family, should the need arise. The Queen and her son were the last to venture this path in secrecy during the worst of the war."

"The King could never make the journey, his belly is thrice the size of the passage."

Lady Esther released a laugh, "The castle was made centuries prior to his reign. The King's of those times were far less indulgent. Come, we make our final descent for thy carriage awaits below."

Lady Esther carefully positioned her footing with each stride as she walked behind the length of the waterfall before disappearing across its veil. I stood to hold my breath as I saw her hand re-appear. She pulled me toward her the moment, she felt my grasp. My compulsion to release a scream in fright was only tempered by her immediate embrace. There we were drenched, standing on the edge of a narrow ledge with the rushing fall beside us thundering down to the ground pushing vast volumes of water outward.

"'Tis beautiful." I said in amazement

"Aye, 'tis indeed this."

She turned and began her way down the precarious hand carved stone steps. I vowed to myself I would hath failed to hath seen them had she not placed one foot after another on each. 'Twas clever to witness from the ground gazing up as it appeared to be an impossible climb to get to the edge of the castle walls. The foresight to carve a route to freedom, which held no visible exit or entry was truly ingenious. To all who were unaware of the castle's secret, this indeed appeared to be an impenetrable fortress.

"How many people know of this passage?" I asked as we reached the bottom.

"The royal family, myself and now thee. 'Tis all."

I smiled, "Anymore and I gather it would no longer be a secret."

She laughed, "Lady Jocelin thou art a charmed one."

I did not know what she meant by this, so I simply thanked her.

A short walk saw us enter the clearing where in the dimness of the moonlight, I could see the outline of the carriage. My face adorned a smile when a sudden movement caught my attention to hath my eyes look upon the white stead fastened to the rear. The gentleman at the driver's helm dismounted to open the carriage door. I pressed forward to greet my horse, but Lady Esther grabbed my hand before I could touch him.

"There is no time. 'Tis with great imperative, I return to the castle before thine absence is noted. The driver shall take thee far away from here after which you may venture by foot or mounted on thine own steed. Please take heed, thou must be taken farther than the news of thine existence can reach. Afford the carriage man the time to get thee to where he has been instructed to travel."

"How ever will I be able to repay you?" I asked.

"Thou hath already Lady Jocelin. I would do anything to restore my Queen to her rightful position. Thy absence grants me this. I am indebted to thee."

With this, I entered the carriage to take my position. The door closed and shortly thereafter we were on our way. I wished I'd held a chance to speak with the Prince to explain what had taken place. Instead, he would be forced to believe a fable told of my running away. I held a burning need for him to know that I truly love him.

She loved him, I thought to myself as I placed the page down and closed my eyes to rest for a minute. The heat being generated from my body's contact with the stone had me now fighting to keep my focus. I only needed a moment.

Cailleach

The cold of the winter winds held an unforgiving bitterness to its passing across my ridged body as I continued the ascent up the rugged mountain side. My hands were numb from the cold. The tattered cloth wrapped around my bleeding fingers had ice particles forming on its surface. White sleet fell so thick I could barley see an inch beyond the rock face. I fought against my body's need to convulse, in fear that I may loose my grip. The struggle was real. I knew I had to maintain my wits and do my utmost not to succumb to my desperate need to shiver madly. "This will pass, this will pass," I continued to say with my eyes shut tight holding on for dear life. Memories of my most cherished moments flashed in my mind's eye while I felt my brain begin the process of shutting down. The nostalgic farewell gave me a sense of knowing the probability for survival for me was now less than a slither of a chance.

My torso thrust forward as I woke gasping for breath. Soaked to the bone I couldn't contain my bodies need to shiver. I tried to stand as my legs gave way causing me to knock my head on the edge of the coffee table as I fell to the floor. I lay there watching the trickle of droplets of blood seeping from the gash on my head create a slowly expanding crimson pool. With no ability to move, I remained there feeling my system tremor, my hands ached from the sharp pain caused by deep lacerations. I was frozen, like ice.

* * * * *

His presence could be felt calmly tending to my wounds while generating a bright light of energy that was penetrating my core and warming me from the inside out. I wanted to say thank you but held no control of my voice as I passed out.

* * * * *

My eyes were closed, but I knew Huckleberry was sitting in front of me patiently waiting. I recognized I was still on the floor in the living room. I felt different, lighter in a sense. My temperature returned to normal. That dream had me transported to a place where I was trapped on the side of a sheer drop face of a mountain during a blizzard. I wasn't myself, yet it felt all too familiar. The memories presented were not mine, they were of Patience. She was trying to show me something. Perhaps this was her way of letting me know how she died. I was present to the trauma of the experience so much so that I was certain I would not survive. During the experience, I retained a sense of myself but also felt present to Patience. When our body reached the point where it was dying, I found the delineation between us had dissipated. It was terrifying.

I slowly opened one eye. Using my hands positioned in front of me as a focal point I waited for my vision to correct itself. The extreme temperature drop compromised my sight causing everything to become blurry. As I opened my other eye, my vision adjusted whereby I could now see the outline of the lacerations on my fingers. I quietly watched intently as they continued to rapidly seal. Once they healed only faint lines remained as a mark of where they had been. I shifted my body, so I could raise them above my head to look at a little closer. Well I'll be damned, I thought to myself, as I jumped up to find a marker. I grabbed a black ballpoint pen from the top draw in the kitchen and began to redraw the scar lines on both my hands. When I was done I stood there looking at it, then took some images with my cell. What if the uniqueness of the human imprint is actually a detailed map defining the pivotal moments within each of our re-incarnations? Perhaps in first birth we all begin with the same imprint and thereafter lifetime upon lifetime the details are added so that each new life holds an audit of where we have been and what is remaining to complete. Maybe this was what Patience was trying to show me.

I stared at my hands in wonder until droplets of my blood falling on the kitchen bench top caught my eye. I placed my hand on my forehead and felt the gash while walking toward the guest bathroom. Distracted by my intent to look at the wound I was not thinking clearly. My body jolted to a halt at the doorway. The sudden rush of the reality of why there was no mirror caused me to gasp. A tear fell down my cheek as I attempted to stop my train of thought from entertaining the horror of what had happened here. I quickly turned away and proceeded to go upstairs.

The cut was deep enough to require stitches. The last thing at this point I wanted to do was leave the apartment, let alone wait in an overcrowded emergency room to get this looked at. I kept poking and prodding its edges convincing myself it wasn't so bad. The sting of the wound held a bite as I doused the area with disinfectant. I placed the handle of my toothbrush in my mouth, so I could clamp down hard before I proceeded to pull the skin taught. Once the sides of the wound were in a reasonable alignment, I neatly layered a row of steri strips across it to hold it in position. I stood there staring at it for a while to make sure it wouldn't reopen. Looking at my healed hands, I felt the need to acknowledge there is a significance associated to my lacerations mending before my eyes while the injury sustained on my head needed time. There may not be answers to all the questions I thought to pose, but I had to proceed in faith that all the answers I need to receive would be presented at the point in time I required to know them. Satisfied that the steri strips were securely holding the skin in place I went into my bedroom to change my clothes before venturing back down stairs to the living area.

I used some disposable toweling to mop up the water puddles and blood from the floor. The sofa was saturated. After I placed towels across every inch of its surface, I pressed down to encourage the absorption of water. While I repeated the process, my mind gave an inkling to a feeling that I through the experience had obtained a deepened sense of clarity that my conscience was yet to be privy to. It was a sense of connectedness but to what I was unsure. All I knew was despite the physical trauma of the dream and my gash on my head, I felt better than I had in a while. My system was humming and there was a sense of abounding strength surging through my core. There was something fabulous was happening within me.

There weren't many pages remaining to read. I was so invigorated I felt torn between heading out for a jog or staying in to complete the story. The concept I held previously about the human fingerprints resurfaced to the forefront of my buzzing mind. I was onto something and felt a confidence of instinctively knowing there's a connection to our hands imprint that no one has deciphered before. There has to be a way to break the code to reveal our lifetimes. I wonder what time it is? I felt a little hungry, maybe I should fix myself a snack before I recommence reading Patience story.

I recognized my mind was racing and seemed to be erratic in the way it was flittering between thoughts but the clarity was there. It felt amazing. Settling on sating my stomach, I made some popcorn while my mind explored a thousand concepts simultaneously. I don't know if it was the knock on the head or the shock to my system of being frozen or perhaps a combination of it all that contributed to this state that I was present to. The increasing strength developing within my body was undeniably euphoric. I felt alive.

Everything about popcorn to me was wonderful, from the popping sound while it cooked on the stove through to the distinctive smell that filled the air causing my mouth to water. I always felt the need to try to ensure every last kernel transitioned to a pop. I had never been successful at achieving this but it didn't deter me from continuing to try and today was no exception. The trick is to give it enough heat while shaking the pot so the kernels stuck down the bottom don't burn. When I figure it is close to complete, I flip the lid to drizzle some extra virgin olive oil, throw in a generous serve of freshly cracked peppercorns, some dried chilli flakes and a pinch of organic pink flaked Himalayan salt. I then shut the lid, give it a final vigorous shake before placing it in an open bowl. This time around by my count, there were at least twelve kernels left un-popped. My best effort still stood at three.

Unceremoniously, I shoved a handful of the warm delicious popcorn in my mouth, savoring the first flavors along with the crunchy goodness. I returned to reposition myself of a dry portion of the sofa. I placed my tall glass of water on the coffee table, the popcorn beside me and finally a fresh blanket over my lap. Huckleberry came to settle in beside me as I prepared myself to commence the final leg of the journey with Patience.

'Twas no longer than a minute into our travels when I felt something was deeply wrong. I placed my head out the carriage window to look upon the driver. He was at the helm with reigns in hand as one would expect. I turned to check on my steed only to realize he was gone.

"STOP THE CARRIAGE." I screamed

"The driver momentarily shifted his head to partially glance in my direction then corrected his posture to continued to look ahead.

"STOP THE CARRIAGE. STEED, I NEED MY STEED." He ignored my plea. 'Twas only when I thrust the carriage door open that he began to reduce his speed. I refused to wait and jumped out stumbling to the ground. Picking myself up I ran down the path realizing in the dimness of the eves available light that Lady Esther was walking toward the castle with my horse in hand.

"WHAT IS THIS?" I yelled as I reached her side.

Startled she jumped as she spun to look at me. "What

possess thee to alight from the carriage? Thee must be on thine way."

"I told thee I shall not leave without my horse. Why has he been retained?"

She tightened her grip on his reign, "He got loose, you were on route so I thought to return the beast to the castle where he belongs."

Immediately I leant in feeling my heart palpitating as I furiously snatched the reigns from her grasp, "He belongs with me. My Prince gave him to ME."

I took witness to the presence of a slyness in her arising smile as the carriage made a turn and was heading toward us. I knew in this instant all was not what it had been presented to be. I gripped my horse's mane for leverage then swung my body to land upon his back.

"YAH, YAH," He flew into a gallop as I made a wide berth bypassing the path to head into the forest where the carriage was unable to follow.

"STOP HER," screamed Lady Esther as I disappeared into the night.

Instinctively I tucked my head level with his neck gripping tightly in complete trust that my steed held the ability to navigate at speed through the woods. My eyes dripped with tears as the branches made mark upon my exposed skin. We flew through the air with each bound. My mind focused on the thunderous sounds of his gallop gliding in lengthened stride as he took me further and further away from my beloved Prince.

Hours passed, my horse lathered in sweat his breath strained while my grip weakened. I knew his ability to maintain his speed would succumb to eventual exhaustion. I mustered the strength to continue to hold, allowing for him to select the pace of travel. The further we ventured the safer we would be.

'Twas only when we hit the edges of a roaring river that he slowed to pace then walked along its edge. Cautious of the way ahead I knew from Nathaniel's teachings, if one was to be lost in a forest they are sure to be found by the water. People regularly gathered at the edges of fresh water he said. If it is to be followed in either direction, it is a certainty to come upon a village for there is always one built within close proximity to flowing rivers.

We traveled in the open until my steed entered a ravine surrounded by cavernous rocks. He ventured in past the point where the break of the morning light upon the horizon could follow. In the darkness, I felt the dizziness of exhaustion. The moment his body ceased motion, ungracefully I felt myself slide off his back onto the hardened ground. My fingers ached from grasping, my legs had seized, I lay there feeling the added surge of pain from my fall. The steed stepped forward gently placing his whiskered muzzle over my face. This was the last image I could recall before my mind blackened.

* * * * *

The fire warmed my skin while I remained still. I could see through the flames flicker my steed was at rest along side the darkened outline of another. As I saw a pair of boots move toward me, my surrounds blackened once more.

* * * * *

I woke to the sound of breathing in my ear. I quickly tried to gather my senses realizing my head was placed on the torso of another. Carefully I shifted my position to attempt to stand but my mind pained me.

"Keep still Lady Jocelin, you need to rest. 'Tis I."

My heart palpated as his voice rang true to my ears. I pushed with my bruised hands to lift my torso. I stared into his eyes as he presented with the warmest of smiles.

I reached out and touched his face, "'Tis this not a dream."

He laughed, "No 'tis not, but I fear we hath entered into somewhat of a nightmare, you and I."

I looked down at the ground and then at my soiled hands, "The Queen was set on having me killed. Lady Esther was charged to aid my escape only to lure me off the grounds and hath me delivered into the hands of the carriage man. The King, thy own father, demands my hand. I fear the Queen feels I hath betrayed her, when I hath not."

"Odette sent a charge in secrecy to pass word of my father's intentions. I immediately returned to address the matter but I was too late, you had already gone. Lady Jocelin, thy words allude to savage intentions of being slain. How did thee come to such a conclusion?"

"'Tis the way the carriage man and Lady Esther exchanged glances. There were previously spoken words of agreement between them, I could tell. When she sought to take my steed, I knew for certain nothing but ill tidings were granted. I challenged her intentions then leapt upon the horses back to journey through the woods."

He smiled as he placed my hair behind my ear.

"Come warm yourself near the fire, you must take nourishment. Days hath passed since thee hath eaten."

"Days?"

"Aye, t'would appear ye hit thy head rather hard. 'Tis why upon my arrival I discovered thee to be in the midst of courtship with a depth of slumber not even my kiss could revive ye from."

I reached up to touch my lips and smiled, "How long hath thou been present?" I asked still dazed.

"I arrived in the morn after the better part of two full days of travel. Thou absence 'twas noted some four days prior to this day, perhaps a thread longer."

"Two day's travel? My steed brought me here in no greater than one. How is that possible?"

Prince René rose to his feet then walked across to where the two horses lay. Once he was positioned behind them, he went to bended knee placing his hand on one and then the others neck. "The steed I gifted to thee my Lady has capacity for speed as I hath never seen any beast to possess. 'Tis akin to the soar of an eagle once he rises to his extended stride he glides across the surface of mother natures soils with nothing able to resist his projection."

"How did thee know to find me here?"

Prince René placed his hand on the black horse to stroke him, "I knew not how to reach thee, 'twas my steed who brought me to this place."

I extended my arms out to warm the tips of my fingers against the rising heat of the flames. "I'm afraid I do not understand. How could thine steed possibly know this location with such precision? Doth they possess the capacity to track for scent?"

Prince René lent in as he smiled, "They are twins. One was born pure black, the other pure white. They hath been inseparable since birth. No matter how far one travels, the other is sure to follow. Their souls are connected. The black can never lose sight of the white tis no matter the distance traveled, they always find their way."

I nodded my head as I allowed a tear to fall. "You gifted the white to me."

"Aye, this I did. The black one is mine. 'Twas my wish

to tell thee upon our exchange of vows of the significance our mounts held."

"Enlighten me now, please if you may," I whispered with a quake in my voice from being so moved by his gesture.

"'Twas my telling of my wish to bind with thee and thereafter never part. We would always find each other no matter the cause of distance. Our souls are bound as one. I recognized from the moment, I first entered the room that I loved thee Lady Jocelin with a depth unparalleled. 'Twas within an instant I knew the white steed was born to be gifted to thee."

I cried as I stared at them all, "My heart is filled with so much love for thee I never thought it to be possible."

He came across and embraced me, "Then why doth thee cry?"

I continued to cover his shoulder with tears, "I thought I would never hold opportunity to express to thee how my heart felt. Everything thou hath said, all the considerations given toward me, hold me steadfast to my already knowing our love is pure."

He held me tight as he whispered, "and still you cry."

"I am happy, my Prince" was all I could say as I continued to release the tears.

Once I settled he insisted I eat the portion of bread and cheese he brought with him. The horses left to graze leaving the Prince, and I remaining.

"What are we to do?" I asked.

"Upon the break of day I must leave to journey back to the castle."

"No," I said grasping at his tunic shaking my head. "Thou mustn't"

"I must. The impending issues need to be addressed, and I am afraid I left my mother there alone bickering with my

244

father. He is a bitter man with cruel intent at times but he has ruled the lands fairly to a point of prosper."

"The way he stared at me."

"Aye, what you fail to know is that my mother and I had made execution of our plan to hold the ceremony in his absence. Father had been away near on six months and was not due for return for another six. When he heard word of a royal wedding he returned to the castle. 'Tis why mother and I were silent during the course of our first meal. He was furious expressing his conclusion of us taking such matters in our own hands as a betrayal. He berated mother and I for hours prior. I can assure thee that his desire to wed thee is nothing more than an attempt to assert his authority, to ensure acknowledgement of his power as the King."

"No, listen to my plead, it comes from knowledge of such things. I hold grave concerns in regard to his intentions. The King holds conviction to remove all who would stand in the way of his access to me. I fear he see's no cost too great to obtain my hand. I hath seen this look many times before, he possessed an obsession, and not even the devil himself would cause him hesitation to step forward and fight to claim me."

"Do not cloud thy mind with worry of such things. I know my father. 'I can assure thee, his actions are merely an aggressive attempt to assert his power. He will come to his senses. I am his only son."

"No, 'tis not as you see it. I swear to thee, he is not of sound mind and will refuse to reason. With all due respect, I fear my Prince in this instance thou art wrong. I beg of thee, take heed of my words." I said resigned to a sense of sadness.

"Let us rest. I need to leave in a few short hours for my return. Lay in my arms so I may feel your warmth."

I lent into him and closed my eyes as he wrapped his arms around me. There was so much I wished to share with him about my ideals of our future, the likes of things I had never thought to dream. Being with child, carrying his progeny within my belly was an ache in my heart, I wished to be fulfilled. He needed to take rest, his journey would be long and I fear he was in a state of oblivion with regard to the challenges placed before him to manage. I so wished he would pay heed to my words.

* * * * *

The noise of the horse's hooves entering the cavern woke us. We found ourselves laying in a manner a husband and wife would find, side-by-side looking upon each other's gaze.

"Good morrow." He whispered sweetly.

"Don't leave." I implored.

He closed his eyes placing his forehead on mine, "I must but I will return swiftly."

All I could do was release a sigh and nod my head.

"Come, I must prepare to leave." He rose to his feet holding his hand out to assist me.

Once we were both standing, he fetched his saddle to place it on his horse.

"No, if the white steed is faster take it so you may address the matters quickly and return even quicker."

"If I take him then you will be without a horse for the black is certain to follow. I will not leave thee here without a steed. The nearest village is a full day's travel from here slightly less if ye hath length of stride and move swiftly. 'Tis far too dangerous."

"Then it is settled. The imminent danger would hath thee hold the desire to return at speed. Please, you must take him."

"Lady Jocelin, do not underestimate the dangers which

lurk here. This is no place for a lady to be stranded I can assure thee."

"Then leave me thy bow and arrow and if thee carry a hunting knife, leave it as well."

His face contorted, "'Tis not as simple as holding them, one must know how to use them, please I hath no time for this folly."

I shook my head as I walked toward him, "Why doth thou insist upon not listening." I said as I took the bow and a single arrow. "Look upon the sapling over yonder." I raised the bow, placed the arrow within my hold and released. As I turned to greet the Prince's gaze he shook his head with dismay.

"Why do thou still look upon me this way?"

"Thy aim seemed true and the form was surprisingly well presented but my Lady you hath missed the target."

"Perhaps the Prince should refrain until he takes a closer inspection. My aim is always true. The sapling is weaker than the strength of my arrows speed so it merely shot through."

The Prince walked across to inspect the sapling. The arrow had passed through embedding itself securely in the heart of the trunk of the tree directly behind.

I walked up to him with the white horse now saddled, "Provide me with a knife if thee can spare it and please accept the steed with no further word of concern in regard to my safety."

"How is it that thou hath mastered the arrow so?"

"The convent I was raised in held a vow of poverty, the only way I was set to be able to repay them for their kindness was to learn to hunt so I may regularly secure meat for storage in preparation for each winter."

"Thou art amazing." He whispered.

His adoration of my capabilities surprised me. In all my

247

term at the convent, I was rarely thanked for my skill by any whose bellies were filled by my hand. Instead, some would chastise my behavior with insistence that a true lady doth not hunt. To feel the warmth of his acceptance made me fall a little deeper in appreciation of his beauty. "Thank you." I whispered in return.

"Here is the knife ye ask for and some coin for supplies. There is enough bread and cheese to last three days. I plan not to be longer than five at the most. I will return for thee Lady Jocelin."

I brazenly stepped forward, "I wish for thee to kiss me."

He took pause and looked at me in a way I had never seen any look upon me before.

"I hold little strength to leave thee as it is. If I do as thou ask, and how my heart desires, then I surely would hold no resolve to part this day."

I stepped in even closer, "If this is true then I demand to receive thy kiss upon my lips for I never want thee to leave."

He smiled as he placed his forehead on mine pressing us together with his hand, "I will come back for thee. Our souls are one my beloved. I make a promise that upon my return, I will grant thee one kiss before we are wed. I make another such promise that post the blessed exchange of our vows I shall never to stop kissing thee thereafter. I will return post haste my love."

"Then I shall wait for thee forever for my heart is gifted to thee and no other. Thou art my one true eternal love."

He mounted the white steed with ease then looked at me smiling while he placed his hand on his heart, "Until next we meet."

I nodded my head executing the same with my hand before he turned and rode away. 'Twas not long before the black steed set off to follow, leaving me standing there alone.

* * * * *

Days had passed and still my Prince had not returned. I prayed for hours upon my knees to the Lord requesting that he may guide my Prince to receive the outcome required to hath him within my embrace once more. I knew from the moment he was to re-enter I would never allow for us to part again. Our strength was in our heart's unity. In his absence, all that consumed my mind was his absence, I could barely endure the pain.

Upon the ninth day, I set toward the village to see if I could find word of what is happening across the lands. In drab hunter's attire with my hair hidden beneath a cap and dirt across my cheek and brow I walked among the people ensuring my eyes were firmly set to the ground. Nearly all conversed in their native tongue some of which I knew from Odette's teachings but they mostly spoke too quickly for me to comprehend. 'Twas only when I reached the markets that I heard some who spoke in English. I followed the sound of the voices, which lead me to some men standing near the fishmonger's cart.

"How could this be?" asked the weathered old man leaning into the young boy.

"'Tis the spoken truth, I swear it. I heard word from my cousin who is assigned to the royal kitchen. The reward for her finding is to be announced by all the town criers across the lands on the coming Sabbath. There will be pictures issued from the private collection, so we may see what she looks like. Any man who delivers her unharmed to the King will be rewarded the title of Earl along with land and other riches."

"Hath thee knowledge of what we are to look for? If you can gain insight prior, then perhaps our early commencement

may bear us fruit before interest is amassed to scour the lands. 'Tis but a woman, how hard could she be to find?"

The fishmonger stepped forward to join the two who were already speaking.

"May I ask what she has done to cause such interest that the King would offer the price of Earl and such?"

"I heard it on good authority through my cousin who works in the royal kitchens that the girl was engaged to his son Prince René. When the King laid eyes upon her beauty he was bewitched causing him madness."

"Such folly no woman holds power over a man, least of all a mighty King."

The young man shook his head, "No, I tell you she is an enchantress who set the King so beholden to her that he beheaded the Queen and then tortured his son to make him confess on where he had hidden her."

"The Prince had hidden her?"

"Aye, 'twas Lady Esther the Queen's own hand who suggested so, stating the word from villages referred to an enchantress seen riding a pure white horse. A carriage man stepped forward to vow to her word and was richly rewarded for his knowledge. When Prince René entered the castle he was upon the very same white horse with a black horse in suit. It was most certainly the work of witchcraft. The King was enraged insisting upon his son's confession to which he did not speak a word. The King beat him with his very own hands then left him to choke on his own blood. Upon the King's insistence Prince René has been buried in an unmarked grave and officially denounced as his son."

"Perhaps the King is simply mad for who would do such an act of atrocity to his own son for a mere woman?" asked the fishmonger.

"This is why there is certainty witchcraft is involved.

They say any who look upon her are converted to slave or stone."

I quietly left the markets returning to the centre of the village where I set out to purchase a horse. I used the coin the Prince had given to buy a spirited brown stallion with anger in his eyes. The man gladly accepted my generous bid, to which he included a saddle with my purchase. I demonstrated no hesitation as I mounted the dancing beast of fury. He reared on his hind quarters then leapt forward as he adjusted to yield to my command. We rode out onto the path for a short way before disappearing back into the forest.

It took a little over two and a half days to travel through the woods unseen. The horse needed to receive frequent rest, while I sat in waiting. When we arrived close to outskirts of the back of the castle, I released the steed, giving it the reward of freedom for service. It stood by and watched as I sulked forward into the darkness to climb the steps toward the waterfall. Once I was secure behind the fall's veil I remained in waiting. My clothes needed to dry so the water would not leave a trail. Patience was required for this hunt.

Entering into the belly of the castle, I used the shadows cast for coverage as I made my way down the passages towards the King's chamber. Knowing his guards would be in attendance, I entered the Queen's chamber, closing the door behind. Foolish men of war only guard what is known. 'Tis to my advantage they hold no consideration to all the entry points. The King and Queen hath separate chambers, but a private access path exists to allow the King to visit the Queen's quarters whenever he felt the desire to spurt his putrid seed. In the absence of the Queen's chambers holding occupancy, they see no need to neither guard the door nor lock it. The idiocy of men was to my advantage this night.

Once in the private access channel, I listened at the secret *doorway into the King's bed chamber. He expelled his rancid breath in deep guttural tones as he slept. Upon the next utterance, I wedged the door open to gain sight to where he was positioned. There was no other in his room. I had hoped Lady Esther volunteered her services to warm his bed, so I may kill them both.*

Carefully, I removed my cap from my head crushing it in my hand while I held Prince René's knife within the other. Upon the moment, the King rolled to his back releasing a snort, I entered the room. Within a single bound I was upon him, my cap wedged within his mouth as his eyes opened to bulge at the feel of the knife enter his throat severing his vocals, before thrusting deeper to severe his spine. The strength in his arms fell to a release while I pressed upon the cap to ensure he would not hold an utterance of noise from his mouth for aid.

I watched the life fade from his eyes and wondered whether he still saw me as beautiful or was I now a monster born with the eyes of the devil looking upon his last breath. Most assuredly, I wished to bestow him with a lengthy torture such to which would pale in comparison to the rage he unleashed upon his own son. This vile man's actions toward his own flesh and blood, birthed a fire of anger in my belly that would not forgive nor find peace with what had transpired. His life alone would not be payment enough. Nothing would appease me the pains of the loss that I felt in my heart.

My years of hunting served me well. I completed what I set out to do and left through the passage as quietly as I entered. By daybreak, I was well clear of the castle, safely perched high above a canopy in wait.

'Twas shortly post the midday sun when I saw the carriage from a distance leaving the castle along the path.

I waited until I held certainty before I took aim. A single arrow shot through the heart, for the man who clearly had none. The horses slowed as he stumbled before becoming limp of life. I watched to see who might alight, but none did. My instinct held steadfast to maintain stillness. An hour passed before her head dared to peer out from the window. I watched, as she looked left and right then upon the illusion of clearance, she gained the courage to alight. I thought Lady Esther might take the path to the return to the castle by foot. Rather she climbed up to take position to drive the carriage forward, pushing the carcass free so it fell to the ground.

As I took aim I made a loud masked call of a bird, so her head rose to glance upon me when I released the arrow. The look of fear on her face gave me no pleasure but the arrow entering through the bridge of her nose causing her skull to rupture from the deliverance of my hatred for all she stood for, did. I climbed higher still to gain better coverage from the canopy to wait for nightfall. The carriage had not been discovered by the time the darkness greeted the lands so I freed the horses and left the carcasses where they fell.

Upon foot, I traveled through the wilds of the forest, returning to the shelter of the ravines. A week had passed before I entered the village once more, this time to seek news of how the King's demise was conveyed. I ventured through all the same places and overheard nothing. I stopped by the fishmonger to purchase a fish while making idle chat I asked if there was further news of the reward to take place on the Lady the King sought to find. He merely laughed and said nothing had come of it, no town criers presented on the Sabbath. He concluded that the boy was caught in a convincing fable.

The King's soldiers searched for me relentlessly. My ease of access to the King made a mockery of all they trained and stood to represent. They seemed to hold little to no regard for the loss of a ruler who treated them poorly. They were intent on silencing me, so they could say as they pleased in regard to the matter with no challenge.

It took me many years to realize the discovery of the King's fate was not released beyond a few. Those who witnessed his bloodied carcass of pulp sprawled on the bed with his skin perfectly removed, scalp intact, hung and stretched by binds for prime display across his majestic poster bed, were sworn to secrecy. None were to breathe a word of such a failure to protect their King. Instead, a conspiracy was weighted in favor to sway the powers that be to remove all reference to his reign. The King, Queen, my beloved Prince René were etched away from reference on any books of bind. With no written historical reference remaining intact and little spoken of them, it took but a generation to hath knowledge of their existence wane. This is how the affairs of lords and Kings govern these lands. The blood spilt, betrayals and lies buried deep beneath the tall tales of the fables they desire to be remembered. Nevertheless, the idiocy of their greed would not see the countless images of me created by the artist in residence Marcel, destroyed. Instead, they were kept within the royal archives and some Marcel himself retained. 'Twas said the artist held an inability to cease painting my image. Upon his retirement, he sought refuge within the village in a small home where he devoted the remainder of his years toward mastering the art of capturing his memory of my beauty on canvas.

I've searched relentlessly for my beloved's unmarked grave each year upon the spring when mother nature softens her soils. I venture from the mountains to the castle grounds where I place my hands beneath the dirt's surface in search of his remains, to no avail. Legends hath been spurred by my presence on occasion being sighted. Men doth speak of a creature described to be part woman, part beast adorned in the skin of a bear with a face of weathered unnatural beauty. 'Twas encouraged by the soldiers of old to seek to hunt the creature that was thought to live within the rugged mountains. Many who tried lost their lives either through the mountains claim or by my hand if they succeeded to venture closer than my comfort would allow. I tried to deter those I could, but some were persistent enough to warrant the receipt of my poisoned arrow.

I cursed the Gods who made me this way. I cursed them for giving me life, providing me the knowledge of how it felt to love and be loved, then without warrant mercilessly tore him away.

I curse them still.

The final page was complete. I ran my fingers through my hair as I re-read Patience's last words cursing the Gods. I wished I could find a way to hold her in my arms to aid her in the release of her anger. To let her cry a thousand rivers of tears, if that's what she needed, just so she could find peace with it all. I know there will never be anything that makes such horrendous experiences any better but that's not the point. It's about not allowing them to define her to such a degree that it becomes the single driver, influencing all decisions and actions thereafter. To do this leaves her robbed of joy while the cycle of pain is sustained. This only provides her a narrow pathway whereby Patience becomes a victim of circumstance.

I felt completely gutted knowing that she momentarily had within her grasp what seemed like that most amazing beginning to the truest of love stories that

I had ever read. I can't imagine what it would feel like to fall deeply in love with someone and then have them torn away. What Patience had with Prince René was real. It tugged on my heartstrings and had me secretly wishing to experience the same. In passing moments within my own life, I have felt my heart ache to fall in love and to be loved like no other in return. I just know this won't happen for me, at least not in this lifetime.

Huckleberry lifted his head releasing a single high pitched bark. I looked at him and smiled, "I'm sorry little fella can you read minds? Present company excluded, I love you dearly my sweet little one." He licked the sections of my arm he could reach as I patted his neck and back. If I didn't know any better, I might have believed that he could hear and understand my thoughts.